SARAH ALDERSON

SEVERED

For John

First published in Great Britain in 2012 by Alula Press

Also by Sarah Alderson
Hunting Lila
Losing Lila
Fated
Shadowed
The Sound
Out of Control

World is crazier and more of it than we think.

Louis MacNeice

1

The headlights of the car punctured the black blanket sky, illuminating rolling countryside which ceded eventually to the sprawl of suburbs and then finally to the brutal glare of the city. But Evie barely noticed. She didn't even ask Lucas where they were going. As she clenched and unclenched her hands, which were still sticky with blood, all she could think about was what had happened back in Riverview. And about the dead they'd left behind.

She stared down at her bare feet, which were laced with dirt and mud and the stomach-churning remains of scorched Thirster flesh, and her teeth began chattering so loudly that Lucas reached over and cranked up the heat in the car to full.

Evie snuck a surreptitious sideways glance at him as he drove, his arms taut as they gripped the wheel. In the dim light from the dash he looked more unhuman than human. His eyes had a wolf-like intensity to them and his skin seemed to gleam and merge with the shadows. He was half human, half Shadow Warrior - able to pass in both worlds. But it was so damn obvious that he had unhuman blood in him that she couldn't believe she'd never noticed it before. What kind of a Hunter was she? Even the way her body reacted when he was around – her heart thrumming in her chest like it was an animal trying to burrow its way free, her breathing running tight and fast - should have alerted her. Her brain and her body had been trying to warn her all along that Lucas was the enemy. But her heart had told her something else entirely, so she'd willfully ignored all the signs and shut out the sound of her instincts screaming.

Other than for the times his eyes flicked to the rearview mirror, Lucas hadn't once lifted his gaze away from the road since they'd got in the car. He hadn't said a word either. He was too focused on driving with his foot to the floor, as though they had an army of Thirsters and Mixen demons on their heels – which quite possibly they did but Evie didn't want to contemplate that. She couldn't. Not right now.

She sunk back into the cool leather of her seat and instead thought back to what Lucas had told her just a few hours ago in Victor's boutique. He'd broken his oath to the Brotherhood for *her*. She knew the penalty for that was death, as did he. But he'd done it anyway, and all because he claimed to love her. *Did he?* Evie felt her heart stutter. He was here wasn't he? He'd risked everything for her. He'd stood by her side as they'd fought off both Hunters and unhumans to escape Riverview. And, what was more, he believed that she was the one who was going to end the war that had raged for over a thousand years between unhumans and Hunters. Evie closed her eyes. Did she believe it too?

'We're here.'

Her eyes snapped open. Lucas had parked up on a dark street. Evie looked out of the window. Where had Lucas brought her? She knew they were somewhere in Los Angeles and, judging from the scruffy state of the apartment block he'd parked in front of, they weren't in the Beverly Hills part, but that was all she knew. She was about to ask him what they were doing there but he had already got out of the car. She watched him as he walked around to her side. He looked as if he'd been in a fight. Several fights actually. To the death. Which would be accurate. His dark hair was matted and sticking together in clumps. His shirt was ripped and streaked with blood – a red bloom just over his heart marked the spot where her own knife had pierced the skin. She shuddered at the memory of the tip scraping the bone and of what she'd almost done.

He opened her door and she climbed out, her muscles cramping then yelling in protest.

'Where are we?' she asked, taking in the deserted street. It was still dark outside. Dawn hadn't even begun to lighten the sky.

Lucas didn't answer her. He just took a deep breath, grimaced, and strode towards the entrance of the apartment block, looking over his shoulder once to check that Evie was following.

'Whatever you do,' Lucas said, shooting Evie a warning glance as he buzzed entry and then led her inside and towards a stairwell, 'don't tell them who you are – or *what* you are. They don't need to know.'

Evie's heart slammed to a standstill. She stared at Lucas, dazed. She had no intention of declaring to a total stranger that she was a half-trained Hunter with zero powers and a debilitating inability to actually slay any demons. And she had even less intention of announcing herself messiah-like as the White Light come to sever the realms. But who the hell were *they*?

She wished now that she'd asked him about his plan back when they were leaving Riverview. But they'd been in kind of a hurry.

Lucas was now leading her down a dingily lit corridor that smelt of cigarettes and burger grease. He stopped in front of a door with flaking paint.

'Evie? Are you alright?'

She blinked, realising that she had come to a standstill in the middle of the corridor, her stomach in knots. She walked slightly unsteadily over to Lucas who was staring at her, his grey eyes dark and troubled. Stress was etched across his face, which was still so pale it made her stomach wrench, remembering.

'Are you alright?' he asked again, more softly.

She nodded in response. But it was a lie and he knew it.

Lucas pressed his lips together, still staring at her with that worried look on his face. His hand hovered for an instant by her cheek and her breath caught. He hadn't touched her since she'd taken his hand and dragged him out of the alley, past Jocelyn, past Risper's crumpled remains and past the scorched and oozing patches of earth where two dead unhumans had lain.

She leant in towards him, suddenly needing to feel connected to him, to get some kind of reassurance that he was still here, that he was real and wasn't about to disappear or dissolve into the shadows. But just as she moved towards him his hand dropped to his side and he turned quickly away from her and slouched against the wall.

Was he having second thoughts? Was that it? After everything that had happened was he realising that protecting her was a losing battle? He'd almost died trying – was he finally starting to see sense? She wouldn't exactly blame him.

She stared at him, frozen with uncertainty, anxiety seeping through her, but before she could say anything or do anything, the door in front of them flew open. Evie turned her head. A girl was standing there with her arms crossed over her chest. She was in her early twenties, Evie estimated – tall, slender but athletic looking. Also angry looking. The scowl on her face was enough to make Evie take a quick step backwards and start scanning the hallway for the exits.

She wondered if Lucas had got the wrong address. But when she glanced over at him she saw that he was smiling at the girl, almost roguishly, his head tipped to one side, looking up at her through lowered lashes. Evie frowned, confused by the smile and the casual but charming pose he was striking, before realising that he was trying to hide his bloodstained clothing and the fang marks on his neck.

'Hi Flic,' Lucas said in a drawl which made Evie wonder even more at how the two of them knew each other. He tilted his head in Evie's direction, 'This is …'

'I know who she is,' the girl snapped back.

Lucas's smile vanished instantly and a shadow flitted across his face. Then just like that, without appearing to have even moved, he was standing up straight, filling the doorway, every trace of charm gone.

The girl visibly flinched, the scowl dropping away and her eyes growing wide as she took in Lucas's ripped and bloodied shirt and his dark scowl. But then she tossed her hair over one shoulder and narrowed her eyes once more in a death glare.

'Can we come inside?' Lucas asked, ignoring her expression. His voice was so low it could easily have been mistaken for a threat.

Evie glanced up the corridor once more, wondering whether this was such a good idea. This girl knew who she was. And if she knew that, how could they be safe here?

The girl didn't move out of the way, she just continued to glower at Lucas.

Evie thought about reaching out and taking Lucas's arm and pulling him back. They could go somewhere else, anywhere – a motel even. She didn't understand why Lucas had brought them here where obviously they weren't welcome. But just as she was about to clear her throat and suggest that they leave, the girl huffed loudly and stepped to one side, revealing a dimly lit hallway behind her.

Evie guessed that was as much of an invitation as they were going to get. She looked at Lucas, who nodded at her without smiling and ushered her forwards, his hand pressed against the small of her back. It was the first time he had touched her since they'd run from the alley and the feel of his hand, the reassurance it gave, overrode her instincts which had started screaming. She ignored them though and let Lucas push her inside the apartment.

The girl stiffened as she passed her, flattening herself against the wall as if Evie was contagious. Evie's gut clenched in response, the hairs on the back of her neck bristling. Something wasn't right. She scanned the narrow hallway, her heart racing. There were five doors coming off it – all closed except for one door at the end, which stood slightly ajar. A thin strip of light was painting the patch of scuffed floorboard in front of it. She paused, her mouth running dry and the muscles in her back and shoulders locking. Her instincts weren't just screaming now, they were yelling at her to turn and run.

There were others here. She could sense it. But more than that, the thing that had made her adrenaline start pumping, the thing that was causing her instincts to fire like rocket jets, wasn't the fact that there were others here, it was the fact that those others were unhuman.

Evie turned instantly on her heel, heading straight for the door, fists raised, ready to fight her way out, but Lucas was blocking her way and she banged straight up against his chest. He caught her by the tops of her arms and the pressure of his hands instantly calmed her. She looked up into his eyes, saw the reassurance in them, and tried to steady her breathing. If Lucas had brought her here, she told herself again, then it was fine. There was absolutely nothing to panic about.

Just then the door slammed and Evie jumped. Lucas's grip on her tightened. The girl rammed home a bolt and then spun around to face them, her whole body resonating with anger. Maybe it wasn't so fine after all, Evie thought. She felt like a rat trapped in a tunnel and cursed herself silently for letting Lucas bring her here – for not listening to her instincts when she still had a chance. This girl was unhuman – she had to be.

Evie studied her in the gloom of the hallway. She looked human enough. There was nothing obvious to say that she wasn't – she didn't have a pale-green tinge to her skin like Shula, and Evie couldn't see a tail. That ruled out Mixen and Scorpio demons. And she doubted Lucas would be friends with any Thirsters. But it didn't look like he was friends with this girl either, from the way they were glaring at each other.

'You brought her to my house?' the girl yelled at Lucas. 'You brought her here?' She stepped towards them, her face blazing, and Evie felt herself shrink further against Lucas's side. 'What were you thinking?' the girl demanded. She held up both hands. 'No, don't tell me. Clearly you weren't thinking. Because if you had been, you wouldn't be showing up here at four in the morning with a Hunter in tow.'

A hard lump of panic rose in Evie's throat. She heard Lucas take a sharp breath. How did this girl know about her being a Hunter?

'Flic, we had nowhere else to go,' Lucas said, before adding more quietly, 'There's no one else I trust.'

Lucas trusted this girl? Evie twisted her head to look at him. The girl snorted under her breath as if she couldn't believe it either.

'I can explain, Flic,' Lucas said, sighing.

'I'm not interested in an explanation, Lucas,' Flic spat. 'I'm interested in how you lost your freaking mind. She's a Hunter. There is no possible explanation for this. I thought you'd joined the Brotherhood to get revenge. Aren't you supposed to be killing Hunters? Isn't that kind of the job description? But no, instead you turn up at my house with Cinderfreakingella here, covered in blood and begging for my help.'

Evie cast a glance downwards at what she was wearing. At the time she'd thought the red Valentino cocktail dress was the perfect outfit to wear for facing down and killing Lucas. Or for dying in, because that had seemed like more of a possibility at the time. It turned out that, despite choosing it for its colour, it didn't hide bloodstains so well. And now she felt ridiculous, standing barefoot, bloodied and bedraggled, being scrutinised by this girl. She ran a hand self-consciously through her knotted hair and then down her dress trying to straighten herself out. *Cinderfreakingella?* She ground her teeth.

'Flic,' Lucas said, his voice a knife wrapped in silk.

Flic ignored him. 'Where are the Brotherhood?' she yelled. 'They won't just kill *her*, Lucas – they'll kill *you*. They'll kill you for this – for running off with a Hunter. Do you realise that?' She paused, her eyes widening, 'Did they follow you here?'

There was a moment of silence, which reminded Evie of floating underwater tangled up in weeds, a silence so deep she thought she was going to drown in it. Then Lucas spoke up. 'There is no Brotherhood,' he said. 'We got in a fight with them. They're all dead.'

Flic's mouth moved but no sound came out. Instead, she closed her eyes and tilted back her head to stare at the ceiling. She sighed loudly. 'Great. This is great. No, really, that's an awesome career move. Killing the Brotherhood. Nice work.' She levelled her gaze at Lucas, her voice shaking with anger. 'There are easier ways to commit suicide, Lucas.'

Evie looked down at her bare feet, staring at the dirt and blood caked all over them. She didn't want to look up. She didn't want to see Lucas's reaction. Here was someone saying out loud what she was too scared to and what had hung between them in the stifling silence of the car. By protecting her, by betraying the Brotherhood, by fighting against them and killing one of his kind, Lucas had signed his own death warrant. She felt guilt beat an acid path through her veins.

'Flic.'

Evie's head flew up. Someone was standing in the shadows at the end of the hallway. He advanced towards Flic, glancing warily at Evie as he passed her, before laying a hand gently on Flic's arm. This one was definitely unhuman. Evie's heart had begun to pound as if someone was playing drum and bass in her head.

Flic nodded at the guy standing next to her. 'This is Jamieson,' she said through a clenched jaw. 'He's my boyfriend. Thanks to you he's probably going to end up as my dead boyfriend.' She took a breath. 'Jamieson,' she said, without taking her eyes off Lucas, 'this is my stupid-moronic-going-to-get-us-all-killed-because-he-can't-keep-his-trousers-on brother, Lucas.'

2

Brother? Evie tried to ram her mouth shut before anyone could register her shock. This girl was Lucas's sister? She stared at Flic in amazement. But of course she was his sister. It was so obvious. The razor-sharp cheekbones and the ridiculously long eyelashes. The thick dark hair and straight eyebrows over those almond-shaped eyes. Except Flic's eyes were a dark-brown colour while Lucas's were every shade of grey. And Flic's eyes were iridescent with rage and Lucas's were right now so guarded she couldn't tell what he was feeling and really didn't want to imagine.

'Flic, don't be so melodramatic,' Jamieson said, putting an arm around her shoulders. He gave Lucas an apologetic shrug.

Flic threw off his arm and turned on him. 'Melodramatic? Is that what I'm being?' she shouted. 'Did you hear this? Did you hear what he just said? My darling brother here has killed the entire Brotherhood. As in killed. As in DEAD!'

Jamieson's face turned ashen. He turned slowly to look at Lucas. 'You killed ...?'

Lucas dropped his gaze to the floor.

'It wasn't really him,' Evie burst out. 'I mean Lucas didn't actually kill anyone.' 'Tonight,' she added under her breath, remembering Caleb. He *had* killed Caleb but that had been a couple of nights ago.

'Well, who did kill them? You?' Flic asked snidely. 'You're not even fully trained are you? Do you even have your full power?'

Evie bit her lip and took a deep breath. 'No,' she admitted in a whisper. Lucas's sister seemed to know a hell of a lot about her. Evie threw a worried glance at Lucas to see whether he was thinking the same thing, but she was distracted by Flic suddenly taking a step towards her.

'Because of you,' Flic said, pushing right up into Evie's face so that Evie could make out the yellowy-gold rim at the edge of her irises, 'my brother is now being hunted down by every unhuman in a seven-realm radius.'

Evie's gut tightened.

'How did you know about Evie?' interrupted Lucas. 'How did you know that she's a Hunter? How did you know about ...,' he paused, glancing briefly in Evie's direction, '*us*?'

'How do you think I knew, Lucas?' Flic snarled.

Lucas's eyes widened slightly. 'She's here?' he asked, dropping his voice, his eyes darting over Flic's shoulder.

Evie glanced between them, trying to work out who they were talking about. Who did Lucas think was here? And then, as if on cue, she heard a girl's soft voice.

‘Hello Lucas.’

Evie spun around as Jamieson edged aside, revealing a girl with hair like sheet lightning falling over one shoulder, reaching almost to her waist. But it was her eyes that Evie was drawn to. They were huge – unhumanly huge – two pale-blue discs in the white oval of her face.

She was a Sybll. Evie knew it immediately. This girl in front of her could see the future. That’s how they knew all about her, and about Lucas being on the run with a Hunter. This girl standing in front of her had seen them coming.

‘Hi Issa,’ Lucas finally answered, his voice taking on an uneven tone.

The girl gazed at him for a few seconds, her face as blank as a corpse, but then her eyes flew to Evie, and Evie could have sworn she saw a shudder run through her before she quickly looked back at Lucas. Did Evie really look that bad? Or was it that she had seen something? Something coming? Was that how it worked? God, she realised she really didn’t know a lot about unhumans. So much for Victor’s training. She hadn’t even thought to bring the book with her which contained all the information the Hunters had gathered on unhumans over the years. It was still at her house, hidden under the bed. All she knew for certain was that she was standing in a narrow hallway surrounded on all sides by demons who she was theoretically supposed to kill.

And it looked as if they'd like to do the same to her, except without the theoretical part.

'Flic, let them stay,' Jamieson said. 'Issa can warn us if anyone's coming. Let's find out what's going on at least,' he added when Flic made no sign of relenting.

Flic pressed her lips together in a gesture that reminded Evie of Lucas and then she exhaled loudly. Without a word she strode past all of them and into the room at the end of the hallway. Jamieson turned to them and with a shrug of his shoulders gestured for them to follow her.

Evie hesitated, convinced now that they'd be better off leaving, but Lucas's hand was suddenly in hers and he was shooting her a pleading look and she was just too tired to argue. The last of her adrenaline had leached away and she didn't think she would be able to even make it back to the car. So she trudged after Flic into the living room.

Jamieson crossed straight away to a beanbag in the corner of the room and flopped down onto it, his eyes darting from Lucas and his crimson-spattered clothing to Evie in her strapless cocktail attire. She watched his eyebrows rise as he took in the state of the dress and her bare legs and feet streaked with blood and mud. She shuffled uncomfortably, aware of how badly she wanted to shower and change into something clean.

There was a sofa against one wall covered in blankets and a small coffee table in front of it scattered with magazines and empty cans. The room was lit by several floor lamps and some candles sat on the windowsill. Flic moved straight to the window and pulled down the blind. Issa stood quietly in the centre of the room – a marble statue, dressed all in black, her gaze glued to Lucas.

Evie inched closer to Lucas. In the flickering glow of the lights he didn't seem so pale but, standing this side of him, Evie could see the dried trickle of blood running down his neck and the two scabs where Joshua had sunk his fangs in. She shut her eyes trying to erase the image that flashed before her, but it remained there, as though seared with a branding iron onto her retina. She didn't think she'd ever manage to successfully rid herself of that one.

'You saw us coming?' she heard Lucas ask.

'Yes,' Issa answered. 'I'm still connected to you, Lucas.'

Evie's eyes flew open.

'And you're sure no one followed them?' Flic asked.

Issa frowned briefly before stepping around Flic and taking hold of Lucas's hand. Evie tensed beside him, watching.

Issa's eyes suddenly glazed over, the blue turning milky-white. Lucas stood stock-still, not breathing. After a few seconds Issa's eyes flashed open. 'You can relax,' she said, turning her back and walking to the sofa. 'You're safe for the moment.'

'But they're coming?' Lucas asked, his voice sounding strained. 'You see them coming for us, don't you?'

'Yes, they'll come,' Issa answered, dropping down onto a cushion.

Evie stared at her, biting her lip. You didn't need to be a psychic to know that.

3

Lucas saw Evie's face pale. Her eyes, the colour of deep ocean, were locked on Issa. For a second his mind flew back to the Mission, remembering another Sybll standing in front of him, clutching his arm. *You die because of the choice you make*, Grace had told him.

Except he hadn't died. He was still here. Even though he'd made the choice to turn his back on the Brotherhood and on his oath, he was still alive. Which made him wonder whether fate was so set in stone and whether Sybll always got it right.

'Sybll predictions don't always come true, Evie,' he said to her softly, shooting Issa a warning look.

Evie turned to him. She looked fragile all of a sudden and unsteady on her feet. He fought the urge to pull her towards him. The last thing he needed to do was give Flic any more reason to lash out – she was already simmering dangerously. And he was acutely aware too of Issa, standing there, observing them both silently. He hadn't expected to ever see her again, least of all here. The last time they'd been in each other's company – the time he'd said goodbye – hadn't exactly been one to store in the memory bank.

Evie was still staring up at him, her body tensed and her chin held high. She was trying to show she was unafraid. But he could hear her heart beating as rapidly as it had done back when they were cornered in the alley. The front of her dress was torn at the hem and there was a bloodied handprint stamped across her collarbone. He kept glancing at it, wanting to wipe it away. It was unsettling, as if an invisible demon was trying to strangle her.

'Tristan told me that Sybll sometimes get it wrong. That things can change according to the choices we make,' he said, trying to reassure her. 'Think about it,' he added. 'Wouldn't they have sent more than just the Brotherhood to kill you if they'd been able to foresee what was going to happen? We wouldn't be standing here now if Sybll got it right all the time.'

Evie chewed her lip, contemplating what he'd just said. She didn't look that convinced.

'It's true,' Issa said.

Lucas looked at her, startled. He hadn't expected Issa to back him up on this one.

'We don't see everything,' she said. Was that a pointed look she threw his way before she turned back to Evie? 'I only catch glimpses. To see someone's future it helps to be near them or touching them. Or to be connected to them in some way.' Another look in his direction, which made him turn his head and start admiring the cushions strewn along the back of the sofa. 'And even then,' he heard Issa sigh, 'Lucas is right, things do change according to the choices that people make.'

That one was definitely aimed at him. He took the hit. He deserved it.

'OK, enough about Sybll shortcomings,' Flic interrupted. 'Are you going to tell us what the hell happened?' She was leaning against the wall by the window, her arms still crossed, shooting daggers at him and something altogether more lethal at Evie. It had been a year since Lucas had seen her. She hadn't changed one bit. She was still sharp as a shadow blade. And just as unforgiving. He was only glad that she hadn't answered the door armed with one.

'Yeah, I'd like to hear what happened, so I know what may or may not be coming,' Jamieson added, winking at Issa.

Lucas studied the boy lounging on the beanbag. He was a Shapeshifter. Easy to tell; the scent of him and the extra-fast heartbeat gave it away. Lucas normally didn't have a problem with Shapeshifters. Neena was a Shapeshifter and the only member of the Brotherhood he actually liked, apart from Grace. He felt a sudden sharp pain in his side as if someone had twisted a knife into his gut. He still didn't know what had happened to either of them – whether he should even be thinking about them in the present tense. He shook his head. He needed to focus. There was nothing he could do for them now. And everyone in the room was looking at him expectantly.

He took a deep breath. 'I was sent to kill Evie.' No one said a word. He continued, 'The Brotherhood had been looking for her for a long time. Seventeen years to be precise.'

'Why?' Flic interrupted, staring Evie up and down, her top lip curling in a sneer.

'She's the last full-blood Hunter,' he answered. *And she's the White Light*, he thought to himself. He carried on before Flic could say anything more. 'We were ordered to kill her before she could gain her full power – before she was fully trained and had made her first kill,' he said, watching the reaction from the others as he spoke.

Jamieson had drawn himself up to a sitting position, and was leaning forwards, resting on his elbows and studying Evie as though she was an exotic beast. Issa was perched ramrod straight on the sofa, as motionless as she was expressionless. Flic, he noted, had finally stopped scowling. Now she was frowning at him.

'The first time we tried to kill her we failed,' Lucas went on, remembering the attack behind the diner and how Evie, still a stranger to him then, had fought back, surprising them all. He remembered Shula lunging towards Evie and how he'd darted forwards and pushed Evie out of the way. Later he'd tried to kid himself that he had only saved Evie from

Shula's acid grasp so that he could kill her himself. Except here she was standing next to him, still alive, and here he was, ready to do whatever it took to keep her that way. Killing her had never been an option. It had just taken him a while to figure that out. He realised he'd stopped talking mid-sentence and that the others were sitting there hanging on his words, waiting for him to finish.

'Tristan sent me back to Riverview to spy on Evie and the other Hunters who were training her,' he said, leaving out the part where he had convinced Tristan to let him go, arguing that as he was half-human he'd be able to pass undetected. 'So I did,' he said, glancing at Evie out of the corner of his eye. 'I spied on her and watched her train.' He paused, swallowing uncomfortably, 'Until one day Tristan told me time was up and I needed to kill her.'

'And?' Flic demanded, hands on hips. 'What stopped you?'

Lucas frowned, not sure how to answer in a way that wouldn't have his sister launch a round of expletives at his head.

'He couldn't do it,' Issa said softly, before he could open his mouth.

Lucas shrugged. It was an answer. And it was the truth. At least, as much truth as he was prepared to tell them. He didn't expect Flic of all people to understand. And besides, it was something that he himself couldn't even put into words. How could you describe a feeling that made every other feeling and thought fade to nothing? How could he explain the reason he'd chosen to walk this line, even though it would inevitably lead towards his death, when it *wasn't* reasonable? It was just a need that ran so deep, that owned him so completely, that no other action was conceivable. There was Evie and there was keeping her safe. And there was nothing else in between. If such a notion had come from anyone else he would have told them they were insane and to seek psych treatment. So he could understand Flic's fury. But there was nothing he could do about it.

'That doesn't explain why the rest of the Brotherhood are dead,' Flic shouted.

'The Brotherhood turned up just as we were leaving,' Lucas carried on quietly, 'and we had to fight our way out.'

'You got bitten?' Jamieson asked, pointing to Lucas's neck.

'Yes,' Lucas said, his fingers reaching instinctively to the puncture wounds there. At the time it had felt as if two sharpened, acid-coated needles had been shoved deep into the vein. 'But I'm fine. I wouldn't have been if Evie hadn't been there,' he added, glancing at her. She raised her eyes and he saw the shadow of a smile pass across her lips.

He only vaguely remembered the sensation of falling, the pull from the shadows, the way it had felt dissolving into darkness. And then Evie's weight on top of him, shocking him back, until he felt the hard ground beneath him once again. His face had been buried in her shoulder, and her hair, falling over them like a curtain, had almost blocked out the soft whisper of steel slicing through air above them.

'Damn Thirsters,' Jamieson said under his breath. 'There's more and more of them coming through.'

Lucas looked up sharply, 'What?'

Jamieson stared at him in wide-eyed surprise. 'They're coming through in droves. You haven't heard?'

Lucas shook his head. At the Mission the Brotherhood had been cut off from everything, focused only on their training and on tracking down Hunters.

'It's making things really difficult for the rest of us,' Jamieson went on. 'We're just trying to get by, you know, trying to keep a low profile, and they keep advertising the fact there are unhumans in town. It's not good for the rest of us.'

'Advertising how exactly?' asked Lucas, simultaneously knowing and fearing the answer.

Jamieson gave him another look, this time noticeably grimmer. 'You know Thirsters – they're not exactly fussy eaters. People are disappearing. Not just humans. There's talk that they're feeding on the rest of us too. Particularly Shapeshifters,' he grimaced.

Lucas nodded. Shapeshifter blood was reputedly the most sought-after blood in all the realms because of the way it tasted.

'It's not just Thirsters coming through. We've seen Mixen around too,' Flic added, her nostrils flaring in disgust.

'And one or two Scorpio. Though it's harder for them to pass.'

'Why are they coming here?' Lucas asked, turning to Issa for the answer.

'Why?' Flic hissed, before Issa could speak. 'Why do you think? Why are we all here? Because the Shadowlands suck. Because the Shapeshifter realm is being overrun by bloodsuckers who've drained their own lands dry and are after a tasty snack. Why wouldn't they all come here? Scorpio can get into fights and actually win. Thirsters can eat whatever they want without getting banished. Mixen can get their freak on and no one bats an eyelid. Everyone's so off their head in this town or so used to seeing crazy shit no one notices them. Who wouldn't rather be here than stuck in their own realm? Even with all this going on, even with Hunters doing their damndest to exterminate us,' she threw Evie a look, 'even with Thirsters and Mixen and Scorpio running around like they own the place, I still choose here.'

'Maybe everyone's trying to get through while they can,' Jamieson muttered.

'What do you mean?' Lucas asked.

'There's a rumour going around,' Jamieson said, his eyes flashing nervously around the room. 'People are saying that the way through is about to close.'

Lucas felt Evie stiffen behind him. 'What else are the rumours saying?' he asked casually.

'I don't know. I think I heard something about some kind of prophecy? But if what you said just now about Sybll not being right all the time is true, then maybe it's bull. Who knows?' He shrugged again. 'All I know is that it's getting really crowded in this part of town. And going out at night's starting to feel about as dangerous as walking naked through a crowd of angry, sexually frustrated Mixen.'

'Aren't Mixen always sexually frustrated?' Flic remarked under her breath.

'What else did you hear about this prophecy?' Lucas asked, ignoring Flic and trying to keep the urgency out of his voice.

'Nothing much really,' Jamieson said, shaking his head. 'It was just talk. I didn't pay it much mind. I mean people are always talking about stuff – who's fighting who, who's bitten who, who's been banished from the realms, who's got connections among the Elders, who's dating a Shadow Warrior ...' He tailed off, his eyes darting in Evie's direction.

'I heard something about a White Light.'

Lucas turned slowly towards Flic.

'Some Shifter at the club said she'd heard a Sybll talking.'

'The White Light will come and will sever the realms,' Issa suddenly whispered.

Flic snorted, 'What the hell does that mean? *Sever the realms*?'

Lucas dropped quickly to his knees by Issa's feet. 'Issa, what else do you know about this?' he asked.

'What's it to you?' Flic demanded, moving invisibly to stand by his side. 'Why are you so interested in this prophecy?' Her eyes narrowed at him in suspicion.

Lucas looked up and held her gaze, 'Don't you think severing the realms would be a good thing, Flic? You're the one who's just been talking about how dangerous it's getting with all the unhumans coming through and *getting their freak on*.'

'Wait up, I'm confused,' interrupted Jamieson. 'I thought Issa and Lucas were just trying to convince us that Sybll prophecies don't always come true – that we can change things. So why's everyone getting worked up about something Shakespeare could have written?'

'This prophecy is different,' said Issa, standing up carefully and stepping around Lucas, careful not to touch him. 'It's never changed. Not through all the ages. It's one of the marked prophecies.'

'The what?' Lucas asked, suddenly on his feet.

Issa had stopped in front of Evie. 'There are some prophecies that were written down thousands of years ago,' she said. Her voice, if he wasn't mistaken, had an edge to it – something similar to excitement, though an excited Sybll was something of an oxymoron. 'There are maybe a dozen, fewer, all from the same Sybll, and every single one of them has come true so far. She predicted the Shapeshifter rebellion almost nine hundred years ago, Hiroshima, the massacre of the Originals, every major event in the last thousand years across all the realms. These prophecies, ones made by her, are known as the marked prophecies.'

Lucas looked over at Evie. She turned her head at the same time and their eyes locked.

'But if the Sybll knew all these things were going to happen why didn't they try to stop them? I'm sure there's a fair few million people who'd be happier and, oh, let's see – maybe *still alive* – if they had,' Flic snorted.

'Sybll don't interfere, Flic, you know that,' Lucas answered tersely.

'It's not our role to change the fates of the realms. We just observe,' Issa added.

'What are you people? UN Peacekeepers?' Flic snapped back. 'So who the hell is this White Light?' she yelled, throwing her arms in the air, 'Does anyone even know? Did this great wise foreseer of the future think to give us a name? Or a date for when this severing might be occurring?'

'No, no one knows when or who it will be,' said Issa. 'The prophecies were broken into fragments and scattered many years ago. I only know one fragment of it, passed down through the generations. You need to find the rest for it to make any sense.'

'How did the Sybll manage to lose the other bits? I mean, you guys actually have foresight. You didn't see this day coming? The day when we might need to know the rest of it?'

'The Sybll didn't want it falling into the wrong hands, Flic,' Lucas spoke up for her, frowning as the pieces of the puzzle all slid into place. 'It doesn't matter, don't you see? To them, it's going to happen anyway whether anyone tries to stop it or not. If people knew who it was or when it was going to happen they'd try to stop it. And, if Issa's right, if it's marked as she says, there would be no point. It would be futile.' As he said this last part he turned to look at Evie. If it was as Issa claimed – if the prophecy was marked – then Evie was safe. She couldn't be harmed. At least, not until she had fulfilled the prophecy. Lucas turned quickly to Issa. 'Do you know where we can find the other parts, Issa? All we have to work on is a verse that we read in a book belonging to the Hunters.'

Issa was staring at Evie now. 'I know only that the White Light was said to be a child of two warriors. The last Hunter.'

Flic's mouth fell open. She rolled her eyes and groaned. 'You have got to be kidding.'

'Are you saying what I think you're saying? Jamieson asked, standing shakily. 'Is it Evie? Is that who the prophecy is talking about? Is it her?'

'Yes,' Lucas answered. 'She's the last pureblood Hunter.'

'She's the White Light,' Issa said in wonder.

'And yet, dear brother,' Flic said, glaring at Lucas, 'despite knowing this, you still didn't find enough reason to kill her.' She moved in a heartbeat, so fast she was just a blur. But Lucas anticipated her and was quicker, his hand reaching and pulling Evie behind him, out of Flic's reach.

Flic tipped her head back and laughed as if it was all a joke but her dark eyes were flashing fire.

'I'm not going to let you hurt her, Flic,' was all Lucas said in response, feeling Evie's fingers biting into his shoulders as she sheltered behind him.

Flic pulled a face at him. 'What about kill her? Will you let me kill her? I'd be doing us all a huge favour. The Elders would probably saint me. Or give me a medal, or whatever it is they do.'

Evie made a noise behind him, something that sounded like a growl.

Jamieson appeared and rested a hand gently on Flic's arm. A faint shimmer rose off him as if he was fighting the urge to shift. 'Flic, come on,' he said, 'we don't even know what this prophecy means for sure. Don't you think we should find out before you start attacking and, er, killing people? Especially if the person in question is your brother's girlfriend?'

Flic glared at him and then, shrugging her arm free of Jamieson's hold, she crossed over to the window where she stood with her back to them, her arms crossed, looking out through a crack in the blind.

'Issa,' Lucas said, still keeping one eye trained warily on Flic, 'can you help?'

Issa regarded him for a moment, before nodding. 'I'm not sure. I could try going back to the Sybll lands to see if I could find someone who might know more. But you can't come with me, Lucas.' She held up a hand, seeing he was about to argue with her. 'It's too dangerous for you to go anywhere near the Gateway. And she certainly can't come,' she said, nodding at Evie. 'You should both stay here.'

Flic spun around instantly, 'They can't stay here!'

'Where are they going to go, Flic?' Jamieson asked quietly. 'You said yourself that every unhuman in the realms is going to be looking for them.'

'The Hunter's not in any danger though, is she? If she's who you all say she is then no one will be able to stop her fulfilling this dumbass prophecy. She's invincible!'

'She can't do this alone,' Lucas answered.

'She needs to be with her own kind, Lucas,' Flic said, jerking her head at Evie. 'Don't look at me like that. You chose your side. Deal with it! Aren't there any Hunters she can run to?' She flashed him a snide smile, 'Surely they'd help her fulfil her destiny?'

'We can't go to them.'

She raised her eyebrows. 'Why not? Did you kill them as well?'

Lucas pressed his lips together. Risper, the only Hunter they could possibly have counted on, was dead. Not killed by him, but by a Thirster. He'd seen her die, torn apart and choked on, limbs discarded and her blood sluicing over the uneven ground, and he hadn't been able to save her because he'd been fighting for his own life and for Evie's. And Victor and Jocelyn, the only other two Hunters left, were alive but not exactly on their side. So no, there was no one else they could turn to.

'What about the rogue Hunters?'

'The who?' Lucas asked, whipping around to face Jamieson.

'There's a band of Hunters,' Jamieson said. 'Trained. Running around like the children of Blade taking out unhumans. They're on some kind of mission.'

Lucas heard Evie draw in a sharp breath behind him. Her fingers gripped his shoulder tighter.

'How do we find them?' he asked, feeling a surge of hope.

'Start a fight,' Flic answered, smiling savagely. 'You're good at that, aren't you?'

4

Evie watched the water drain first red, then pink and finally run clear down the drain, and only then did she stand up under the steaming shower and stop shaking. She rinsed her hair, took a few deep breaths and then turned off the tap. Putting the nail file down on the side, she grabbed a towel and wrapped it quickly around herself. The mirror was fogged up. She could make out her body distorted and smudged with purple bruises through the clouds of steam, but she didn't want to look down and measure the events of the last weeks in each of the marks left behind.

She hesitated before unlocking the door and stepping out into the darkened hallway, trying to pull herself together. She could hear the others talking in hushed voices in the living room as she crossed silently into the room opposite – the room that Jamieson had pointed out to her. She closed the door, feeling suddenly terrifyingly alone and wondering whether taking a shower in the house of a girl who wanted to kill her had been a wise thing to do. She'd half expected Flic to pull the shower curtain back and go all Norman Bates *Psycho* on her. Hence the nail file she'd pilfered from the cabinet and taken into the shower with her as a defensive measure. She was just about to drop the towel when someone cleared their throat behind her. She spun around. It was Lucas. He'd appeared out of the shadows by the closet.

'Here, I brought you a change of clothes,' he said, keeping his gaze level with hers and holding out a pile of black clothing towards her. 'I borrowed them from Flic. She's a bit taller than you but they should fit.'

'Thanks,' she said, reaching for the clothes. Their fingers touched as she took them, and she felt a jolt, like a static shock, shooting up her arm. She clutched the towel tighter to her body.

'I'll go,' Lucas murmured, glancing at the ground before raising his eyes to meet hers once more. He seemed nervous all of a sudden. 'You can sleep in here,' he said, nodding at the bed. 'I'll take the sofa.'

'We're staying?' Evie asked, surprised.

'Yeah, we can stay one night. Jamieson got Flic to agree. We'll leave tomorrow.'

'And find these rogue Hunters?'

Lucas nodded. 'Yes.'

Evie swallowed. What choice did they have? They couldn't stay here. Flic hated her and staying here was putting all of them in danger.

Lucas had crossed to the door and was turning the handle.

'Lucas?' Evie called out before he could leave.

He turned, his eyes settling on her face, as if he was making a concerted effort not to look down.

'Can you stay? With me? I mean, I don't think I'll be able to sleep otherwise.'

What with your crazy-ass sister threatening to kill me and all, she added silently.

He bit his lip softly, before letting out a long sigh. 'I don't think that's such a good idea.'

She felt herself flush. 'Oh.' She stared at the ground, cringing.

'Not if you're only wearing that towel. Maybe if you put those clothes on.'

She glanced up and saw the tentative half smile playing at the edge of his mouth. She smiled back, feeling a rush of relief soothe the burning in her cheeks.

'OK, turn around,' she ordered.

He did. She dropped the towel and, keeping her eyes on his back, quickly pulled on the long-sleeved top and black leggings that Flic had lent her.

'You can look now,' she said, gathering her wet hair up into a ponytail.

He turned around slowly and this time his gaze fell to her body and her heart started hammering in response. Could he hear it? He raised his eyes to hers and she could see by the look in them that he could. He was biting back the smile.

'I should shower first,' he said. 'I mean, before sleeping,' he added quickly, a blush seeping across his cheeks.

She smiled. He was still wearing his blood-soaked shirt. It was sticking to him in places like a rancid second skin. He was right. He did need a shower.

'I won't be long,' he said, sensing her unease at being left alone. He headed towards the door and then, all of a sudden, he vanished from sight. Evie stared at the empty space where he'd just been standing, wondering how he could do that – disappear at will leaving not a trace – when, just as suddenly, he reappeared, standing right in front of her. She lifted her face to his, noticing the dark trace of stubble along his jaw and the rust-coloured flecks of dried blood spattering up his neck.

'I really wish you wouldn't do that,' she whispered. 'I don't like it when you disappear – when I can't see you.'

Lucas studied her for a moment before bending and kissing her gently on the lips in reply. She felt her pulse spike into one long elevated line. Then he turned and walked out of the room leaving the door partly ajar.

She collapsed onto the bed and looked around. She guessed this was the spare room. There were boxes stacked untidily in a corner and a bookshelf stood against the wall piled high with books and magazines. A bicycle with flat tyres was leaning against one wall and an old, dust-coated computer was sitting on a desk under the window, opposite the bed.

Evie got up and walked over to it. Taped to the wall beside it were a couple of photographs. Evie leant in closer. There was one of Flic posing with her arms around Jamieson. Evie had to do a double take to make sure it was really Flic in the picture because she was grinning and not scowling. She peered more closely at Jamieson and wondered again what he was, other than insane to be dating someone so clearly psychotic. A Shapeshifter, she figured. There weren't many other options.

The photograph beneath was more battered. One edge was torn and the colour had faded. But the girl in it was recognisable as Flic. She looked about ten in the photograph. She was beaming a gap-toothed smile and had long dark hair hanging in braids. Evie wondered what had happened to make her change from the sweet and happy-looking child in the photograph to the laser-tongued fury next door. Then she remembered what Lucas had told her about his childhood. They had lost both their parents, just like she had. She couldn't suppress the surge of sympathy.

Beside this sweet, ten-year-old, alternative-universe version of Flic stood a boy, staring darkly at the camera as if suspecting it of sinister motives. He had eyes the colour of storm clouds and unruly dark hair. *Lucas*, she thought with a smile, tracing a finger over the picture. Between the two of them, kneeling down, was a woman. She had straight brown hair, almond-shaped eyes and a smile that lit the picture better than a camera flash. Their mother, obviously. Just a few years after this picture had been taken, she had been killed by Victor. Lucas had watched her die.

Victor. Evie shook her head, trying to clear it. It was still hard to believe that the man who'd walked into Joe's diner a month ago and informed her that she wasn't Evie Tremain but Evie Hunter, the last pureblood demon-hunter on the planet, the man who'd trained her – well half-trained her, half-tortured her – was the same man who'd killed her real parents too.

Evie closed her eyes. Images, jumbled and fractured, pierced through with the sounds of screaming, filled her head. She pictured Victor flat on his back, Lucas's knife pressed to his throat, blood bubbling chemically against the metal. And she pictured herself telling Lucas to let him go. What the hell had she been thinking? Victor was out there now. Looking for them. Looking for her, so that she could fulfil this damn prophecy, which no one seemed to have a clue how to do, not even a Sybll. If only they could find the other fragments of it, that might help.

A sound made her eyes flash open. She tiptoed to the door and poked her head around it. From the living room she could hear the hum and hiss of voices speaking in raised whispers. She couldn't make out what they were saying but undoubtedly it was about her. And seeing how she was the odd one out in this situation and the idea of killing her had already been voiced, she decided it was only wise to find out what exactly was being said. She eased open the door and stepped silently out into the hallway. It was Flic who was the loudest, her whisper stepping over the line into a shout that had probably woken the neighbours over in the Shadowlands.

'I can't believe you're doing this, Lucas. When you ran off and joined the Brotherhood I thought that was stupid enough, but this? This is beyond stupid. Way beyond. This is crazy!'

'Flic,' she heard Lucas respond, exasperation and tiredness flattening his voice.

Flic ignored him. 'Are you trying to save her because you couldn't save mum? Is that what this is all about? You think that if you save Evie it will make all your guilt go away?'

'Don't,' Lucas hissed through clenched teeth.

There was a brief pause before Flic spoke again, quieter now. 'Lucas, you're my brother. Do not ask me to stand by and let you do this. I'm not going to allow you to kill yourself. For who? For what? For *her*? For some ridiculous notion you have of love? Of saving this world?'

'Flic,' she heard Lucas say, 'you knew when I joined the Brotherhood there was a risk of something happening to me. There was always a possibility – a strong possibility – that I was going to die. Look at dad. It's not a career choice you make with a pension and retirement to the Shifter realm in mind.'

'Yes, but at least that was about revenge, Lucas. That I could understand. This – this I refuse to.'

'It's about more than revenge now. Don't you see that at least? The realms should be severed. We don't belong here.'

'Speak for yourself,' Flic shot back.

'We're not human, Flic. Not fully. We don't belong in this realm,' Lucas answered calmly.

'Well, where do we belong?' Flic shouted, 'The Shadowlands? We wouldn't be welcome there even if a grey wasteland with no housing and no sanitation was somewhere I actually wanted to live. And now you say I can't live here. So where am I supposed to go? Where do I belong, Lucas? Where do *you* belong?'

Evie could feel her palms sweating. She felt like one of the helplessly frozen mannequins from Victor's boutique, standing there helplessly behind the door.

'Flic, this whole conversation is pointless,' Lucas answered. 'The realms are going to be split. The prophecy is marked. It's going to happen.'

'OK,' Flic said. 'If it's going to happen as Issa says, it's going to happen with or without you. If she's it, if she's the White Light – she'll sever the realms without you. So why do you need to help her? Answer me that.'

He didn't answer her that. No one answered in fact. Everyone had fallen silent and suddenly the only noise Evie could hear was the waterfall rush of blood in her ears. She shrank further back into the shadows, holding her breath, waiting, wishing she could turn invisible like Lucas.

Finally she heard Jamieson mumbling something and under the cover of his mumble she started tiptoeing quickly towards the bedroom.

She closed the door behind her, turned around and let out a scream.

5

'Jesus!' she said, clutching a hand to her heart and falling back against the door.

Lucas was standing in the centre of the room, arms crossed over his chest, fixing her with a cool stare. He'd showered. His hair was brushed back from his forehead in wet streaks and he was wearing a faded black T-shirt and a pair of dark sweat pants.

'How did you ...?' she stopped. She understood. He'd done his turn-invisible, slink-into-the-shadows and pass-her-in-the-hallway trick. Damn it. So he knew she had been eavesdropping. Was he angry? She couldn't tell. She took a step towards him and then stopped. She didn't want to get too near. It would put her off. Just looking at him was putting her off. Even through her tiredness, even with her heart still beating as though it could see a finish line up ahead, she couldn't help but register how much she longed to be in his arms. Proximity would only make saying what she had to say harder.

'You can't do this,' she blurted. 'Flic's right. It's insane. It's like she said – if the prophecy is marked, if it's meant to happen, then there's no need for you to be involved. It will happen with or without you.'

Lucas regarded her for a long moment, his head tipped slightly to one side, then he took a step towards her, his hands coming to rest lightly on her shoulders. 'Do you want me to stop?' he asked in a neutral voice, his eyes locked on hers. 'Do you want me to walk away?'

She drew in a breath and tried to drop her gaze but it was impossible – he had her hypnotised with those slate-grey eyes of his. 'No,' she said, shaking her head. 'But Lucas, that's just me being selfish – worse than selfish.' She swallowed down the wedge of guilt that had got stuck in her throat. It didn't budge. 'I just don't want to do whatever this is I'm doing alone.'

'You won't have to,' he said, his lips so close to her own that it made her lose her focus. 'I made my choice and you're it.'

Her stomach dropped away, whether through relief or something else she couldn't tell.

'Even if you sent me away I wouldn't go,' he continued, his hands tightening on her shoulders. 'Ever since I first saw you there's been something holding me to you. I don't know what. And I don't fully understand it. All I know is that I couldn't walk away now even if I wanted to. I told you before that I would do whatever it took to keep you safe, that I would fight whoever was trying to hurt you – human or unhuman, demon or monster – and I will.'

'But what if ...?' she stuttered before falling silent. All she could hear in her mind was Flic telling Lucas that he was going to get himself killed.

Lucas's fingers squeezed her tighter. 'I'm not going to die,' he said in such a low voice it came out as a growl.

Evie took a deep breath. 'Lucas, if there's a chance,' she said, 'even the smallest chance, that by fulfilling this prophecy you'll get hurt then I don't care how marked this prophecy is, I don't care whether every damn Sybll in the world tells me it's going to happen, I won't let it.'

He didn't say a word. He just considered her, his face inches from her own, their breathing running in unison.

'OK,' he finally said.

'OK,' she repeated, hearing the wobble in her voice. 'Glad we're clear about that.'

Slowly he drew her into his arms, pulling her close until her head was buried under his jaw. She felt his lips press against the top of her head, could hear his heart beating loud and strong beneath her ear. She pushed back suddenly so she could look at him again.

He wasn't smiling. But then neither was she. She studied him – the iron cast of the shadows under his eyes, the paleness of his skin under his tan. He took her hand and led her to the bed. She sat down beside him, their shoulders brushing.

'So, the way through?' she asked. 'I didn't want to give your sister any more reason to shoot me her Gorgon stare, so I didn't ask earlier, but what was

Jamieson talking about when he mentioned the way through? Is it the same thing Issa was talking about – this Gateway?'

Lucas nodded. 'Yes. It's how unhumans get here. How, all unhumans travel into this realm. The way through. Some people still call it the Gateway.'

She couldn't help but snicker. 'The Gateway? What does it look like?'

'I've never seen it. I've never been through it. Tristan explained it to me once as a break in the fabric of the universe.'

Her eyebrows rose another inch.

He laughed gently. 'Imagine it like a rip in a blanket.'

'And what's on the other side of that rip?'

'The Shifter realm. And from there, there are other Gateways through to the other realms.'

'How were they made – these rips?'

Lucas drew his shoulders up and then let them drop, shaking his head, 'No one knows. They've just always been there.'

'What are the Shadowlands like?' Evie asked next.

Lucas frowned, his gaze dropping to the floor. 'They're wastelands – barren, wild. It's a place where the sun never seems to rise or set. Permanent dusk. It's nothing like here. There are no cities or houses to speak of. It feels like waking up on the dark side of the moon – everything's in shadow, freezing cold.'

He shuddered, then looked up at her, 'It's the most lonely I've ever felt.'

Evie took a long, slow breath. 'You've been there?' She shook her head. 'When?'

'The accident that killed my mother.'

Evie stared at Lucas's hands gripping the edge of the bed. She reached out and placed her own hand over his.

'I was thrown clear when the car flipped. I don't remember it clearly – I was in the car one second and then I was gone. I think I must have passed out because the world wasn't spinning and I wasn't in the car anymore, I was somewhere else. And I knew, it was funny, I knew straight away that it was the Shadowlands, as if a part of me deep inside recognised it as home.'

He was staring straight ahead at the door, his eyes glazed. Evie's hand tightened around his. 'You must have been terrified.'

A small frown line appeared between his eyes. 'Yes, I was scared. It was just a desert as far as the eye could see, and so cold and so grey, and I was completely alone. But I wasn't afraid of that. The only thing I was scared of was not being able to find a way back. I was only there a minute – maybe less – but it was the most scared I've ever been.' He broke off again, his jaw tensing. 'And then I was back. Just like that, without any warning. I was lying on the ground – in some wet leaves, the taste of earth in my mouth.' He closed his eyes. 'The car tyres were still spinning, which is how I knew I hadn't been gone long. I crawled. I couldn't walk, I couldn't get up, so I crawled. And my mum was ...' He broke off and swallowed and Evie realised she'd been holding her breath. 'I sat there and I held her hand and I watched her die.'

Evie squeezed her eyes shut. When she opened them again Lucas was staring at the door opposite. She reached a hand up and brushed her fingers softly along his jaw. 'You came back,' she whispered. 'You didn't stay there. You're meant to be *here*, in this world. This is where you belong.'

He looked puzzled for a moment. Then he lifted his hand and pushed a loose strand of hair out of her eyes and tucked it behind her ear. With a sigh he pressed his forehead against hers. 'We have to find a way of closing the way through,' he said. 'Mending the tear so to speak. I can't imagine what else it means when it says severing the realms.'

They fell into silence.

'It's not going to be as simple as stitching it shut is it?' Evie eventually asked, trying to break the tension.

He didn't answer her. He didn't need to.

'Do you think Issa will find anything useful out?'

He shrugged, 'I hope so.'

'Was she your girlfriend?' The question was out of her mouth before she could stop it.

Lucas tensed beside her. ‘If you want to call it that,’ he said. ‘We were briefly involved. It was never serious. It never is with a Sybll. When they can foresee your every move, your every word before you’ve even thought it, it kind of kills the romance. But for a time, yes, we were together.’

‘So you broke up with her?’ she asked, swallowing.

‘Not exactly. She saw it coming. That’s why she left me first.’

‘She saw what coming?’

Lucas paused for a long time before speaking. ‘You,’ he finally said. ‘I think she saw you coming.’

6

For a long time he watched her sleep. Watched the rise and fall of her breathing. She was quiet now. Earlier she'd been dreaming, calling out Risper's name, calling out for him too. He'd held her tighter, reassuring her with words whispered in her ear and his arms wrapped tight around her, that he was still there, until her body had relaxed and she'd fallen back into a deeper sleep.

He lay in the bed beside her, one arm wrapped around her and the other hand wrapped tight around the hilt of his blade. He couldn't sleep. His mind kept turning over the events of the last day and night, running through them again and again, trying to figure out how he could have played things differently, thinking of what Evie had told him about Neena and how she had died. He couldn't stop picturing the scene, trying to fathom why Neena had sacrificed herself so that he and Evie could escape.

The dawn had come and gone, the sun had arced across the sky and fallen low once more. Long mauve shadows were stretching themselves across the room, like fingers trying to enfold Evie in their grasp. Lucas moved, positioning himself so that they fell on him instead of her. She moaned lightly in her sleep. Her hair was falling in a dark tumble over her face. It reminded him of the picture he'd first seen of her, with a strand of hair caught like a spider's web over her eye.

He brushed it away. She looked like a normal teenage girl sleeping peacefully before waking up to a world where the only horror might be a looming exam. Well, not normal, he thought, she was far too unusual – too striking looking – for an adjective like normal to describe her, and even if she wasn't a Hunter there would still be something marking her as different, something that stood her apart from her peers. It was partly her eyes, Lucas thought. The flare of challenge within the blue. The defiant way she always stood with one hip jutting forward and her chin slightly lifted. The way she took on the world expecting it to back down and not the other way around. He smiled to himself. Then slowly eased himself out of the bed and, checking once more that she was still sleeping soundly, he crossed to the door and left the room.

Issa was back. He'd felt her return a few minutes before. She'd been gone an entire day. He hoped she'd managed to find something out in that time because they needed to move soon. The Elders were probably right this minute sat in a meeting in the Shadowlands discussing how to retaliate, lining up Shadow Warriors and sending them through the Gateway to find him and Evie and to kill anyone who stood in their way.

Lucas walked into the living room. Jamieson and Issa were sitting on the sofa. Flic was standing with her hands on her hips, tapping her foot impatiently.

'Finally,' she said, when she saw him. 'Did you sleep well?'

The inference in the word *sleep* didn't pass him by. He ignored it. 'Yes. Evie's still sleeping.'

Flic's mouth was set in a grimace. 'Well, you need to wake Sleeping Beauty. It's time to go.'

He ignored her again and instead turned to Issa. 'Did you manage to find anything out?' he asked.

She looked up at him from the sofa, her long blonde hair hanging in a twisted rope over one shoulder. 'I couldn't find anything out about the prophecy. No one knows where the other fragments are.'

Lucas studied her, trying to tell if she was lying. After all, the Sybll had no interest in the fragments being found. They were content to let fate play out while they sat and watched from the sidelines. Was Issa playing him?

'Tell him what you did find out though,' Flic urged Issa.

He saw the wary look pass across Issa's face. She cleared her throat. 'The Sybll are all seeing one thing,' she said softly.

A static charge leapt through Lucas's body. He knew from the way Issa was looking at him, with her lips pressed together so tightly that they were bleached as white as her skin, that whatever the Sybll were seeing wasn't something good.

'What?' he asked Issa, his body tensing in apprehension. 'What are you seeing?'

'An army. We're all seeing an army, Lucas. Coming through into this realm. To find her.'

It took him a while to find his voice. 'An army?' As he said the words, he suddenly remembered what Tristan had told him the last time he'd seen him – that the Elders had wanted to send an army to hunt down Evie.

'Yes. They're not recruiting a new Brotherhood,' Issa said. 'This time they're recruiting an army.'

Lucas shook his head. An army? That was impossible. The Elders had trouble recruiting one member from every realm to even make up the Brotherhood. That explained the barrel scrapings like Joshua whom he'd had to train alongside. There was no way an army was coming through. He narrowed his eyes at Issa, wondering whether she was lying in order to scare him, put up to it by Flic, who had fallen strangely silent. At the very least, Issa had to be exaggerating. An army? When had the last army been raised by the Elders? Five hundred years ago maybe? During the Shapeshifter rebellion? A thousand years ago when the Originals were culled?

'How are they recruiting an army?' he asked. 'They couldn't even recruit enough members for the Brotherhood.'

'I'm just telling you what I'm seeing,' Issa answered.

'But if the prophecy is marked,' asked Flic, 'why are they bothering to send an army? It won't change anything, will it?'

'No. But that's never stopped anyone from trying. That's why we don't get involved,' Issa answered with a frustrated sigh.

Lucas continued to study her. She was staring innocently back at him, her enormous blue eyes clouding over as if she had cataracts. He wondered what else she could see. Could she see his future? Could she see where it intersected with Evie's and the point at which it diverged? He fought the urge to ask. 'Issa,' he said instead, 'I need to find someone – another Sybll. She was in the Brotherhood. She might be able to help. I ...'

'You mean Grace,' Issa interrupted before he could even finish.

'Yes,' he said, realising she must have anticipated this question.

Issa shook her head. 'She vanished around the same time that the Elders took Tristan.'

'They took Tristan?' Lucas asked, his stomach dropping. Tristan was the man in charge of the Brotherhood. The man who had trained him and ordered him to kill Evie. 'What have they done with him?'

'They banished him to the Thirster realm,' Issa answered. And then, as she anticipated his next question, she added in a quieter voice, 'They blamed him for what happened to the Brotherhood – to the others.' She paused, 'For your betrayal and for Evie escaping.'

Lucas was acutely aware of the three of them watching his reaction, so he blanked his expression. But all he could see now in his mind's eye was Tristan, a Shadow Warrior, but a wounded one, banished to a land where he would be easy prey. Unless he found some allegiance with the Originals – the older Thirsters who no longer fed. There were worse fates, but right now Lucas couldn't think of any. And it was his fault. He was the one who should have been banished. The crime had been his, but Tristan was the one paying. He squeezed his eyes shut.

'Look,' he heard Flic say, 'we need to get going.'

'Where to?' Lucas asked, trying to clear his head of the images that were now racing through it, trying to shake off the molten layers of guilt that were settling over him.

'The Tipping Point,' Flic answered.

'What's that?'

'It's a club.'

'And there'll be unhumans there?' he asked.

'Oh yes,' Flic answered with a slow smile. 'You'll have your pick. Last time a fight broke out between some Scorpio and some redneck Thirsters and the rogue Hunters arrived and broke it up quicker than a Shapeshifter can shift. Let's just say the place is now a charred relic, as are the bodies of those unhumans.'

'You don't need to come with me,' Lucas said. 'It's going to be dangerous. Just tell me where the place is.'

'No. We're coming,' Flic snapped.

'Issa says it's fine,' Jamieson added when Lucas opened his mouth to protest.

'You'll need someone to get you past the doorman,' Flic said. 'You can't walk in there and show your face. You'll have to stick to the shadows.'

'Word's out, Lucas,' Jamieson said with a grin. 'Everyone's talking about the Shadow Warrior who ran off with the Hunter. You're famous.'

'And you have a price tag on your head.'

Lucas looked at Issa. She seemed vaguely amused. 'How much am I worth?' he asked.

'Enough for me to reconsider family ties,' Flic quipped, though Lucas wasn't entirely sure she was joking.

'Six figures dude,' laughed Jamieson.

Lucas smiled grimly. 'Let's see if we can up that.'

7

Evie looked up at him when he walked in. She was crouched on the ground, her hair dishevelled and her hands buried deep in the pockets of the blood-spattered trousers he'd been wearing the night before.

'I need a phone,' she said as soon as he appeared in the doorway. She sounded afraid. Her bottom lip was trembling slightly.

'What's up? Who do you need to call?' he asked.

'My mum,' she said, stumbling to her feet. 'My mum, Lucas! I forgot to call my mum. Crap, what time is it?' she asked, her head whipping side to side.

'It's nearly seven.'

'In the evening?' she asked, confused.

'Yes, you slept a long time.'

'Damn. You should have woken me up! I need to call her, Lucas.' She dropped once more to her knees and started rooting through the pile of discarded clothing. A sob erupted from her chest. 'If anything's happened to her ...'

'Nothing's happened to her,' Lucas said, dropping to his knees and taking her hands in both of his. 'It's OK. She's OK. I called her this morning, just after you fell asleep. I knew she'd be worried.'

'You called her?' Evie whispered, turning pale. 'What did you tell her?'

He stood up slowly. 'I told her you were with me, that we'd decided to take a little trip and would be back soon.'

Evie sucked in a breath. 'You told her that?' she said, falling backwards onto her haunches and staring up at him.

'Yeah,' he answered, with a small shrug.

'And you thought that would help how exactly?' Evie yelled. 'Are you trying to make me an orphan twice over? Did she have a heart attack?'

'No.' He paused. 'Though I don't think she likes me as much as she used to.'

She glared at him. 'I'm not sure I like you as much as I used to.'

He gave her his roguish grin in reply, pushing his hands deep into his pockets. She tried not to, but she smiled back anyway.

'I said you'd call her when you woke up.'

'And what am I supposed to tell her exactly?' Evie asked.

'Tell her the truth.'

Evie's eyebrows rose another inch in disbelief. 'The truth? What – you think I should tell her that I ran off with a boy who's half-demon because we're going to save the world together by ridding it of the really mean demons who are out to get us?'

'No,' Lucas said softly, taking a step towards her. 'Tell her you love me. Tell her that I love you and that I'm keeping you safe. And,' he paused, 'tell her we're coming home soon.'

Evie stared at him in amazement, her mouth falling open. He held her gaze, unfazed. She shook her head slowly, the blush sweeping across her face. 'But I need to tell her to get out of Riverview, Lucas. What if the Brotherhood comes looking for me? Or any of the unhumans that Flic mentioned. What if they come looking for us there? What if she's in danger?'

'She's not in danger,' Lucas answered calmly.

'How do you know?'

'Because I called Jocelyn too.'

Evie's face drained of colour. 'You called Jocelyn?'

'Evie, she's the only one who can protect your mum right now. And despite everything she's done to you, she does care about you.'

Evie grimaced.

'She told me it was already handled. Your mum's safe.' He walked to the desk and picked up his father's blade, testing the point against his thumb, more out of habit than anything else. It never lost its razor sharpness. 'Look,' he said as he sheathed it in a leather holder on his waist, 'can we talk about this when I get back?'

Evie's head flew up, 'You get back from where?'

'We're about to head out to this club. You're staying here. It's safer. Issa says you'll be fine. She doesn't see any danger for you.'

Evie jumped to her feet. 'No way. I'm coming with you.'

'No you're not.'

'Yes I am. Lucas, I'm coming with you.'

There she was, tilting her chin, standing with one hip jutting forward, taking him on as if he was the world. He sighed inwardly. The world never won against Evie Tremain. He should have learnt that by now.

'We know the prophecy is going to happen,' she said squaring up to him. 'So we know that I must survive whatever happens tonight. Theoretically, therefore, I should be the one going and *you* should be the one staying.'

He raised one eyebrow.

'But I know that's not going to happen,' she conceded. 'So I'm coming. Besides,' she said, her tone becoming more wheedling, 'you said you'd never leave me alone again. You promised.' She took a step closer towards him, sidling up to him, until she was so close her stomach was brushing the hilt of his knife. He let out a long sigh and pulled her close, feeling her smiling victory against his shoulder.

8

'Where are we going?' Evie whispered to Lucas as they hurried down the block.

Jamieson looked over his shoulder and answered her, 'The Tipping Point. It's an unhuman club.'

'Where is it?' she asked. She was still having to do a double take every few seconds, sneaking peaks out of the corner of her eye at him.

'It's downtown. It moves every night to a new location so that the humans can't find out about it and claim it for their own enjoyment.'

'You shouldn't be bringing her,' Flic muttered as she strode past them. She was wearing a see-through leopard print top and dark jeans. In heeled boots she was almost Lucas's height. Under the glow of the orange streetlights, with her geometric cheekbones, she looked like some mutant wildcat escaped from a lab and prowling the streets for dinner. Tonight her eyes were violet coloured. Last night they'd been brown, but Evie was fairly sure that both colours had been achieved by contact lenses. She had a sneaking suspicion that Flic's actual eyes were yellow. Maybe it was some Shadow Warrior gene that had skipped Lucas by. Thankfully.

Evie pressed herself closer against Lucas's side, her hip rubbing comfortingly against the hilt of his blade. She was distracted. In her mind she was still playing over the phone call she'd just had with her mother. It had contained a lot of *disappointeds*, a dozen *what about schools?* And had finished up with a cheek-flayingly cringetastic *Please, dear Lord, don't come back pregnant.*

Evie sneaked a glance at Lucas. He was walking fast, his arm tight around her, his eyes focused on the street ahead. She mentally added pregnancy to the list of things they were trying to avoid, along with being killed by demons. Her mother would be better off praying to the Lord for her to come back alive – never mind the pregnant part. And besides, it wasn't as if she and Lucas had actually done anything beyond kissing anyway. The only time they'd even properly kissed had been in the basement of her house, just after Lucas had killed Caleb. Now that the whole world seemed to be after them, trying to kill them, kissing seemed like frivolous behaviour. Having said that, now she was thinking about it, remembering what his lips had tasted like, what his hands had felt like against her skin, and what Lucas had looked like without his shirt on, maybe it wasn't so frivolous after all. Maybe kissing was exactly what they should be doing right now, rather than going out to start a fight with some unhumans. But from the looks of it, Lucas wasn't contemplating frivolity. Judging by the expression on his face and the tension running in taut lines across his shoulders, it looked as if he was contemplating a fight.

Every slight tensing of a muscle in Lucas's body she felt too, as if transmitted to her by electric current, and every step was making her feel more and more jittery, as if she was being charged with static and at any moment lightning was going to strike through the top of her skull. Sensing her unease, Lucas slowed his pace and pulled her closer, his fingers curling around the nape of her neck. A vague memory jostled in her mind of the last time she'd felt the pressure of his fingers on her neck. That time he'd done something to her that had made her black out. This time though he laid off on the Vulcan death grip, instead brushing the tip of her wounded ear with his lips. Her whole body shuddered in response and she stumbled against his side.

Flic had lent her – well, thrown at her – a pair of black high heels which she was finding it hard to walk in. Together with the pair of borrowed black jeans, which were restricting her circulation, and the spaghetti-strapped black camisole top she was wearing, she felt as if she had left the house half-dressed, late for a dancing session with a pole.

Another shudder suddenly rose up her spine, goosebumps chasing their way down her arms. It felt as if a million icicles were crystallising rapidly against her skin. She inhaled sharply. She knew it wasn't the cold that was making her shake as if she had hypothermia, or Lucas's arm around her. She was sensing what felt like thousands of unhumans close by. She squared her shoulders and forced herself to keep walking straight with her head held high. There was no way she was going to give Flic the pleasure of seeing her freak out.

Lucas sensed her fear. 'Nothing's going to happen to you, remember,' he murmured softly, his lips brushing the top of her head.

She nodded absently. Didn't he know already? It wasn't herself she was worried about.

'I have to disappear,' Lucas suddenly said, giving her waist a squeeze before letting go.

Evie turned to him, frantically grasping for his arm, but he had already vanished. She stopped in her tracks, shivering, staring in disbelief at the space beside her where he'd been just a moment before.

'Keep walking,' she heard him whisper suddenly in her ear. 'I'll just be a few steps away. I need to stay in the shadows.'

She took a faltering step forward, rounding the corner and almost stumbling to a halt when she saw the mass of unhumans before her. A line stretched out ahead of them that was so long it continued all the way around the block. They were in what looked like a film studio's back lot. Warehouses lined the street and stretched in every direction. The one before them had a metal fire escape criss-crossing it like an exoskeleton. A thin, uneven alleyway, like a knobbly spinal cord, ran between two squat-looking buildings and it was down this alley that the line snaked.

Evie darted what she hoped was a casual glance sideways. They were passing a screeching group of unhumans dressed in shimmering neon. Just as they drew parallel, one threw back her head and cackled loudly, exposing her face to the dim orange street light above her. The girl's skin was a pale shade of green. Evie eyed the others – also green. But even if Evie had been colour blind the halo of bare tarmac around them was signal enough that they were Mixen demons.

Flic strode on past them without a second glance and headed straight towards the front of the line. Evie froze uncertainly on the sidewalk.

Issa was beside her in the next moment, slipping her arm casually though her own. 'Don't just stand there. Walk!' she hissed, dragging Evie forward while simultaneously raising her arm and waving at someone in the line.

Evie clutched at Issa's arm. 'Was that the Olsen twins?' she whispered, trying to look back over her shoulder at the two short blonde girls with enormous panda eyes, wearing purple kaftans, whom they'd just passed by. 'As in, the *real* ones?'

'Who knows,' Issa shrugged, still walking, trying to keep pace with Flic. 'Most of the time it's Shapeshifters. They like to show off. Don't stare like that,' she warned, yanking Evie's arm. 'They'll realise you're not one of us. And besides,' she said with a sigh, 'it only encourages them.'

As they neared the entrance Evie felt her heart rate upping and beads of sweat starting to slide down her back. 'Is this going to work?' she asked Issa nervously.

'So far, so good,' Issa answered. 'But who knows? Everything hinges on one snap decision. You stare too long at those Mixen over there then who knows which way this could turn.'

Evie swallowed and kept moving forward, head down, eyes averted. She wished she could feel Lucas, wished even more that she could see him. She tried to sense him like she had done the other night, when he'd been fighting Shula, but there were too many unhumans around and she couldn't focus. With the suffocating panic that had a hold of her, it was all she could do to follow Issa's orders not to stare and to keep putting one foot in front of the other.

They reached the head of the line and Flic burst her way through the crowd, planting herself in front of two doormen who were standing in front of a metal door. A stream of profanities and growls erupted from the crowd behind them.

'Hey Jules,' Flic drawled, completely ignoring the protesting crowd and flashing the doorman a wide smile, 'I brought some friends. Can we skip the queue?'

9

Lucas waited in the shadows ready to pounce. The Thirster behind Evie was growling unpleasantly. Lucas's fingers were clasped around the hilt of his blade. He watched the Thirster. If it made the slightest move it would find itself missing a head. And then it would find itself on fire. He was tempted to start the fight here and now. But taking it inside was the sensible thing – away from any prying human eyes – and somewhere he could contain the mess. His training from Tristan was coming back to him instinctively. He had already scanned the entire crowd on his way past, assessing who potentially posed a threat, who would run, who was armed, who would go down easily. There were no Shadow Warriors, thankfully, besides Flic. No one who could see him hidden here in the shadows.

He rolled his shoulders, trying to loosen them up, never taking his eyes off Evie. He didn't like it – being this far from her. It reminded him of how he'd felt standing on the bank of the pond watching her dive down into the darkness – that stomach-curling sensation of having her just out of reach, the freezing fear that he might not be able to reach her in time. From over here in the shadows he could barely scent her, her heartbeat was just a rapid whisper, an undercurrent to all the other noises he was picking up – the shrieks of the Mixen further back in the crowd discussing the downfalls of getting intimate with the male of the species, and a couple of Scorpio talking in hushed voices about which realm was best for scoring drugs. Some young Shapeshifters near the front of the line were still talking about him. Apparently the rumour had it he had slaughtered a whole army of Thirsters, drunk the blood of the Scorpio whose tail he'd chopped off and had made into a belt, and was now off enjoying a romantic honeymoon with the Hunter he'd rescued.

He laughed under his breath, imagining what Evie would say if she could hear. No doubt she'd ask to see the Scorpio-skin belt. She was looking around nervously now. From the way her eyes kept skirting over the alley he guessed that she was trying to sense him, but her eyes flew right by him. Issa had stepped between her and the Thirsters and was shielding her partly from sight. He stared at Issa's blonde head, half masking Evie's darker one, and another wave of unease washed over him. What if Issa had been right about the army? What if she wasn't trying to scare him?

He didn't have time to think about it, however. Whatever Flic had said had worked. The doorman was standing aside to let her and the others into the club. Lucas readied himself, waiting for Jamieson's signal. As soon as he saw it, he moved, crossing the alley unseen and ducking beneath Jamieson's arm as he held the door open wide for Evie and Issa.

He moved fast down the corridor, the neon lights affording no cover. He would be a dark blur, a shadow flickering against the wall. The girls sitting by the cloakroom were busy though. Their heads were bent and they were giggling over something. They didn't look up as he flew past and slipped behind some Shapeshifters, following them through a heavy fire escape door and into the club.

He found himself on a concrete landing, at the top of some stairs. There were at least five hundred unhumans beneath him, all lit ghoulishly by strobe lighting. He scanned the crowd, his eyes lighting on a group of Thirsters hanging around the edge of the dance floor. They were slightly anaemic looking, clearly on the prowl, even though it was forbidden. A group of young Shapeshifters, barely old enough to shift, were dancing right next to them, totally oblivious to the fact they were being eyed up like dancing entrées.

Lucas spotted the leader of the Thirsters easily – a skinny boy in his early twenties with auburn hair, wearing a dirty white tank top. The saliva was dripping from his fangs. He'd do, Lucas thought to himself, already at the top of the stairs. One fewer Thirster in this world. Not exactly a tragedy. The Shapeshifter kids would live to shift another day.

Lucas was down the stairs and moving swiftly through the crowded dance floor towards the Thirsters before he noticed the projection on the wall. A wildly dancing Shapeshifter bumped into his shoulder and lurched with a confused yelp backwards, unable to figure out what the invisible obstacle in his way was, but Lucas kept standing there unmoving, staring at the wall.

Staring at himself.

10

They started walking down a narrow corridor towards another door at the far end. Evie could hear the thump of loud music and the tribal drum beats of what sounded like a thousand unhumans stampeding just the other side of it. The sweat was turning to ice against her spine. A blast of wind whipped past her, making her shiver. She kept walking, Issa ushering her forwards. Just before the door there was a cloakroom. Two girls were sitting outside, heads bent over an iPad.

'He's so freaking hot,' one said, grasping the screen and pulling it closer. 'I really hope they don't kill him. Maybe they could just banish him. Hell, I'd take banishment, even to the Thirster realms, if I got to stare at him all day long.'

Evie peered over Jamieson's shoulder trying to see who they were talking about, but Issa pulled her back out of sight, frowning hard at her.

'Oh hey, Flic!' the other cloakroom girl said, glancing up and noticing them. 'Watch out tonight, there's like totally loads of Scorpio deviants wandering around looking for some action. Jules keeps letting them in.'

'Thanks for the tails up,' Flic said, moving swiftly past them. 'Think I can handle a Scorpio.'

'Flic, no fighting!' the girl called after her. 'You know the rules.'

'Hey, Jamieson, looking hot, I like the shift,' the other shouted.

'Brad Pitt – if only it was actually him,' the other girl sighed.

'Hey, how do you know I'm not the real Brad Pitt?' Jamieson asked, laughing.

'As if Flic could land Brad Pitt,' the first girl said, snorting through her nose.

Issa was already pushing her way through the door, so Flic's answer was muted by the noise that boomed out. As she followed after them, Evie glanced down at the iPad the two girls were looking at and felt her heart smash into the roof of her mouth. She had guessed right. They were looking at pictures of Lucas. Even upside down there was no mistaking those sullen grey eyes and razor-sharp cheekbones. A hand on her arm alerted her to the fact she had stopped walking and was staring dumbly, her mouth hanging open. Issa yanked her through the door before the two girls on cloakroom duty could notice.

'Did you see that?' Evie gasped. 'They were looking at pictures of Lucas. Why were there photographs of Lucas on Face ...' She stopped mid-sentence, her words evaporating instantly into the whirl of noise and flashing lights that assaulted her. Before them was an enormous concrete shell of a room. Strobe lights strung from the ceiling were flashing pink, red and green over the pulsating crowd below. The entire floor space looked like a heaving sea of hurricane debris – green gyrating bodies forming a mass in the centre around which a five-metre radius of empty dance floor had opened up.

Running along one wall, with a crowd three deep pushing against it, was a makeshift bar. The bar staff behind were shimmering like heat mirages as they flipped bottles and slapped drinks and change down onto the counter.

Evie scanned the crowd immediately below her, spotting three or four famous faces, whether Shapeshifters or the real thing she couldn't tell. Over in one corner was a small group of pale-looking kids. They were noticeable because they were the only people not moving in the entire place – they were just standing there rigid, dressed in an assortment of questionable clothing. Only their eyes were moving, roving across the crowd as if searching for something. Or someone? Evie could make out the pinprick irises of the girl closest to her and then the flicker as a tongue darted out and licked a pointed incisor. She gripped Issa's hand. 'What are they doing in here?'

Issa followed her gaze. 'Thirsters are allowed in too. So long as they abide by the rules.'

'The rules?'

'Yes. No eating on the dance floor. Or anywhere else for that matter.'

'But they look like big cats eying up the impalas at the watering hole.'

'They won't dare,' Issa said, nodding up at the ceiling. Evie glanced upwards. Hanging from the beams above them were rows of industrial-sized stage lights.

'UV?' Evie asked.

'Yes,' Issa nodded. 'For emergencies. The way things are playing out I think they're going to be used tonight.'

'Where's Lucas?' Evie asked. She scanned the crowd again trying to see him or sense him, but with the flashing lights and all the unhumans it was impossible to feel anything other than the icy drip of terror coagulating in her veins.

'He's down there somewhere,' Issa answered. 'It's OK,' she added. 'In about two minutes Flic's going to start a fight with that boy over there.' She jerked her chin in the direction of the Thirsters on the edge of the dance floor. 'And Lucas is going to end it.'

Evie turned her head. Issa was pointing at a wiry boy with auburn hair and a pointy chin, dressed in a grubby tank top and skinny leather trousers. All of a sudden Evie's attention was caught by something else, something far more alarming than the group of Thirsters below them. 'Oh my God!' she cried out.

Flic, who was standing on her other side, whipped around, her mouth twisted in a snarl.

'I'm on the wall,' Evie said, pointing with a trembling hand to the wall behind Flic.

'Jesus!' Flic swore as she spun back around and looked in the direction Evie was pointing. 'I told Lucas we shouldn't bring her here!'

'Why am I on the wall?' Evie asked, trying not to panic at the sight of her face projected ten metres high onto the warehouse wall.

As she watched, the image dissolved in a cheap slideshow effect of snowflakes and, pixel by pixel, a brand new image formed over the top. This time Lucas was staring out at them, his face twenty metres wide, his dark-grey eyes seeming to burn a hole right through her. Evie registered in some recess of her mind that several people had started whooping on the dance floor below. The image of Lucas fuzzed out and dancing psychedelic swirling hearts appeared in its place. At the same time the thumping house track that had been playing scratched to a stop and a new track started up – a souped-up version of a Celine Dion song. The dance floor went wild. Evie shut her eyes and tried to wake up. When she opened them she saw the psychedelic hearts were no longer swirling. Now they were bleeding, raining great crimson drops, which together with the red strobe effect that had ramped up to full throttle, created the sensation that the entire warehouse was filling up with blood.

'Jamieson, get her out of here!' Flic shouted over the music and the whoops.

'No, I'm not leaving,' Evie answered, pulling her arm out of Issa's grip.

Flic was suddenly right there, in her face, her violet eyes flashing. 'Do not think,' she hissed, 'that because your photograph is on the wall in high-definition glory surrounded by love hearts you are welcome here. Though those imbecile Shifters down there might think it's the most romantic thing since Edward Cullen impregnated Bella Swan do not be fooled into thinking you are safe. You are walking meat. You are the impala. In fact, you are a lame impala, dripping blood. And if they scent you, they will each and every one of them – Thirster, Mixen, Scorpio, Shadow Warrior, Shifter – take you down. Do you understand?'

Evie swallowed and nodded.

'Jamieson,' Flic said, not taking her eyes off of Evie, 'take her and leave. Now please.'

'Take her out the back way, Jamieson,' Issa cut in. 'There's a crowd of Mixen about to come through that door up here – in thirty-eight seconds from now to be precise. You take her that way and Evie gets recognised.' She paused, shooting a nervous glance at him. 'It doesn't end so well for you. If you go out the back, you'll be fine.' She smiled at them reassuringly as they headed for the stairs. 'Just remember to duck!' she called to their backs.

11

He was dissolving into a sea of bleeding hearts while a song about love lasting a lifetime played in the background. And now Evie had appeared on top of him, thirty metres high. It was the same photograph that Tristan had given to the members of the Brotherhood, right before he'd ordered them to kill her.

Lucas turned quickly back towards the stairs to head Evie and the others off before they got inside. If Evie walked in here she'd be recognised in seconds. Why the hell hadn't Issa seen this? It wasn't exactly hard to miss. Damn the Sybll and their faulty, inexact visions. He wove through the crowd, his eyes on the door, willing Evie not to walk through it, but it was already too late. She was standing at the top of the stairs, staring open-mouthed at the photograph of herself projected onto the wall. He watched her grab Issa's arm and point, and then saw Flic spin around and bark an order at Jamieson.

But Evie wasn't moving. Instead she was throwing back her shoulders and arguing with Flic. *Damn it.* Lucas pushed past a crowd of Scorpio, ignoring their flicking tails and grabbed the banister. They needed to leave. Now. Before someone spotted her. The fight could wait. He was about to launch himself up the stairs three at a time when he finally saw Evie nodding in agreement and Jamieson taking her quickly by the arm. Lucas froze, waiting for them to turn and leave. But instead Jamieson was pulling her towards the stairs, heading in his direction, down into the club. What was going on? Why weren't they leaving? He looked up at Flic and Issa, wondering if maybe Issa had seen something coming. And, as if on cue, the door behind them exploded open and a swarm of Mixen burst through screeching with laughter, their green skin pulsing a toxic warning under the strobe lights. Lucas thanked Issa silently for the heads up.

He let Jamieson and Evie pass him by, resisting the urge he had to reach out and take Evie by the arm and pull her towards him. Instead his fingers trailed the air behind her. He didn't want her distracted. He wanted her to keep walking and get the hell out of this place. If he let her know that he was there, right next to her, shadowing her every move, she might change her mind. Knowing Evie, she *would* change her mind. So he stayed invisible, following them as they made their way across the dance floor towards the rear exit.

Jamieson skirted wide of the Thirsters and the Mixen, pulling Evie through a group of Shifters whose wall of shimmer offered some cover. Finally they broke free of the crowd and he could see them heading towards the green glowing exit sign up ahead. He was wondering whether it was now safe to leave them and head back into the club to start this fight when a curtain of shimmer erupted suddenly out of nowhere blocking their path. Evie stumbled backwards, almost banging into him. The shimmer faded almost instantly and two Shapeshifter girls appeared. Lucas was already beside Jamieson and Evie, standing there invisible, sword raised.

'Oh my God!' shrieked the first girl. 'You're so that girl! You're so her. Aren't you?'

'Aren't you?' squealed the other in unison, jumping up and down.

'Er – what girl?' Evie tried.

'That girl,' the first one said, pointing one arm at the pixelating picture on the wall behind them. 'The one who Lucas Gray is going to die for!'

Lucas was holding his knife at chest height, pointing it at just the right angle to slide between the ribs and into the left chamber of the girl's heart. They were completely unaware that the person they were talking about was at that moment standing right in front of them, ready not just to die, but also to kill for *that girl.*

'Girls,' Jamieson suddenly burst out laughing, 'do you really think an on-the-run Hunter would come to a place populated by demons who want to rip her to shreds and scatter her body parts to all corners of the realms?'

The girls stared blankly at Jamieson and then frowned at Evie.

'But you look just like her,' the one with the knife against her ribs said unhappily.

Lucas didn't want to kill them. It would be like killing puppies. He took a breath, calculating whether he could knock them out instead and drag them somewhere without anyone noticing. Maybe it could look like they'd had too much tequila – be a lesson in under-age drinking. But before he could sheath his knife and bring his hands up to squeeze the nerve at the back of their necks, he caught sight of a ball of shimmer just to his left.

For half a second Lucas wondered what the hell Jamieson was doing and then he started praying that his sister's boyfriend was shifting into something good – a lion or a three-metre tall bear, anything that would send them running, screaming, in the other direction.

But Jamieson went one better.

Evie turned to look at Jamieson but he had vanished. There was just the mirror on the wall opposite and her own reflection smiling back at her. It took her a good five seconds to register that she wasn't staring into a mirror at all, but at Jamieson. He had shifted. Into her. He'd copied every detail, from the camisole strap that had slipped down her arm, to her mussed-up hair, which she'd swept over to one side in an attempt to obscure her face. The only visible difference between them was that he looked a whole lot calmer than she knew she did. And he was smiling. She was fairly certain she wasn't smiling.

'It's like totally our thing,' Jamieson said, turning to the two girls. Evie's jaw dropped. Was that what she sounded like?

'So don't copy us, OK?' Jamieson said, planting one hand on his hip. That was so drag queen. She'd have to talk to him about that. She never stood like that.

The first girl's mouth fell open like a dead fish. 'OH, MY ...'

'GOD!' the second girl chorused.

They both started shimmering wildly, like faulty Christmas lights, and in the next instant Evie was surrounded and staring back at two more reflections of herself. She felt dizzy, as if she'd been led unexpectedly into a hall of mirrors after a wild turn on a teacup ride. The two Shifters standing opposite were now admiring their arms and legs – *her* arms and legs – and groping each other's butts – *her* butt. Then, once they were done groping her body, they turned to each other and started admiring each other's eyes and eyelashes.

'I am so totally hot like this,' declared the first.

'I call dibs on the first Shadow Warrior.'

'Do you think we'll be able to bag someone as hot as him though?' the first one shrieked, grabbing hold of the other Evie's hands and pointing up at the photo of Lucas, which had appeared once again on the wall behind them.

'Ahhhhh!' they both squealed, before running off into the whooping crowd.

Evie turned to Jamieson. 'Please tell me I do not sound like that,' she said.

Jamieson gave her a lopsided grin. 'Freaking you out?'

'Yes. But thanks,' Evie said, still blinking in amazement at him. 'I think you saved my ass.'

'It's a cute ass,' Jamieson said, groping his own behind admiringly. 'Definitely worth saving.' He took her hand and started off towards the fire exit. 'Now, let's get out of here.'

'No. Let's stay,' Evie said, pulling her hand free. 'Come on, you created a great cover.'

Jamieson grimaced at her and she made a mental note to never grimace. It wasn't a good look.

'What about Flic?' she tried. 'She might need our help. Look, there she is!' Evie pointed at Flic who she'd spied wading through the crowd in their direction. Jamieson spun to look just as Flic hit the edge of the dance floor and vanished.

'Where'd she go?' Evie asked, craning her neck to see over the crowd.

'Over there,' Jamieson said, pointing.

Flic had reappeared on the other side of the dance floor. She was standing in front of the group of Thirsters, hands on her hips, smiling flirtatiously. The skinny one with auburn hair gave her a crooked smile and flashed his fangs at her. Flic smiled back – a long, seductive smile that elicited a few loud whistles from the group of Thirsters.

'What's she doing?' Evie asked, clutching Jamieson's arm.

'Oh, she's starting a fight. She claimed Lucas was good at it, but let me tell you, Flic's a pro. Normally they have her work the door at this place.'

'Seriously?' Evie asked, looking up at him in astonishment.

'Just watch,' Jamieson said, nodding his head back at Flic.

'But she's unarmed,' Evie whispered. She'd seen Lucas fighting a Thirster and it had been violent, brutal and bloody. She'd tried to kill one herself. Three crossbow arrows, including one through the brain, still hadn't been enough to finish off Joshua. She glanced at Jamieson, but he didn't look at all worried.

The auburn-haired Thirster was swaggering towards Flic now, his fangs fully out. What was that? Some kind of Thirster mating ritual? Display teeth and impress the ladies? Next he started to gyrate his pelvis in Flic's direction. She didn't look all that impressed by his moves. Evie heard Jamieson snort as Flic gave the Thirster a bored stare, raised one eyebrow, and turned swiftly on her heel.

The Thirster's friends all collapsed laughing at the brush-off Flic had given him, but the auburn-haired one hissed through his teeth, rounded his shoulders and sprung like a cat at Flic's back. Somehow though, Flic anticipated it and moved in a blur, spinning fast and delivering a kick to the Thirster's head that for certain, Evie thought, would have decapitated any human.

As it was, the Thirster flew backwards, his head snapping viciously to one side and lolling there for a second until he grabbed it in both hands and cracked it back into place.

13

Lucas had watched Flic fade and cross the dance floor. He had hesitated before following her, not wanting to leave Evie. But then he'd seen what Flic planned to do, and he dived instantly through the crowd trying to head her off. By the time he'd made it to her side, Flic was aiming a perfect roundhouse kick at the red-haired one. Lucas heard the sickening crunch of bone as her foot made contact with the Thirster's face and watched him fly backwards, his head cranked at an unnatural angle. The dance floor immediately erupted around them as people started screaming and trying to get away from the fight. Lucas forced his way through the crowd, stepping in front of the Thirster, who had wrenched his head back into position and was marching towards Flic with murder in his eyes.

Lucas didn't hesitate for even a second. His blade was out of his hand before he could even think. It flew silently, slicing through the marble flesh of the Thirster's throat as if it was no more solid than air, embedding itself up to the hilt in the concrete pillar on the edge of the dance floor.

14

Jamieson was tugging Evie through the crowd, his fingers wrapped tight around her arm. Someone bowled into her, and she felt a stinging pain as something sharp scratched her above her left eye. She and Jamieson shoved a path through the screaming people. The crowd was thinning as it streamed towards the exits and they were finally able to push their way free, when suddenly a shadow fell over them. Evie glanced up, remembering Issa's words almost too late.

'Duck!' she yelled, reaching a hand out and grabbing Jamieson, pulling him down just as something hard smashed to the ground by their feet, making a crater in the concrete floor and sending a cloud of dust up into the air.

Evie opened her eyes slowly, almost too afraid to look. It took her several seconds to piece together what she was seeing. The Thirster with the auburn hair was staring back at her unblinking. His mouth was frozen in a silent shriek, his blackened tongue lolling out of his torn-out throat. She was still staring at the frayed edge of skin and the white rope of spinal cord that was visible when someone lit the place up in a blaze of UV. She curled into a ball and closed her eyes, sealing out the light as well as what was in front of her.

When she opened her eyes again, the head was still there, the mouth still open in a rictus of terror, the teeth still glinting moistly with saliva while the skin turned slowly black and fizzled.

In the next second Evie was on her feet, stumbling backwards, away from the head. She'd made the mistake before of thinking a Thirster was dead when it hadn't been and it had come back quite literally to bite them. Even a decapitated head that was slowly cooking wasn't something she was going to get too close to.

She glanced around, blinking away the harsh lights that were making her eyes water. The warehouse had emptied in the few seconds it had taken her to open her eyes and stand. A few stragglers were dragging unconscious friends who'd been trampled in the stampede through the exit at the top of the stairs. Six Thirsters lay in heaps around the dance floor, steam rising from their bodies as if they were drying themselves over heating vents.

A hand on the back of her neck made Evie jump.

Lucas steadied her, his hands coming to rest on her shoulders. His eyes were searching hers frantically, as if he was looking for something in them. Evie realised that he was probably just checking that she was the right Evie and not a

Shapeshifter. She took hold of his hands and realised he was shaking. No. That was *her* shaking.

'Are you OK?' Lucas asked, his hands suddenly cupping her face, pushing back her hair. Ouch. She let out a yelp and put a hand up to her forehead, which was suddenly stinging like crazy. She pulled it away and stared at the blood on her fingertips.

'It's OK, you'll live,' Lucas said, as he checked her carefully for other bruises and cuts, his hands running the length of her body. She wanted to stay like that for ever, feeling the gentle pressure of his fingers, letting them anaesthetise her body and her mind. But Flic was suddenly looming between them, tugging at Lucas, pulling him away. She was handing him something. Lucas took whatever it was and followed Flic across the dance floor. The two of them started dropping things onto the heaps of hissing Thirsters and Evie frowned for a moment, not understanding, until the flames started whooshing and she realised they were dropping matches. Jamieson kicked the Thirster's head towards Lucas who caught it with the edge of his foot and then dropped a lit match into its open mouth. The head burst into a ball of flame.

Through the black smoke that had started billowing over them, Evie saw Issa reaching for something stuck in one of the far pillars. She was tugging at it, trying to get it free, and when she did and turned back towards the light, Evie saw that it was Lucas's blade. She kept staring at it, glinting blue, as Issa walked towards her.

'Are they coming?' Evie asked her when she got near. 'The rogue Hunters? Are they coming?'

'Yes,' Issa nodded, handing Evie the blade before turning on her heel.

Evie stared down at the blade in her hand, wondering why Issa had given it to her and not to Lucas.

'Incoming,' Issa suddenly shouted.

The door at the top of the stairs flew open. Evie had been expecting the rogue Hunters, but it wasn't them. It was the two Scorpio doormen. They came bursting through the door, coats swinging, tails lashing behind them, as if they'd only just figured out that the screaming exodus from the club might require investigation. They skidded to a stop at the top of the stairs, staring down at Evie and Lucas, their mouths making odd gurning shapes, which Evie read as surprise.

Evie glanced over at Lucas. He hadn't bothered to fade, he was just standing there waiting, watching the two Scorpio with a weary expression on his face. He cricked his neck and shook out his arms like a boxer readying himself for the next round. Flic had paused only briefly to look up at them but had already gone back to flinging matches at the Thirsters, whose bodies were squealing and popping in response to the flames.

Evie watched the two Scorpio exchange a look, as if silently agreeing their next move. And then she saw what they were planning to do and swore under her breath. Because, even to her, it was obvious that they were going to lose. Why be heroes when they could live to be doormen another day? Obviously this thought hadn't occurred to them because they launched themselves down the stairs anyway and straight towards them.

Flic sighed as the first one came flying off the bottom step. She moved almost lazily to one side as he skidded past her and then jump-kicked him from behind, sending him sprawling to the floor. The second one, the one called Jules, dived left, his tail flicking out behind him.

Evie felt herself shoved backwards and realised that Lucas was pushing her, trying to force her out of the way. She saw his head turn left, searching the pillar for his blade, which he didn't realise that she was now holding in her hand. And in that same second she caught a flash of the future. She saw exactly what was about to happen and she hated Issa.

Before she could even open her mouth to yell, Evie watched Issa step calmly and deliberately forward into the path of the oncoming Scorpio. Evie registered Jules's tail arching over his head, and vaguely she heard Flic screaming at Issa to move. She was aware of Lucas turning and she knew that nothing he or Flic could do would be fast enough to save Issa. She watched as Jules's tail slashed down in an arc towards Issa and in the same instant Evie, knowing she had no choice, sent Lucas's blade flying like an arrow into the Scorpio's chest, just below the ribs, exactly where Victor had taught her to aim.

She watched Jules falter and stagger sideways, his hands grasping at the hilt, trying to pull it out, and she felt a vicious stabbing pain in her own chest, as if the blade had impaled her as well. The Scorpio fell to his knees, still clutching at the knife, a funny gurgling sound erupting from his throat. Thick black liquid started pouring out of his mouth, dribbling down his chin, and then the Scorpio finally fell face forwards, his head smacking the concrete with a crack. Evie raised her eyes and looked at Issa who was still standing exactly where she had been, unmoving, her eyes locked onto Evie, the faintest of smiles playing on her lips.

Evie felt like she'd fallen into a tar pit. Her limbs were suddenly so heavy she couldn't move them. She couldn't tear her eyes away from Issa. And there was just silence all around, as if everyone had breathed in and was now too frightened to breathe out. Even the Thirsters had stopped hissing and spitting. She could feel everyone staring at her, Lucas's gaze burning the back of her neck.

And then, an electric shock against her skin. She looked down. Lucas had put his hand on the back of her arm. She stared at it, feeling every millimetre of contact as if he was stroking her with feathers. Her head flew up. She heard Issa stepping towards her from across the room, her foot crunching on broken glass. Then came the sound of Flic and Jamieson breathing out in unison.

Issa stopped in front of her, a foot away. Evie's gut tightened, her blood seemed to rush faster through her veins, the metronome beat of it pulsing in her neck. She could feel every point of contact Lucas's hand was making against her skin, the heat washing up her arm.

'Why did you give me the knife?' Evie asked in a voice that didn't sound like her own.

The smile that had been threatening to vanish grew bolder. 'Why d'you think?' Issa answered.

Evie didn't respond.

'I did it to make you who you were meant to be, Evie. And believe me, things will work out better this way.'

Evie let the words sink in and then frowned at Issa, shaking her head. 'How did you know I'd do it?'

'I'm a Sybll,' Issa answered. 'I saw it.'

Evie stared into the two pale-blue abysses in front of her. Had Issa seen the future, or had she created it? There was a difference. A big difference.

Evie opened her mouth to ask her, but Issa had already turned away. 'Time to go,' she announced, stepping over the dead Scorpio's tail and heading towards the stairs.

Flic and Jamieson followed her without a word. Evie watched them all disappear through the fire exit, only Jamieson turning and lifting his hand in farewell.

15

Lucas walked straight to Jules's body, rolled it over with the tip of his boot and then crouched down beside it. Evie watched him, with the continuing sensation that a plasma screen divided them and that this wasn't happening in real life but in some alternative universe that she was observing on celluloid. The sounds around her were amplified, as if coming at her from speakers set into the corners of the warehouse. The colour of the blood pooling at Lucas's feet was brighter than blood ought to be, as though someone had mixed additives it. She could smell it from here, a rotting meat smell that smacked the back of her nose. She gagged and then vomited onto the ground, narrowly missing emptying the contents of her stomach onto the smouldering remains of a Thirster.

She wiped the back of her hand against her mouth and lifted her head. Lucas had one knee on the chest of the Scorpio and was twisting the hilt of his blade trying to pull it free. She heard the cracking snap of a bone breaking and then a squelching, sucking noise as Lucas yanked the blade out.

He paused to wipe the worst of the blood off on the side of the Scorpio's sleeve and then he stayed crouching as the body vanished, leaving just the pool of blood it had been lying in as evidence that it had ever been there in the first place. She had seen this happen before – unhuman bodies disappearing right in front of her eyes – but she still blinked in disbelief. One minute there. One minute gone. It was so neat. All evidence of what she'd done removed. Except for the blood. And the knife Lucas was holding. And the image indelibly stamped on her mind of the Scorpio's face as the knife sliced its way through his shirt, through skin and bone, and plunged straight into his heart.

Lucas stood slowly and turned to Evie, and she felt the air suck out of her own chest as if he'd just pulled the knife from her body. His expression was furious. His mouth, usually soft even when he was sad, was drawn into a long hard line. His eyes were blazing with anger. She felt a rage of her own flare in response, though it was instantly muted by the voice in her head that was screaming at her about what she had just done. What had she done? She tried not to let her gaze fall back to the floor, to the pool of blood that she could see out of the corner of her eye. She kept her gaze firmly on Lucas instead. Why was he looking at her like that? It wasn't as if she'd had any choice – or had she?

Her heart was now beating in her mouth. She could feel it – a solid object, pulsing thickly against her tongue. And her skin felt as if it had been coated in metallic paint. The air around her was charged as if a storm was about to break, making her skin tingle and itch.

Her head flew up at the same time as Lucas's, both of them turning towards the stairs. Without thinking, Evie moved, so astonished at her own speed that she stumbled to a standstill, her arms flying out to balance herself. The doors at the top of the stairs burst open and the rogue Hunters appeared.

In that first second she took in all three of them – their height, weight and clothes, what weapons they were holding and what weapons they were carrying concealed. She clocked the girl as the one to watch, the boy at the front as the leader and the boy standing just behind him as an expert in hand-to-hand combat.

The three of them stood on the landing, their eyes flickering over the scene below, taking it in as quickly as Evie had taken in them. Then, as one, their eyes flew back to her and Lucas, who had stepped out from her shadow and was standing beside her, his blade at his side.

The one at the front, the one Evie had marked as the leader, strode forwards and rested his hands on the balcony in front of him. 'Six dead Thirsters,' he said, his voice carrying easily across the empty warehouse. 'From the looks of it, two dead Scorpio. And the two most wanted people in the realms. This is a pleasant, yet unexpected, surprise.'

Evie looked up at him, studying him properly. He was in his early twenties, she guessed, maybe younger, well built, definitely well trained by the look of his arms under the close-fitting white T-shirt he was wearing. He had brown hair streaked with blonde and it was tousled – but carefully; he'd probably had to use a protractor to angle all the tufts that perfectly. Evie made a mental note to throw a lighter at his head in the event of any falling out. With that amount of product in his hair he'd undoubtedly go up in a big ball of flames. Before either she or Lucas could answer, he was suddenly on the stairs, halfway down them, heading straight towards her and Lucas. The other two were hot on his heels, fanning out as they hit the last step so that they formed a triangle around them.

The leader stopped in front of Evie, examining her as if she were some prize animal at a barn-raising, about to be taken off to slaughter. His gaze flitted over her body, weighing her, assessing her in a way that made her feel he wasn't only checking her for weapons. Then he looked up. His eyes were the first thing she noticed. They were deep-set. Green-blue in colour, with a slash of brown cutting across the iris of the left one.

'Interesting place for a date,' he said. 'Don't you two have some balcony in Verona to be hanging out on?'

'We were trying to get your attention,' Evie said, by way of explanation. 'We needed to find you.'

'Well, you found me,' the one in charge said, stretching his arms out wide. 'Here I am, baby. I'm all yours.'

Evie felt her nostrils flare in response.

'What's the matter?' he asked, coming closer until his chest was filling her field of vision. Evie held her ground, refusing to step back, tipping her chin up instead. She found herself staring at his jaw. It was blunt, what some people – her mother for example – would call chiselled.

'You don't like the familiarity?' he asked, stepping backwards so he could see her properly, or maybe he just wanted to give her the chance to check him out properly. 'How about Evie – or just plain Ev? No?' he said, taking in her glowering stare. 'Cupcake?' He smiled mockingly and then sidestepped swiftly so he was standing in front of Lucas. 'And you, what do we call you? Lucas, Luke, Lukey-baby? Dead unhuman walking?'

'You can call me anything you like,' Lucas responded evenly. 'Just depends if you want me to answer. Or if you want me to finish wiping off the blood on this blade using the inside of your throat.'

The leader turned his head sideways to look at Evie, his expression puzzled. 'Friendly guy – you actually dig this?' he asked, jabbing his thumb at Lucas. 'For real?' He shook his head in amazement but stepped back nevertheless and started studying her again, more carefully this time.

Evie felt her impatience growing. Her eyes slid downwards. Two could play this game. He was wearing scuffed-up jeans she noted, but brand new sneakers and had a tattoo on the inside of his wrist, though she couldn't quite make out what it was of. He was an inch or so shy of Lucas in height and maybe a few pounds heavier, though all muscle, testified by the ridges of his stomach, clearly outlined through his T-shirt. He bore several scars – one visible on his neck that looked like it could be a Thirster bite, another on his forearm that looked like a Mixen burn. She recognised it because she had a similar scar on her own arm in the shape of a hand. There was a battered leather sheath on his waist, the hilt of a knife visible, but otherwise no other weapons.

'You seem to know all about us,' she said, raising her eyes and forcing herself to look indifferent. 'So are you going to bother introducing yourself?'

'We're the rogue Hunters,' he said, flashing her a smile.

She arched an eyebrow. 'Is that what it says on your driver's licence?'

The boy on her right snorted through his nose.

The leader tipped his head to one side, his eyes narrowing, but the smile remained on his lips. 'I'm

Cyrus,' he finally said. 'This,' he indicated the girl on his left, 'is Vero.'

Evie glanced over. The girl was short and slight, with a shock of black hair sticking straight up on her head, shorn at the sides. She was wearing a floral dress with a lace frill, a studded collar, and fourteen-hole Doc Marten boots with bright green laces. Evie frowned. There was something weirdly, disturbingly familiar about her. She tried to think what but her focus was distracted all of a sudden by the shiny silver thing poking over the girl's shoulder, which at first sight she'd thought was a rucksack. Evie now realised with a start that it was in fact a sword. A scimitar to be precise – the word slinging itself unannounced into Evie's brain. It had a curved blade and a long handle, had probably been forged during the Crusades and looked to weigh more than the girl herself did. Evie glanced at the girl again, more nervously this time. The girl was glaring back at her, her tiny white teeth bared. Now, that was familiar too – where had she ...?

'And this is Ash,' Cyrus said, nodding at the boy to his right.

Evie dragged her eyes off the girl. She saw immediately that she had been right about the boy. He was narrow-shouldered and slight but he looked like an anatomy project of a body sculpted from wire that someone had then thoughtfully draped skin over. He was all sinew and muscle. And the way he was standing, one leg forward, bent slightly at the knee, arms hanging loosely at his sides with fingers curled into fists, only confirmed her first impression that he was some sort of martial artist. She had seen enough Bruce Lee movies with her dad to recognise the look of someone who could kill with one kick.

'And now we're through with the introductions,' Cyrus announced, 'are you going to tell us why you were looking for us or shall we just get on with killing you?' He paused, leaning into Evie, 'Well, maybe not you, but definitely him,' he said, nodding his head in Lucas's direction.

'He's on our side,' Evie burst out. 'I mean ... he's ...' She stopped. She wasn't sure whose side they were on. Were she and Lucas on the same side as these three now?

'I'm on Evie's side,' she heard Lucas say before she could figure out how to finish her sentence.

Cyrus's eyes darted to Lucas. 'Hmm,' he said, 'that's not what I hear. I hear you're one of the Brotherhood. And let's see, that would mean you and her aren't on the same side at all. It would make you and her sworn enemies, wouldn't it? Oh, and *us*.' He shrugged, rolling back his shoulders, his hand reaching for his knife and pulling it free from its sheath. 'So maybe we should ready ourselves for a fight to the death.' He spread his legs wide, pointing his knife at Lucas's throat. '*Your* death that is.'

16

Lucas made no move to counter him. His hands stayed by his sides. 'I have no allegiance to the Brotherhood anymore, nor to the Hunters,' he said in a voice that sent a shudder up Evie's spine. 'I have no fight with you.'

'Is that because you're scared?' Cyrus said. 'Sounds to me like you're scared.' He jabbed the knife in Lucas's direction.

Lucas didn't flinch as the blade grazed the air in front of his cheek.

'I think I'll have the upper hand,' Cyrus taunted. 'You're probably tired after this latest killing spree. And it's also three against one. Sure you don't want to give up now? I'll make it nice and painful if you do.'

'Three against two actually,' Evie snarled, taking a step forward and closing the distance between her and Lucas.

Cyrus hopped back, the knife dropping, regarding her with an expression that made her want to wipe it off his face with her fist. 'You're half trained, so I hear,' he said. 'You didn't get your first kill yet unless any of these are yours, which I'm doubting.' He pointed to the corner, 'So why don't you just stand to one side and observe how it's done?'

If it wasn't for the fact he was holding a knife Evie was sure he'd have patted her on the head. 'And then,' he continued, 'we'll sit you down and set you straight on the rules of being a Hunter. First one, thou shalt not get confused over which side you are on.' He turned to Ash, 'Ash, do you remember the second rule?'

'Thou shalt kill members of the Brotherhood and not sleep with them,' Ash offered.

'Yeah, that joke's kind of wearing thin,' Evie interrupted. 'And by the way, just so you know,' she said, looking back at Cyrus and pointing her thumbs at her chest, 'full power.'

Gratifyingly, his eyes grew round and his mouth gaped open for half a second. But then he recovered and the sneer was back in place. 'OK, pleasantries are over.'

Evie caught the flash of steel in the corner of her eye as the girl unsheathed her sword.

'One last kiss goodbye?' Cyrus asked, pointing his knife between them.

Evie stared at him, eyes wide. 'Whoa, are you not even going to listen?' she asked. She felt Lucas move ever so slightly, shifting himself an inch to the right, blocking her with his shoulder. Would he fade? Would he move for Vero first or Cyrus? She could probably outpace Cyrus, duck fast enough to avoid Ash's first kick or punch, but then what?

She didn't have time to process any further. Cyrus took a blindingly fast leap forward, bringing his knife to Evie's chin. She looked down. Lucas had moved too in the same instant. He was standing against her side, holding his own blade low, the tip pressed against Cyrus's stomach. She glanced up. Vero had raised the sword above Lucas's head executioner style.

'Checkmate to us I think,' Cyrus said softly. 'Now listen to me,' he said, dropping his gaze to Evie. 'If you want protection you can come with us now. Your boyfriend, however, is one of them. And what's rule number three, Vero?'

'Kill all unhumans,' the girl answered flatly.

'Jesus,' Evie said, bringing her hands quickly to Cyrus's chest and pushing him hard. He fell backwards a few steps. 'This is not Fight Club,' she yelled. 'You can break a rule for Chrissake.'

He squared his shoulders and came back at her, 'Says the master.'

Evie let out a growl of annoyance. Why had they even bothered trying to find these people?

'Look,' said Cyrus, raising his knife again and pointing it at her. 'Give me one reason why we shouldn't kill your boyfriend over there. Come on. The dark scowling face is reason enough in my book.'

She could have sworn she heard the sound of Lucas's eyes narrowing to slits.

'Come on, just one reason,' Cyrus repeated, 'and it better not include the words love, eternal or soul.'

'Whatever you might have heard,' Evie spat back, 'this is not about love.'

Even as she said it she was aware of the projection of her and Lucas on the wall above them. It had faded in the blinding UV lights but she could practically feel the hearts bleeding onto their heads.

'Ah, ah, ah – you used the love word. I warned you. Vero,' Cyrus barked. Vero stepped forward, the sword still raised above her head.

'We're trying to close the realms for good,' Evie blurted, holding one hand up to avert the blade, her other hand reaching desperately for Lucas before he could fade or do something rash like kill the girl first. Another massacre wasn't what was needed right now.

Cyrus did a double take, holding up his hand to still Vero. 'And how are you planning on doing that exactly?'

'She's the White Light,' she heard Lucas say behind her.

Vero dropped her sword with a bang to her side. Cyrus took an unsteady step back and Ash exhaled loudly. Evie stared at them all. She wasn't sure what to make of their reactions. They'd obviously heard of the prophecy though. Vero was looking at her like she was a ghost, as if she could see all the way through her. Why was she looking at her like that?

'Is it true then?' Vero asked in a shaking voice.

Evie glanced at Lucas. He was staring at her too. The anger from earlier seemed to have dissipated.

'Yes,' she answered, 'it's true.'

Vero turned to Cyrus. 'Risper said it might be true.'

Evie drew in a sharp breath. *Risper*. That's who Vero reminded her of. She looked just like Risper.

'If Risper was right, if she's this White Light – it's the prophecy,' Vero continued, turning back to Evie, her face now bright with excitement. 'She's the one who's going to sever the realms.'

'So are you going to help us or not?' Evie heard herself snap, suddenly tired of hearing the word *sever*. And the word *realm* for that matter.

Cyrus regarded her for a long moment. 'You need our protection,' he finally said. It wasn't a question. It was a statement.

'Yes.'

'Lover boy can't manage it by himself?' he asked, cocking an eyebrow at Lucas.

'We've got half the realms after us,' she answered through gritted teeth, 'in case you hadn't noticed.'

'We need to find the rest of the prophecy – we need to know how to close the way through,' Lucas cut in.

'But we don't know where to look,' Evie added.

Ash coughed and then cleared his throat. 'Cyrus, what about your mum?' he asked. 'Won't she be able to help?'

Cyrus frowned. Then he looked Lucas and Evie up and down one more time, his eyes coming to rest finally on Lucas. Lucas looked straight back at him through heavy lids, his shoulders locked with tension.

'Let's get one thing clear,' Cyrus said after a beat, sheathing his knife with a dramatic flourish. '*We* are not joining *you*. It's the other way around.' He strode off, pausing briefly to look over his shoulder at them. 'And, Romeo and Juliet, just so you know – I'm in charge.'

17

The one called Cyrus, the one who couldn't take his eyes off Evie, the one who thought he could actually fight a Shadow Warrior and win, was beginning to really irritate Lucas.

They had followed him back to his so-called hide-out. Though it was less a hide-out and more an apartment that a small child had been given free rein to decorate. It was downtown, in a warehouse not three blocks from the building The Tipping Point had occupied for the night. They had entered through a small metal door, crossed a dusty abandoned workshop, and taken a cranking goods lift to the top floor. The grille had pulled back to reveal a high-ceilinged loft space. Windows filled two walls. Exposed brickwork had been spray-painted with what Lucas assumed was an ironic attempt at graffiti art – at least, he hoped it was ironic. A kitchen took up one end of the space and an open doorway led through to a hallway that had several other doors coming off it. The floors were wood, sanded down and smooth underfoot, strewn with beanbags and items of furniture Lucas wasn't sure were for sitting on or for eating off or just for looking at. An air-hockey table took up one corner of the room, a trampoline another. The ceiling was latticed by metal air vents and pipes, over which ropes had been slung, as well as several punch bags, making it look like an ape enclosure at a zoo.

'Work-out space,' Cyrus had said, nodding his head up at the ceiling when they walked in.

Lucas hadn't replied. He hadn't said a word yet in fact. Sometime soon he thought he and Cyrus were going to have a falling out, so he was trying to restrain himself until that time came.

Evie's hand was still in his. He kept noticing the three rogue Hunters staring at them and their linked hands, as if something unfathomable, like a unicorn, had appeared in the room and they had to keep checking that it was real. The girl, Risper's sister he'd figured, was the one to watch. Her dark eyes kept tracking to him every time she thought that he wasn't looking. But he saw her. And possibly he was just suspicious but he wasn't about to let his guard down where she was concerned. There was an edge to her that he was sure was lethally sharp and given the slightest provocation she'd strike. The boy Ash looked like a fighter – as in a real fighter – someone who would probably make him break a sweat, even while he was invisible. The boy had instincts, he could tell from the way he moved and the way he listened, his head pricking up at even the slightest sound that the others weren't noticing. He was the quietest, the most contained emotionally too – hard to read. But Lucas didn't sense any immediate threat from him. At least, not yet.

He'd been wary at first of coming back with them, but what choice had they had? Flic and the others had disappeared without even a goodbye, and he knew that door was shut. There was no going back. He felt a momentary twinge of regret and maybe anger that it had ended that way with Flic but there was nothing he could do about it now. He and Evie seemed to have reached a tentative truce with these self-styled rogue Hunters. Not that he had any faith in it holding. Given the choice, he would have preferred to strike out on his own with Evie because now he felt like he was having to watch his back from every direction. But they needed to figure out the prophecy and fulfil it, and the only person who might be able to help them, other than Grace, who seemed to be missing in action, was Cyrus's mother. *Scorpio's law*, as they said in the realms.

The three rogue Hunters were facing them. There were no invitations to make themselves at home or to take a seat. He waited, Evie brushing up against his side. She did it every so often, as if checking he was still there. His fingers tightened around hers. He was there.

Vero was the first to speak. 'You know my sister? Risper?'

'Yes,' Evie answered.

The girl's bottom lip trembled. She tried to hide it. 'What's happened to her?' she asked.

Evie swallowed audibly beside him.

'She's dead, isn't she?' Vero asked in a rush.

Neither he nor Evie said anything. Evie made the slightest movement of her head. A nod.

'How?' Vero asked in a small, broken voice.

Evie took a breath. 'We were trying to get away from the rest of the Brotherhood. Risper was with us,' she said quietly.

Vero's jaw tensed, her nostrils quivering. 'What happened? What killed her?' she demanded.

'A Thirster.'

For a second Vero stood there unblinking and they watched a landslide of emotions rush across her face. Evie's hand started crushing his own. And then Vero turned her back, her shoulders heaving, and Ash stepped forward in the same instant to catch her. She fell against him sobbing, her head buried against his chest. His arms wrapped around her, and Ash half carried her out of the room, murmuring to her softly as they went. Her cries reverberated in the high space long after they'd left.

Cyrus stalked over to the window, pausing to kick the sofa on his way. He rested his head against his fist and leant against the glass.

'So they're sisters,' Evie finally said.

Cyrus turned to her slowly. 'Twins.'

It was the first time he wasn't wearing a smirk on his face.

'Oh, God,' Evie murmured.

'It wasn't your fault,' Cyrus said quietly, his eyes on Lucas.

Lucas ground his teeth and forced himself to stay silent. Cyrus gave him one last glare and then strode past the sofas towards an open-plan kitchen at the far end of the room.

'They hadn't seen each other in a while,' he remarked as he opened the fridge. He was waiting for one of them to ask why but Evie didn't say anything and Lucas wasn't about to fill the silence either.

'They fell out,' Cyrus explained as he walked back over holding two water bottles in his hand. He gave one to Evie, pointedly ignoring Lucas, and then went and dropped onto the nearest sofa, kicking his feet up onto a plastic block that seemed to serve as a coffee table.

'What did they fall out over?' Evie asked.

'Over you,' said Cyrus holding up his water bottle as if toasting her.

'Me?' Evie asked.

'Yes. Risper and Vero were both part of the original Hunters. They were only kids when Victor found them – fifteen or so – hanging out at a skate park in Baltimore.'

'Victor? You know Victor?'

'I don't know him. I know *of* him.'

'Risper and Vero – what happened?' Lucas asked suddenly. 'How did they fall out over Evie?'

Cyrus glanced up at him. 'They fell out over the White Light. Victor expected them both to protect you,' he said, his eyes lingering on Evie. 'To train you. But Vero didn't think they should risk their lives protecting something – someone – who she didn't believe in.'

Evie's head flew up.

'What evidence was there that it was you?' Cyrus shrugged, taking a swig from his water bottle. 'Vero thought it was a suicide mission. But Risper wanted it to be true. She wanted it to be true badly – she'd had enough – she wanted out and thought that if they'd found the White Light the end was in sight. So Vero walked away alone. She found us – joined us.' He put the bottle down on the table. 'For the last three years we've banded together in LA, trying to keep an eye on the way through, trying to limit the numbers of unhumans coming through. Waiting, I guess.'

'Hold up,' Evie said. 'Vero walked away? She left? Just like that? And Victor didn't come after her?'

'No.' Cyrus shook his head.

'But Victor said no one ever left. He said no one ever got away.' Her fingers were gripping the sides of the sofa. 'People ... people were killed trying to leave. He told me.' She was talking about her parents but Cyrus didn't need to know that.

Cyrus shrugged again. 'Well, Vero got away. She was one of the lucky ones. My mum too. He never managed to find her either – not for want of trying.'

Evie's voice was a hoarse whisper. 'Your mum? She was a Hunter too?'

'Yes.'

'Who is she?' Lucas asked.

Cyrus looked up at him, an annoyed expression on his face as if he'd only just remembered that Lucas was in the room. 'Her name's Margaret,' he answered.

'Margaret?' Evie said, her head flying up.

Cyrus nodded.

Evie turned to Lucas with a stricken look on her face and he dropped to her side, kneeling in front of the sofa.

'I know her. I know the name,' she said, reaching for him. 'She was in the book. The book Victor gave me with the family tree in it. She was scratched out. He told me she was dead. He made out that he'd killed her.'

'Well, she's alive,' Cyrus shrugged. 'Last time I checked anyway.'

Lucas turned instantly to Cyrus, 'Who's your father?'

'What's it to you?' Cyrus shot back, jumping abruptly to his feet so he was looming over Lucas.

Lucas stood slowly so he was standing taller than Cyrus. 'Nothing,' he said.

Cyrus turned away and started heading towards the door that Vero and Ash had disappeared through.

'Are we going to see your mum?' Evie called after him.

'In the morning. First I think your boyfriend needs some beauty sleep. There's a guest room you can use.' He turned to Evie smirking, 'Or you can bunk with me.'

Lucas lowered his head and fought the overwhelming urge to fade and reappear right in front of Cyrus brandishing the sword that Vero had dropped by the door on her way in. It was tempting. Seriously tempting. But Evie had a tight hold of his hand as though she'd guessed what he was thinking, and she was looking up at him wide-eyed and pleading – or maybe she was warning him not to react, so he ignored Cyrus and, leaning down, kissed Evie on the lips.

18

Evie stared at the bunk beds. The phrase *who's on top?* was on the tip of her tongue but she couldn't bring herself to utter it. She stood there in silence instead. The whole night had been so surreal and now it was ending with them standing here in a room with kids' bunk beds shoved against one wall and a Space Invaders arcade game pushed against the other, while Vero's cries seeped through the thinly partitioned walls.

'Do you ever have times when you just don't want to deal with what's in front of you?' Evie whispered as they stood there, hand in hand, in the centre of the room.

'Yes,' Lucas answered, laughing softly.

She looked up at him, shaking her head slowly. 'You're so lucky. You can just disappear.' She moved to face him. 'I'm always scared that you're never going to come back.'

He smiled sadly at her, tracing the back of his hand along her cheekbone. 'I'm always going to come back,' he said, before he kissed her, sending a shiver all the way through her body that almost lifted her off the ground.

She broke away after a minute and looked up at him again. 'What's it like when you fade?'

He thought about it for a few seconds before he answered. 'It's like sheltering from a storm.'

'Do you prefer it – being invisible?'

He studied her, his eyes narrowing slightly. 'I used to.'

'What happens when you die?' The question tumbled out of her before she could stop it. She instantly regretted it and her gaze fell to the floor.

'Hey, hey.' His hand was under her chin, forcing it back up. His eyes were the exact same colour as an early winter sky. 'I'm not going to die. At least,' he smiled at her, 'not for a while.'

'But when you – I mean unhumans – when you die, what happens?'

'Our bodies cross back to the Shadowlands or whichever realm we come from.' He shrugged slightly, 'I'm not sure where I'll go, being half human.'

It was her turn to frown.

'Why are we talking about this?' he asked quickly. 'Let's focus on staying alive, OK? Not on dying.' He let go of her hand and started pacing the room. 'Cyrus's mother, Margaret,' he said as he walked. 'She must have known your parents – your real parents.'

Evie tipped her head to one side. 'My parents?'

'Yes, in the book,' Lucas said, stopping in front of her. 'I remember seeing it too.'

Evie shook her head, scrunching her eyes shut. When she opened them he had started pacing once more – moving so fast he was a blur. 'You read the book? When?' she demanded.

Lucas stopped pacing. He looked guiltily her way. 'I was spying on you, remember?' he answered, giving her a tentative smile.

'You went through my stuff?'

He weighed his answer. 'It wasn't like I went through your underwear drawer.' Colour slowly infused his face. He had *so* been through her underwear drawer, and she knew it. That was where she'd hidden the damn book before she'd moved it under her bed for safer keeping.

'OK,' he admitted, 'I went through your underwear drawer but I wasn't looking for your underwear, I didn't even notice your underwear.' His head was ducked and he was looking up at her through his lashes, giving her a cheeky half smile. He had *so* noticed her underwear.

'Aha,' she said nodding. 'What else did you spy on?'

His face turned anxious but then he saw her amused smile and his shoulders visibly relaxed.

'Nothing,' he answered, holding her gaze. 'I do have some notions of chivalry. I wasn't about to follow you into the shower.'

She raised her eyebrows at him.

'Anyway,' he said, clearing his throat, 'I think you should be glad I was spying on you; otherwise you might have lost more than the tip of your ear out in that cornfield. Not to mention the fact you would have drowned if I hadn't been at the pond.'

Her gaze dropped instantly to her left hand, on the ring finger of which was a thin gold band. Her mother's wedding ring, which Victor had tossed into the pond and made her dive for. The ring that Lucas had gone back for, risking hypothermia to retrieve.

A silence fell. Vero's cries seemed to grow louder to fill it, making Evie wince and her stomach squeeze tight. Suddenly she was buried against Lucas's chest, her mouth pressed against the warm skin at the base of his throat. 'I'm sorry,' he murmured, his lips brushing her hair.

She rocked back on her heels and looked up at him. 'Sorry? About what?'

'About Issa. About what happened. I'm sorry I couldn't get to that Scorpio first.'

Evie took hold of Lucas's forearms and pushed him backwards. His hands fell to his sides and a look passed across his face that made her want to kiss him or, at the very least, to press her fingers to his lips and make him stop talking. There was so much guilt and pain in his expression.

'Lucas,' she said with a sigh, wondering if he'd ever be free of all that pain, 'you can't stop any of this. It's happening. There's nothing you or I can do about it. I'm sorry too. I hate Issa for what she did. But maybe she was right.' She let go of Lucas's arms and walked away, towards the bed so he wouldn't see her face.

'About what?' Lucas demanded, appearing in front of her again, blocking her path.

She stepped around him and sank down onto the bottom bunk, dropping her head into her hands.

'Maybe she's right about who I am,' she murmured. 'There I was thinking that my real parents were right, that I could choose who I was, that I could choose not to be a Hunter, that the whole White Light thing was just a load of crap.' She looked up suddenly and saw he was frowning hard at her, his eyes almost black in the darkened room. 'But who am I kidding? It *is* who I am. It's exactly who I am.' She paused.

Lucas didn't say a word. He just continued to stare at her.

'Anyway,' she said, forcing lightness into her voice, 'now you don't have to worry about me so much. I can look after myself. I can fight.' She pushed her hair back from her forehead where the cut had already faded to just a faint pink line. 'Look, I've almost healed. Victor said I would be stronger, quicker, better able to heal.'

Lucas dropped to his knees, pulling her hand away from her forehead and taking it between both of his own. 'Evie ...'

She shook her head. 'It's done, Lucas. What's the point in talking about it? I feel fine. I feel great in fact.'

She turned away so he wouldn't see that actually she didn't feel fine at all. She felt like she had a knife buried in her chest and that someone was slowly cranking it three sixty. She had killed someone. It didn't matter that it was a Scorpio. She had killed someone. But having a breakdown or getting all existential about it wasn't exactly tactful in front of someone who killed for a living. Who'd killed for her in fact – to protect her. And besides, it was better this way. She really believed that. If she was stronger, then Lucas would be safer. He wouldn't have to watch her back all the time like he had been doing.

'Evie, your first kill,' Lucas said, his voice strange-sounding, 'it does something to you.'

'Yeah, I know,' she said bouncing to her feet. 'I feel amazing. It's like I just got contacts or something after being short-sighted my whole life. And my body – it's buzzing. I can hear everything – I can hear the fridge humming for Chrissake – I can hear the faucet dripping in the bathroom. Do you hear that?' She left out the obvious sound of Vero's sobs coming at them unevenly through the walls because you didn't need supersonic hearing to hear those. 'It's amazing,' she said, spinning around. 'Victor was right. I wonder why? Why is that? Why does killing someone make you suddenly into this superhuman? That's weird, right? Does that not strike you as a little odd? It shouldn't endow you with power. It should take it away. It doesn't seem right.' She was aware she was pacing the room as she talked, could hear her voice getting shriller and shriller and wished she could shut up.

Lucas appeared in her way once more, causing her to pull up short. She trailed off, her head turning left and right as she unconsciously tried to figure out how to get around him so she could continue pacing. 'Yeah, strange,' she muttered to herself.

'Evie, it's OK,' Lucas said gently.

'I know it's OK,' she snapped at him.

His face fell.

'I'm sorry, I'm sorry,' she said quickly. 'I just ... I ...' She stopped and looked up at him, unable to find the words.

'I know,' he said softly. 'I felt the same after my first kill.'

She tilted her head to study him better. They'd never really spoken about Lucas's life before she met him. Now, looking up at him, she realised how completely self-centred she was being. Here she was yapping on about how her life sucked because, boohoo, she had killed something with a tail – *with a tail for God's sake* – something that was only three steps away from using it to slice someone in half, when Lucas was standing right in front of her not exactly an advert for happy, well-adjusted youth.

She let Lucas pull her over to the bed and slumped down on it. He sat next to her and put his arm around her shoulders. His fingers began massaging the base of her neck, rubbing away the tension.

'Tell me about you,' she said after a minute or so had passed. 'Tell me what it was like for you.'

He took a deep breath. She leant into him automatically, breathing in his smell, layered now and more complex; smoke and a faint metallic hint of blood rising over the normal, warmer summer scent of citrus. Through the thin cotton of his T-shirt she could feel the pulse of his blood beneath his ribs. Her fingertips stroked the inside of his wrist up to his elbow, feeling his skin contract in a shiver. There was a fine, almost invisible lattice of scars running over his arms that her fingers began tracing almost without thinking. She felt his heart rate increasing beneath her ear, his breath on her neck becoming shallower and faster.

'I always knew I was half Shadow Warrior,' he began quietly. 'My father had to start training me young. And Flic. To make sure we didn't make a mistake and give ourselves away. He wanted us to grow up in the human world – be human – or as human as we could be.'

'How did he meet your mother?' Evie asked, her head buried beneath his chin. She liked sitting like this, hearing his heart strong and loud beneath her ear and the rough texture of his voice in his chest.

'He met her here in LA,' he answered. 'He was young. He was a bounty hunter at the time.'

She sat up. A bounty hunter? Images borrowed from apocalyptic films involving men with bushy beards, large motorcycles and semi-automatic weapons leapt into her mind. She didn't think that was what he meant though. 'What exactly is a bounty hunter?' she asked.

He smiled at her. 'They're unhumans, operating outside the Brotherhood, kind of like policemen, but for our kind. They hunt down those unhumans who have broken the rules and they bring them back to face justice.'

'There are rules? There's a justice system where you come from?'

'Kind of. I mean not in any sense of the word that you understand. The rules are things like: don't eat other unhumans, don't kill without justification, don't let a human see you shift, Sybll aren't allowed to interfere in others' lives – that sort of thing. You break them, particularly the revelation law, and you have to answer to the Elders. The punishment is usually banishment to another realm. Normally the Thirster realm.'

'What's the revelation law?'

'No unhuman is allowed to reveal himself to a human.'

Evie grinned. 'Who are the Elders?'

'The Elders are a council of older unhumans,' Lucas continued, choosing to ignore her grin. 'One representative from every realm. They preside over all the realms. They have done ever since the massacre of the Originals.'

'The what?'

'Roughly a millennium ago the Originals tried to gain control of all the realms, including this one.'

'They exist? Originals? I thought they were just a myth.'

'No, they exist, but only a few of them are left. It took a whole army of Shadow Warriors and Shapeshifters to put them down. The Originals are like Thirsters, only ten times stronger. It was the first time that the realms all had to unite to fight one common enemy. After, what was left of the Originals were banished to the Thirster realm and the Elders were elected to oversee the Brotherhood, which was created to put down any threats to unhumans or to the realms – namely Hunters. Now they're ...' he stopped suddenly.

'They're what?' she asked.

'Nothing,' he answered quickly. 'Just that they're going to be looking for us.'

Evie studied him carefully, suddenly unsure. Was he hiding something from her? She looked into his eyes, searching, but all she could see was herself reflected in the grey. She put both hands on his shoulders and leaning against him pushed him backwards onto the bed. He resisted at first, shooting her a puzzled look. But she ignored it and kept pushing until he eventually gave in and lay down. She scooted over and lay down next to him, feeling his arm come automatically around her. She was struck by just how quickly and how easily they'd fallen into being with each other – completely comfortable in each other's arms, with no inhibition or embarrassment. It was like she belonged there.

'Tell me about when you were younger,' she whispered. 'What were you like?'

He laughed under his breath. 'What was I like? A loner. I mean, my mum and dad moved us to Iowa to live with my grandmother when I was about five.'

'Why?'

'Flic didn't get on so well in school. We were living here in LA at the time. She's a year older than me. She started school first and she's a little hot headed – in case you hadn't noticed. Her first week at school she managed to give another kid concussion and disappear a few times. It was a hard one for the teachers to overlook, so my parents decided to homeschool us both from that point on.'

'Oh,' Evie said, not knowing what else to say.

'And homeschooling for my dad meant teaching us how to fight. My mum was all about the Shakespeare but my dad was all about the kickboxing.'

'Why?'

'Because I guess he saw that one day we'd need it. Your dad did the same, right? Taught you self-defence?'

'Yes, but not because he thought one day I might need to protect myself from unhumans.'

'No, just from boys with less than honourable intentions.'

Evie smiled against his shoulder, 'You better watch out then,' she whispered.

Lucas laughed under his breath. 'My intentions are fully honourable,' he answered, his lips pressed to the top of her ear.

'And your mum? How did she feel about it?' Evie asked, trying to suppress the shivers riding up her spine. Now was really not the time.

Lucas sighed, 'She wasn't happy. I mean, who would be? We were kids and he was teaching us how to fight. But I think she understood that he was just trying to keep us safe. You see, he'd broken the rules by marrying a human. And by having us they broke another rule. No cross-breeding with humans. It's absolutely forbidden.'

'Wow,' Evie said, 'that's a liberal and progressive bunch of Elders you've got there.'

She felt Lucas shrug. 'It's not just the Elders. The Hunters too forbid it.'

Evie took a deep breath in. Lucky she was no longer a Hunter then.

'I think my father knew that one day the Elders would catch up with him,' Lucas continued, 'but in the end it was the Hunters who found us first. Victor. And he didn't kill my father – not then, at least. He killed my mother.'

Evie tried to keep her breathing steady. 'Is that why your father joined the Brotherhood?' she asked. 'To get revenge?'

'Yes. And no. I think he was torn between going off and trying to hunt Victor down and staying with us and trying to protect us. But then the Elders found out about us ...' Lucas paused.

'What happened?' Evie asked after a few moments of silence.

'Instead of punishing my dad for breaking the rules – which would have been banishment for him and God knows what for us – they gave him the choice to join the Brotherhood. They needed a Shadow Warrior and with him they had a Shadow Warrior with a cause. He left Flic and me in Iowa with my grandmother and he went off to fight. Then he got killed too.' Evie heard the catch in his voice but he moved quickly on. 'Flic and I moved to LA as soon as we could. She wanted to come here and I didn't want her to be by herself. I finished High School here.'

Evie smiled to herself at the thought of Lucas in High School. She could just imagine the stir he must have caused among the entire female student body.

'When I was eighteen, I joined the Brotherhood,' Lucas continued. 'And then I met you.'

There was a long pause before Evie spoke. 'I'm sorry,' she said. It was the only thing she could think to say.

'There's nothing for you to be sorry about,' Lucas said, clasping her fingers in his own. 'Sometimes in life you have to choose one path over another. The hard path over the easy one. And the hard one leads us past places we don't necessarily want to go. But at the end, you realise that if you hadn't taken that path, past the bad stuff, you'd never have got to the point you're at. To the place where you're supposed to be.' He took a breath, rolling onto his side to look at her. 'And right here, with you, is exactly where I'm supposed to be.'

Evie pressed her lips together and took in the expression on his face, the sadness buried deep in his eyes, but the layers of warmth on the surface. Then her gaze tracked to his lips and lingered there. She let out a long, slow breath. 'So, who's on top?' she asked.

19

Evie padded her way down the hallway towards the kitchen, stepping between the squares of sunlight thrown onto the floor. Judging from the shortness of the shadows and the white glare of the light it was late morning already. She'd left Lucas sleeping, had uncurled herself from his arms and prised herself off the bed. She'd never before seen him sleep. Watching him unobserved felt like she was stealing something from him. There was an innocence about Lucas when he slept. He seemed like a child – his brow smooth, his breathing regular, his lips parted ever so slightly. Though when she swept her eyes over the rest of him, Evie decided that there was also something languorous and fully adult about him as well. The way his body lay when fully relaxed, one arm flung across his chest, the other dangling over the side of the bed, his legs kicked out, one bent at the knee. When he was awake he was always so fully alert, the lines of his body locked rigid and taut, his eyes always darting this way and that, watchful and suspicious.

In sleep she caught a glimpse of another Lucas. It made her stomach stretch and tie itself into knots to contemplate him this way. A sadness weighed her down – that there was this other Lucas buried beneath the surface who she'd never get to meet. Who he'd never get to be.

As soon as she rolled away and inched herself out of his arms she felt the loss, not just of him but of whatever peace she felt when she was close to him. In its place came a rush of adrenaline and a storm of worry and fear. She was tempted to lie straight back down again and let the peace enfold her, go back to pretending that they were both something else, that they weren't lying in the bottom bunk in a stranger's house, being hunted by demons. But she didn't. She got up and walked to the door and headed to the kitchen, intending to make some coffee and wait until Cyrus woke up, at which point she was going to demand that he took them straight to see Margaret. She couldn't wait any longer. Every minute, every second in fact, that they waited to figure this out, was another minute or another second in which someone else might get hurt.

She walked into the kitchen area and stood transfixed by all the chrome shininess. She could see her own reflection stretched balloon-like across the surface of the toaster and shied quickly away from it, heading instead to the fridge and pulling open the gigantic door.

'Looking for something?'

Evie spun around, her heart flying into her mouth. Cyrus was standing in the centre of the room by the sofas. He was wearing only a pair of sweatpants and boxing gloves. Her gaze dropped straight away to his chest but only for a fraction of a second before she realised what she was doing and hauled her gaze northwards. It was a long enough glimpse, however, for her to have noticed the corrugated six-pack of muscle running across his torso and long enough also for him to have noticed she'd noticed and to start smirking.

'Just getting something to drink, if that's OK?' she answered, turning back to the fridge and cursing herself silently. Encouraging Cyrus's ego in any way was tantamount to flaying oneself alive. She straightened her face and turned back, throwing him a bored look. 'When are we going to see your mother?' she asked.

He rolled his eyes at her, 'Later,' he said. 'Want to work up a sweat with me first?'

She threw him one of her dirtiest looks. He grinned in response and pointed with his gloved hand towards a punch bag slung from one of the beams across the ceiling. 'Training. Boxing. What did you think I meant?' he asked, raising his eyebrows innocently. 'You should train – it'll be different now. You'll enjoy it. It'll be pretty intense.'

'I'm not sure there's much point,' Evie muttered as she filled a glass to the brim with milk.

'Why not?'

She slopped some milk onto the counter as she looked up at him in surprise that he'd heard. Damn.

She'd forgotten. Supersonic hearing. She would have to watch that. She set the glass down on the counter and started wiping the milk up, not sure how to answer.

'You're a Hunter,' he said, using his teeth to loosen the laces of his gloves, 'and last time I checked you were the most sought-after object in all the realms. If I were you I'd be training. Or is it that you think you're too important for that and expect us to protect you instead?' He dropped the gloves to the floor.

Evie stared at him for one second before slamming her glass down on the side and marching straight over to him. His goading expression transformed into a bemused smile as she headed towards him but she also caught the spark of uncertainty flash across his face as she got nearer. Just before she reached him she sidestepped, bringing her arm back and punching the bag in a fast one-two movement that forced Cyrus to jerk sharply out of its path. He swore loudly, catching the bag as it swung towards him on the rebound.

She waited until he was looking straight at her again, with a gratifyingly wary expression. 'I don't need protection,' she told him. 'I'm fine. That's the one thing I am sure of.' She gave him a terse smile. '*I'm* going to be fine.' And with that she walked away, hearing the angry slap of her bare feet against the wooden floorboards.

'Ooh, sure of yourself,' Cyrus called to her back.

She paused mid-step, reeled around and then strode back towards him. 'That would be a little ironic coming from you, wouldn't it?' she asked, smacking the punch bag again. God, it was good to hit something. Her body felt amped. She was fairly sure she could punch the bag into orbit without even trying. Cyrus ducked in time and caught the bag, twisting it high and holding it up out of her reach, as though he was dangling a bone above a starving dog.

'I'm not sure of myself,' she said, glowering at him. 'I just know because the prophecy is marked.' She saw his eyebrows draw together in a frown and a question form on his lips. 'You know what?' she said quickly, before he could get the question out. 'I'm so bored of hearing about this damn prophecy. Can we talk about something else instead?'

He frowned at her some more, his lips pursing, but then he released the punch bag. 'Sure,' he answered with a shrug.

She took another swipe – this time a cobra strike that Victor had taught her. Cyrus grunted and steadied the bag against his shoulder, leaning into it as she punched it another dozen times. She liked hearing the smack as her fist made contact with the leather and she liked the fact that Cyrus had to dig his heels into the ground to keep his balance.

'So, what are you doing here?' she asked, when she had finally stopped to catch her breath.

'I'm getting my butt kicked,' he laughed, rubbing his shoulder and trying to hide the wince.

'Yeah, other than that,' she said, deciding to try a jump kick without warning him. 'You know what I mean,' she said, spinning with her leg outstretched so the sole of her foot slammed into the bag sending Cyrus flying backwards, his arms flailing.

Getting his balance, he stared at her for a few seconds, his eyes narrowing slightly, before he turned and walked to the sofa to pick up a towel he'd flung over the arm. Evie watched him wipe the sweat off the back of his neck, and whipped around quickly before he could catch her looking. If she had to see him smirk just one more time she'd do away with the punch bag and start using his face instead. 'Why are you hanging out in a loft space slash playboy den?' she asked between punches.

'I need somewhere to bring the ladies,' he answered with no trace of irony.

'Ladies, plural?' Evie asked. Cyrus was running the towel across his chest now, watching her the whole time. Feeling suddenly self-conscious, she stopped punching and crossed her hands over her chest, aware of the sweat that had started to run down her collarbone and trickle towards her navel. She was still wearing Flic's black camisole top and jeans from the night before. Neither left much to the imagination in the cold light of day.

Cyrus dropped the towel, and leant over the sofa for a glass of water he'd placed on the table. She noted the long scar running across his back – a lash from a Scorpio tail it looked like – and then the ripple of muscle as he set the glass down. Her eyes were back on the punch bag, admiring the stitching, when he looked back.

'My mum,' he said, 'she had some money. She *has* some money I should say. We fixed this place up.' He wiped his arm across his face and then crossed to two ropes hanging down with hoops dangling from the ends of them. He took hold of one in each hand and pulled himself upright so her face was suddenly level with his crotch.

'Where does your mum live?' Evie asked, tilting her head back so she was looking at his face. 'Not here, I take it.'

'No. She lives about half an hour away, depending on traffic.'

'And what does she do now?'

Cyrus was stretching his arms out wide, pulling his legs up behind him to form a horizontal cross. Evie noted with annoyance that he wasn't even shaking with the tension of holding the pose. 'She has a few stores,' he grunted. 'They do pretty well.'

Evie stared at him, blinking slowly. It was possible then, she thought in amazement, to get away and create a life outside this, to be something else other than a Hunter – to be normal.

'I have a question,' she asked.

'Shoot,' he answered, moving fluidly into a handstand.

Evie momentarily lost her train of thought watching the way he moved, his arms locked straight, the muscles in his shoulders glistening with sweat. On the inside of his left arm she spied the tattoo again. It looked like some sort of bird, but upside down she couldn't see enough detail to make out what type of bird it was.

'If she was a Hunter and she ran away from all that, why are you one?' she asked. 'Why, when you have all this and could be staying at home impressing the ladies with your mad air-hockey skills or your gymnastic routines, are you out there hunting unhumans?'

Cyrus landed in a silent crouch in front of her. 'I was wondering when you'd get around to asking that,' he said with a grin.

20

Evie waited but he didn't give her an answer. Instead Cyrus reached into the back pocket of his sweatpants and drew out what looked like a white bandage. He took hold of her left hand and pulled her towards him. Evie tried to snatch her hand back but he held fast, his fingers gripping her wrist. 'You're going to hurt yourself punching like that,' he said by way of explanation as he started binding her hand and knuckles. 'You're healing quickly,' he said, lifting his eyes to her forehead.

She felt with the fingertips of her free hand along her hairline.

'Mixen burn?' he asked, his thumb stroking the uneven patch of skin on her forearm.

'Yes,' she nodded, looking down at it. It had almost faded to nothing. His thumb stopped tracing and went back to tying a knot in the bandage. 'So are you going to tell me why you're a Hunter when there's no need for you to be?'

He finished bandaging her right hand then let go of it. It flopped to her side feeling weirdly mummified. He considered her for a moment as though he was bemused that she didn't know the answer already. Then finally he spoke. 'Because, Evie, we can't fight who we are.'

She frowned at him. Victor had used those exact words just a few weeks ago. She opened her mouth to shout something back at him about screwing *who we are*, but Cyrus had already grabbed hold of a rope and was starting to shimmy up it like a spider monkey.

She watched him. 'Why does everyone keep saying that?'

Cyrus reached the top and jumped to the ground – again landing silently in a crouch beside her. 'Maybe because it's true? Listen, my mum would just love for me to go to Harvard or Yale. Hey, what's so funny?'

Evie bit the inside of her cheek to kill the smirk.

'I could have got the grades,' he went on, 'if I'd finished school. I could totally have gone there. I just chose not to – wasn't my thing. Ever since I was a kid I knew I wanted to be this. To do this. It's in my genes.' He walked over to her and pressed a finger to her chest. 'Just as it's in your genes, Evie. You're a pureblood. It's even more in your genes than mine. For you, being a Hunter is as undeniable as having blue eyes and a tight ass.' He winked and spun on his heel once more.

'But how did you know it was even who you were?' she asked, trying to twist so that her behind was out of view. 'I had no idea. If Victor hadn't come along and told me I wouldn't have just *known*. I never had an impulse to go out and kill people. I never even knew unhumans existed for God's sake. I'd have just kept living in blissful ignorance. I would have finished school, moved to New York, probably studied journalism. My life would have been normal.' Though normal, she realised as she said it, wouldn't have included Lucas.

She started punching the bag again. Cyrus was right; the bandages actually gave her more strength, more power. It would be frightening quite how much she'd grown in strength if it wasn't so exhilarating. She almost wished that Victor was there in the flesh so she could rip him a new one.

Cyrus was leaning against the sofa with his ankles crossed, watching her. 'Well, wave goodbye to the dream of normality,' he said. 'Normality is boring. You wouldn't have been happy.'

'You didn't answer the question yet,' she snapped back, angry that he was presuming to know what made her happy. Though maybe he was right. She hadn't been happy back in Riverview. But was she any happier now living this life? Her hands fell to her sides. Weirdly, and wrong as it felt to admit it, she *was* happier. But not because she was a Hunter. She was happier because Lucas was in her life. Before he'd arrived she'd been hollow, a remnant of the girl she once had been, her heart carved out by grief. Now it felt whole again. *She* felt whole again.

'How did you know you were a Hunter?' she asked, switching the conversation away from her, unwilling to share anything so personal with Cyrus.

Cyrus shook his head. 'I can't remember a time I didn't know what I was or where I came from. Other kids got told fairy tales before bed. I got told about all the unhumans out there wanting to suck my blood, slice me up and rip my head off.' He grimaced. 'My mum believed in honesty. She told me as soon as I was old enough to understand why we were running and what we were running from. I guess she thought if she told me who I was – what my history was – then there was no chance I'd follow in her footsteps.' He laughed. 'But she got that wrong. Maybe if she'd never told me I would have grown up, finished school, gone to Harvard, become a doctor or a lawyer – had that normal life you're so keen on having. But she didn't. She told me about the alternative. And, frankly, this life sounded way more fun. I mean, killing demons? Can you think of anything better?'

Evie wondered if he was being sarcastic but then she realised with a sense of unease that he wasn't joking. His face had transformed, his eyes lighting up, brimming with excitement.

'But what did your mum say?' Evie asked.

'What did *your* mum say when you ran off with a demon?' he shot back.

She frowned. 'He's not ... he's not like that. He's only half anyway. And even if he wasn't, he's ....' She faltered. What was the point of trying to explain how good Lucas was? Or how she felt about him? How could she explain to a boy who was clearly only interested in notches on his bedpost that being with Lucas made the world stop spinning out of control? That he was the one that made her believe in herself? She raised her head wearily. 'You need to give him a chance.'

'No, I don't,' Cyrus answered, walking over to the ropes.

'You're wrong about him,' Evie called after him, hearing the note of defiance in her voice.

'I'm not wrong about anything,' Cyrus answered, taking hold of the rope in both hands and sliding up it.

'Wow,' she said. 'Truly, your modesty astounds me. I bow before your humility.'

He glanced down at her, grinning, and then he let go of the rope, somersaulting twice and landing like a gold-medal-seeking gymnast right by her. She rocked back on her heels feeling his proximity and the heat from his chest, but not about to cede an inch of floor space to him.

'Why should I be humble? I am good at this.' He was leaning in towards her now, his eyes on fire, the dark slash in the left one burning like an ember. 'Really, really good at it. If you gave me a choice now I'd choose this life every time.' He paused, flashing her a knowing smile. 'And you're good at it too.

You're strong. Tell me, what did killing that unhuman feel like? It felt good, right? You feel good now too, I bet.'

She spun away.

'Tell me you didn't enjoy it,' Cyrus called after her.

She came to a sudden halt, took a deep breath and turned around to face him once more. 'I was forced to. I didn't want to.'

'How were you forced?'

'A Sybll. She gave me the knife. She deliberately put herself in danger knowing that I'd have to act.'

'Did she force you or did she just see what you were going to do anyway?'

'She set me up,' Evie yelled, amazed at the anger that had erupted out of her.

Cyrus moved quickly again. He was standing right in front of her all of a sudden and this time the smile was gone, the smugness too. His expression was full of concern. 'You're afraid,' he said softly. 'But what's done is done, Evie. You need to learn to be accountable, because from here on it's going to get messy. If you're scared to think about what you've done, if you're scared to admit what you are, you'll fail.'

She stood there as if paralysed, his words playing over and over in her head. Cyrus didn't move either. He just continued to stare at her, sweat trickling down his chest. Finally, Evie exhaled loudly and started tearing the bandages off her hands, tugging at the knots he'd made. 'Look, forget it. Forget I asked anything. All I wanted to know was why you chose this life. I mean, if you had a choice. But I guess I got my answer.'

He took hold of her wrists. She resisted again, annoyed with him. He pulled her nearer, ignoring her token protest, and started unpicking the knot he'd made, his fingers moving deftly. His body was a fraction from hers, his bare feet either side of her own. She focused on a spot on the wall over his shoulder and tried not to fidget.

'Listen,' he said. 'I didn't really choose this life. It kind of chose me. That's what I'm trying to tell you.'

She scowled at him. 'That's not true. You chose to become a rogue Hunter. You could have gone to Harvard. Apparently.'

'I became a rogue Hunter because I couldn't join the actual Hunters. Not after my mum had run off. So this was the alternative. And besides, the Hunters are old school; they fight archaically – see, big word. Plus, I'm in charge. No one tells me what to do.' He dropped her hands.

'You don't say,' she answered. 'Hey, hand me the towel.'

He flung it to her. She caught it in one hand, biting back the smile.

'I started out on my own,' Cyrus carried on, rolling the bandages up between his hands, 'hunting the streets at night, mainly targeting Thirsters who were out prowling for fresh meat. That's how I met Ash. He was picking fights downtown with Thirsters. He had some issues. One of them ate his best friend.'

'How did you know Ash was a Hunter?'

Cyrus shrugged, 'Easy. You can just feel it. There's a buzz. A chemistry.' He pocketed the bandages and leant towards her, his voice dropping so she could almost feel it reverberating in her own chest. 'You feel it between us, don't you?'

Evie crossed her arms over her chest and smiled sweetly. 'You mean that overwhelming desire I have – to punch you?'

Cyrus grinned. 'Feisty. I like that in a girl.'

She rolled her eyes. 'Just finish what you were saying.'

He paused to lick his lips, a small smile of amusement still on his face, 'You can feel it. When someone's the same as us. Like I can feel you, Evie. Something pulsing off you. It's strong.'

'That would be the waves of irritation,' she answered.

He was obviously deaf because he leant in even closer towards her so he was almost brushing her chest. 'We're like magnets. We're naturally drawn to each other.' His gaze, if she wasn't mistaken, was very much on her lips.

'Aha. Is that so?' she answered. 'Some magnets are repelled by each other you know.' And before he could make another move she marched straight past him towards the kitchen.

'Don't fight it,' he called to her back as she walked off.

She spun around, blazing, 'Oh, believe me, I'm not.'

He shrugged and she felt the low growl build in her throat.

'So you and him then?' Cyrus suddenly asked. 'What's that like?'

It took her a second to register the question. She shook her head in total disbelief. 'None of your goddamn business.'

'Does he disappear every time you get down to it?' The smug smile was back.

'Wouldn't you like to know?' She turned clumsily away hoping he couldn't see the blush spreading across her cheeks. Why in hell was everyone so interested in her and Lucas's business? First her mother and now Cyrus. She could feel another wave of blood rushing to her cheeks as she remembered the last night at Flic's. Lucas hadn't disappeared, but he had pulled away, disentangling himself from the rumpled bed sheets and her wayward limbs and getting up and crossing to the window as if there was something of vital interest hanging outside in the dawn light. She'd eventually gone to stand by him and he'd wrapped an arm around her and pulled her close. Then, after a few moments, he'd taken her hands in his and told her something along the lines of *no*.

But how was it supposed to be then? Cyrus had a point. There was no more normal. There was going to be no prom night, no series of dates and movies and desperate kisses on the veranda while her mother hovered just inside the screen door. This was it. Time was running out. But more than that, there was this feeling she had that was beyond reason. She wanted him. She wanted Lucas more than she'd ever wanted anyone or anything in her life. It wasn't even *want* she realised. It was *need*. Want was for ice cream or a chance at living a normal life. This was need. As in oxygen and red blood cells and a pumping heart. When she was in his arms she felt nothing of the fear that was slowly encroaching on them. All of that fell away, became a dream she could barely recall. But she could just imagine Cyrus choking on laughter and vomit if she told him any of this.

As if he'd read her mind Cyrus suddenly spoke. 'You think this relationship has longevity?'

'Did you have to use a dictionary for that?' she snapped back.

'You're planning marriage and babies then? Long-term commitment?'

She took a deep breath and tried not to let the irritation come out in her voice. 'I'm seventeen. I'm not planning anything.'

'Except ending a war that's been going on for centuries.'

She turned around and stared at him. He was leaning nonchalantly against the kitchen counter. 'Why do you think it involves closing the way through?' he asked.

'Well, it's not going to involve a UN delegation to the shadow world, a friendly powwow and then a signing of a treaty outside Versailles, is it?'

He grinned. 'Did anyone ever tell you you're incredibly sexy when you're being sarcastic?'

'All the time.'

His eyes darted over her shoulder towards the hallway. 'By the pricking of my thumbs something wicked this way comes,' he whispered under his breath, giving Evie a last lingering look and then strolling back towards the living-room space.

Evie frowned after him and then whipped around.

Lucas had appeared in the doorway looking tousled and disorientated by sleep. He paused to pull his T-shirt on over his head, and for a brief moment his stomach was on view. Her eyes fell to the two shallow dips either side of his hips, her breath caught, and then the T-shirt covered them.

'Issa's here. I can feel her,' Lucas murmured.

Evie's head flew up, her senses sharpening instantly as if someone had pushed the mute button off. She cursed herself. She'd failed to pick up on the fact there was an unhuman in the vicinity. She glanced guiltily at Lucas – other than him, that was. But now he had mentioned it, it was obvious. Her adrenaline had cranked up, her hands were sweaty, her breath was coming in short bursts. The problem was that she had the same reaction whenever Lucas was around too.

'How did she even find us?' Evie asked. 'Why would she come here?'

'To pour her spirit in your ear.'

Evie spun around at the same time as Lucas. They stared at Cyrus. He was standing at the window, glancing down at the street, glowering.

'What did you say?' Lucas asked.

Cyrus glanced around, smiling innocently. 'Nothing.'

Lucas turned back to Evie. 'I don't know why she's here, but I'll go and find out. You stay here,' he said, throwing a dark look Cyrus's way before vanishing.

21

It was the same every time he saw Issa, a gnawing in the pit of his stomach – an unshakeable sensation that something bad was about to happen. Maybe it was just the unease of knowing that she knew things about himself that he didn't. Or maybe it was guilt making him hug his arms around his body as he walked towards her. As if covering his heart could somehow stop her seeing inside him – seeing everything he was or was ever going to be.

She was standing in a broad patch of sunlight in the alley running in front of Cyrus's building. He wasn't going to bother asking her how she'd known where to find them. As he walked, his eyes scanned the alley, adjusting to the light, calibrating distances and depth of shadows. In daylight it was harder to hide. He needed the cover of shadows to fade completely and so automatically he assessed his environment, to check where the shadows lay – just in case. But for now he and Issa were alone. There were no other unhumans around. Or humans for that matter.

Issa was wearing large sunglasses, the kind that covered most of the face and made the wearer look like an alien. Her skin was gleaming like wet stone, and, combined with the paleness of her hair and the sky-blue dress she had on, it made him squint against the brightness.

'Why are you here, Issa?' he asked before he'd even reached her. His tone was more aggressive than he'd been aiming for, but less aggressive than he realised he was feeling.

'I needed to talk to you,' Issa answered calmly.

'What about?'

She sighed. 'Lucas, she needed to make her first kill.'

Her words brought him up short. He hadn't been going to mention that – had he? Now she'd said it though he realised that was exactly what was fuelling his anger. And he saw that inevitably the conversation would have swung to this. Issa had known that and had pre-empted him.

'Did she?' he shot back, gathering himself.

'I thought I was doing you a favour – keeping you alive – even though you seem hell bent on suicide.' Issa's voice had taken on a different tone. She was angry now too.

'What are you talking about?'

Issa ripped off her sunglasses and looked him dead in the eye. He struggled, as always, to hold her gaze. 'Without her power she was too vulnerable, Lucas, too weak. It made you weak. Now you don't need to protect her anymore – she can take care of herself.'

'It wasn't your call to make, Issa. You had no right to do what you did.'

Issa shook her head in defiance. 'Lucas, I didn't force her. She had it in her. She's a Hunter. I just tipped her towards her fate. Do you think I would have done it if I hadn't been sure of what she'd do – of how she'd react?'

He shook his head hard. 'You created her fate. You didn't give her a choice.'

She glared at him, one blonde eyebrow arched. Then she took a deep, measured breath. 'Well, you were going to get yourself killed doing what you were doing – protecting her. I saw it. So I did what I needed to do.' She shrugged as though that was the end of the discussion.

'And now?' Lucas shouted, not ready to let it go. 'Do I get to live happily ever after? Did it change anything?'

He didn't know why he was asking or why he was shouting. He didn't want to know. Did he? He wanted to turn away, vanish and head back inside to find Evie. Just trying to stay in the present was hard enough. But he couldn't move. His eyes were locked on Issa as he waited for her to respond.

She nodded almost imperceptibly. 'Something changed, yes,' she said. 'Everything's different now.'

He froze, the air sucked out of him.

'Before,' Issa said, her voice barely a whisper, 'I saw you dying.' Her blue eyes were turning milky opaque, as if she was sorting through visions, stirring them up trying to find lost images. She looked up at him suddenly, her eyes clearing back to blue. 'You were trying to protect her and there were too many of them and she didn't have her power. She was helpless and you died because of it.'

He swallowed, feeling his blood starting to hammer in his ears. 'And now?'

She chewed her lip. 'It's blurry.'

He took a deep breath and tried to keep his voice even. 'Blurry?'

'Yes. But I don't see you dying any more,' she added.

'Though that could be because you can't see anything at all? Right? On account of it being blurry?"

Her nostrils quivered.

'And Evie?' Lucas asked. 'Do you know what happens to her? Or is that all blurry too?'

Issa's gaze fell to the floor. 'I don't know.'

Lucas narrowed his eyes. Funny that her precognition should fail her now. He ran his hands through his hair, his fingers digging into his scalp, suppressing the howl of rage he wanted to let out. 'So you came here to tell me that I'm not necessarily going to die any more but you're not totally sure, and that you've no idea what might happen to Evie? You know, you're not going to be winning any Sybll awards for your predictions, Issa.'

'Usually,' Issa said, ignoring his sarcasm, 'when things are blurry it's because there are still choices to be made that could change the outcome.' She hesitated. 'You walking away, for example, leaving right now with me, could change things, make things clearer.'

'Or not, as the case may be,' he answered back.

A hurt look crossed her face. 'It would change things. I know it would. Don't do this, Lucas,' she said, her voice breaking as she spoke his name. 'It's futile, you know that, you said it yourself. That's why the Sybll hid the prophecies, to stop people from trying. From trying and failing to change what will be. Enough people have died, Lucas, because of you interfering.'

She seemed to realise she had gone too far as she stopped abruptly, biting her lip.

It felt like a thorn was stuck in Lucas's throat when he tried to swallow. 'Every single second of my life,' he said, 'I will have to live with remembering what happened to the others. With the knowledge that I could have stopped it. I see Neena and Tristan's faces every minute of the day. I hear Grace's warnings. I see Risper dying. And I know it's all on me. Because of the choices I've made, people have died. And people are paying for my crimes. And don't think for a second that I don't hate myself for that. That I don't wish I could change it. But I can't. Whatever fate is pulling Evie in this direction is also pulling me. I'm as marked as she is. This feeling I have for her isn't something I can fight. I've tried that. It's pointless. As futile as trying to change the prophecy.' He drew a breath, and let it out slowly, holding Issa's gaze. 'So the only thing I can do is keep moving forwards, make sure it does happen, sooner rather than later, and make sure that no one else gets hurt.'

A tear tracked a lonely path down Issa's cheek.

Lucas let the ache inside him subside and took a breath. Then he smiled at her. *It's OK*, he wanted to say to her, *it's OK*. But a noise made him turn his head, his ears pricking at the sound of footsteps across the concrete floor of the warehouse. He could feel Evie. She was coming towards them, getting closer. He turned quickly back to Issa. 'You should leave,' he said.

She opened her mouth to say something, then shut it and nodded once. 'Here, take this,' she said, pushing a bag quickly towards him.

He glanced down but before he could ask what it was Evie had walked up behind him and slipped her hands around his waist.

She pressed her cheek against his shoulder. 'Hi,' she said.

Lucas breathed out, feeling the heat of her body seeping into his, feeling his sense of certainty returning. 'Issa just came by to see we were OK,' he said, inclining his head towards Evie.

'I'm just leaving,' Issa added.

'Wait,' Evie called, as Issa made to leave.

Issa turned slowly back to face them, her shoulders stiff, her eyes flickering to Lucas.

'Did you see something?' Evie asked, her voice shaking. 'Is that why you're here? Is something going to happen to Lucas?'

Issa shook her head. 'No,' she said, 'I didn't see anything. I just came to bring you that.' She pointed to the bag by Lucas's feet. Then, without another word or a backwards glance at either of them, she walked off.

They watched her go and when she rounded the corner Evie turned to him. 'Did she see something? Is there anything you're not telling me?' she asked.

'No. She didn't see anything,' Lucas lied.

Evie studied him, her eyes blazing dark blue in the sunlight.

He held her gaze for as long as he could, then grabbed her around the waist and spun her towards the door. 'Come on, let's get inside.'

She hesitated for a moment as though she wanted to ask him another question but then she took his hand without a word and let him lead her back inside.

It was only in the elevator that he noticed she didn't have any shoes on. And that she was looking hot. In both senses of the word. Tendrils of hair were slicked against the white of her throat. Her thin camisole was sticking to her body, her cheeks were flushed. She looked like she'd looked last night – unbelievably desirable.

It had taken every ounce of control he possessed to back off yesterday, at just the point he thought chivalry might have completely deserted him. But he didn't want to mess things up or rush anything. He wanted her to be sure. Which reminded him, he still needed to offer Cyrus some polite warnings about what he'd do if he ever heard him call Evie sexy again.

Evie noticed him looking at her and ran a hand self-consciously through her hair. 'I need a shower,' she said. She pulled the damp top away from her body. 'And a change of clothes.'

The elevator cranked to a halt and Lucas drew back the grille, sighing under his breath as he saw Cyrus standing there in front of them. A towel was slung loosely around his waist and he was dripping wet from the shower. He looked as if he had poured half a litre of baby oil over himself and then taken up position by the elevator, waiting for them to come back.

'I don't have anything else to wear though,' Evie murmured, not appearing to have noticed Cyrus standing there half-naked and glistening in front of them. 'We didn't think of that.'

'You can borrow a shirt of mine if you want,' Cyrus grinned.

Definitely a warning was on the cards. Maybe not such a polite one either, Lucas thought to himself. He gritted his teeth and looked down, trying to stay calm, and then he noticed the bag that he was holding. He looked up, smiling. Issa's visions weren't all that faulty after all. 'No, it's OK,' he said, offering the bag to Evie. 'Issa brought us a change of clothes.'

22

She thought Cyrus was stopping for coffee, so she leapt out of the car and stood on the sidewalk, hands on hips, and blocked the entrance to the café and bookshop he'd pulled up in front of.

'We've had breakfast. We've had lunch. We've had coffee. I don't need to buy any books today and, sorry to disappoint you, but it doesn't look like they sell comics or porn in here, so can we just get going and see your mum already?'

She had never known a man take so long in the bathroom. It was nearly five o'clock and it had taken Cyrus until then to prettify himself, arrange his hair, select his outfit, drink two cups of coffee, play a game of air hockey, rile Lucas with a dozen jokes about unhumans, and then finally locate his keys and drive them across town in his top-of-the-range Prius. Evie had sat in the front feeling the pressure coming at her from all sides like over-inflated air bags. She wasn't even sure how Cyrus had managed to drive straight seeing how he'd been permanently looking in the rear-view mirror as he engaged in some sort of one-way blinking contest with Lucas.

Cyrus tipped his head to one side, cool, sea-coloured eyes appraising her. He checked his watch.

'That's where I'm heading now. You're making us late.' He nodded at the door.

Evie turned around. 'Oh,' she said. 'She works here?'

'No. She owns here.'

'Oh.'

Cyrus gave her a condescending smile and then breezed on past. Evie turned to Lucas. He gave her a small shrug and then they followed Cyrus who was holding the door open for them, one foot tapping impatiently. Cyrus waited until she'd passed, then let go of the door so it caught Lucas on the shoulder.

She heard Lucas make a sound in response, which could have been a curse, could have been him just clearing his throat. She didn't need to guess which.

'Hi Cyrus!'

Evie looked up. A tall, skinny waitress with long braids was waving at Cyrus from behind the counter. Cyrus raised a hand in greeting. Then, from out of nowhere a squealing thing came barrelling towards them on platform heels. It pulled up in front of them and Evie saw it was a small blonde girl wearing a tight, midriff-exposing white shirt.

'Hey Cyrus,' the girl said, thrusting her chest out and up towards his face. She was holding a tray on which were balanced two cups of coffee and a chocolate cupcake. Behind her, Evie could see two customers frowning at their delayed order.

'Hey beautiful,' Cyrus said, his eyes grazing the girl's breasts.

'Here to see your mum?' she asked, looking up at him with an expression that was one part hope and two parts desperation.

'Nope, I'm here to see you, Marcy,' Cyrus answered, flashing her a wide smile.

The girl's face fell. 'Marissa,' she said.

Cyrus swallowed his laugh. 'Marissa,' he said, shaking his head. 'I knew that.'

The girl scowled at him, her face scrunching up. 'Sure you did.'

Cyrus grinned, then lifted the cupcake off the tray, leaning forward as he did so and planting a kiss on her cheek. 'Is my mum here?' he asked.

'She's upstairs,' the waitress replied slightly breathlessly. Evie tried to control the eyeball roll, which around Cyrus seemed to have become an automated response, similar to a gag reflex.

They followed Cyrus's lead through the café part of the shop, between smart LA couples nursing their coffees while playing with their iPads, towards a door behind the counter. Cyrus stopped to punch a code on the security system on the wall and Evie found herself suddenly being elbowed aside by the skinny waitress with braids who planted herself securely against Cyrus's thigh.

'Hi,' she smiled, her lip-glossed lips reflecting Cyrus's nervous expression. 'Did you lose my number or something? You said you'd call,' she said. Then bending closer towards him she dropped her voice. 'The other night was ...'

Cyrus cut her off, putting both hands on her shoulders and manoeuvring her away from the door. Evie noticed his gaze fall quickly to her name badge. 'I promise I will call you, Darcy.'

The girl smiled, delirious that he'd remembered her name. Evie suppressed the third eyeball roll in as many minutes and a groan as well. Or maybe she didn't suppress the groan because Darcy the waitress suddenly turned, seeming surprised to see them there. 'Who are your friends?' she asked Cyrus. 'Are they new band members?'

Band members? Evie gave Cyrus a look and he pulled a *just drop it* face before he turned back to Darcy.

'Yeah, that's right. New band members.' He paused, before nodding his head in Lucas's direction. 'Well, he's on tryout.'

Darcy gave Lucas a quick head to toe, her eyes dilating when she reached his face. Evie felt her impatience getting the better of her. She cleared her throat and Darcy glanced at her, smiling nervously when she saw Evie's scowl.

'When are you going to be playing? When's your first gig?' she asked, bouncing on the tips of her toes.

'Oh, you know, we're still practising,' Cyrus coughed, 'gelling as a band. The new bass player needs some practice.' Cyrus punched in the rest of the code and yanked the door open hard, blocking Darcy from sight.

'Well, call me!' Darcy yelled from the other side of the door.

'Yeah, sure,' Cyrus mumbled, urging Evie and Lucas through and slamming the door shut behind them.

'A band?' Evie asked, trying not very hard to keep a straight face.

'It's a neat cover,' Cyrus answered sullenly.

She nodded, smiling. 'Sure it is.'

He was leading the way up some stairs. She watched him swagger through another doorway. Not even rock stars had egos as big as his, she suspected. He stopped outside a final door, heavily plated in some kind of metal, and leant casually against it.

'Mum, it's me,' he called. 'I'm standing outside, so put down whatever weapon you have pointed at the door. I'm coming in.'

He waited a few seconds, then, shooting a smile at Evie, he pressed down on the handle and the door swung open.

Evie inched forward to see, peering around Cyrus's shoulder. A woman was sitting facing them, leaning against a desk. In her hands was a crossbow, similar to the one Victor had given Evie to train with. It had three arrows lined up ready to fire and was tilted slightly upwards so that an arrow was aimed at each of their heads. This was Margaret then.

'Good morning to you too, mum,' Cyrus said.

'What's he doing here?' his mother asked angrily, not taking her eyes off Lucas.

She must have sensed Lucas was an unhuman. Evie appraised her. The woman's instincts were good. 'He's with me,' she said, stepping forward quickly to shield Lucas from the crossbow.

'He's with her,' Cyrus concurred.

'And who is *she*?' Margaret growled, her eyes barely flickering to Evie before returning straight away to Lucas. Evie could see the swallow of fear she tried to hide, the way her nostrils were quivering. She noted the tension in the white knuckles of her hands, wrapped around the firing mechanism. Quite clearly twenty-odd years hadn't dulled either her senses or her fear.

'I'm Evie Tremain,' Evie answered softly, her gaze glued to Margaret's hands.

Margaret's mouth tightened into a brief grimace. 'Where'd you find this one?' she barked at Cyrus.

'Oh, this one found me,' Cyrus answered, crossing over to a cabinet on the wall which seemed, from the quick glance Evie gave it, to contain a whole load of weapons. The door to the cabinet was open and Cyrus reached inside.

'You still haven't told me what *he*'s doing here,' Margaret spat, tipping her head in Lucas's direction.

Evie noticed that Margaret had the exact same eyes as Cyrus – all except for the slash of brown across the iris. She was young-looking for a mum, though Evie's frame of reference for parents was warped by her adoptive parents' ages. They had been a good decade older than most of her friends' parents. But Margaret looked to be in her mid-thirties.

'Why are you with him?' Margaret demanded.

'Um ...,' Evie cleared her throat.

'They're lovers,' Cyrus suddenly piped up, turning around with a switchblade in his hand. 'They're getting their freak on, doing the bad thing, making the sign of the two-backed demon. You name it, they're doing it.'

'Cyrus,' his mother snapped.

Lucas cleared his throat and stepped forwards. 'I'm Lucas Gray,' he said.

23

Evie turned her head slightly. Lucas had stepped silently from behind her and was now standing in the centre of the room, his head slightly bowed, his arms by his side, palms facing forwards, making it clear that he was unarmed. Though he *was* armed. She could see the shape of his knife pressed against his spine, hidden under his T-shirt.

'Why are you here?' Margaret demanded.

'These people wanted to meet you, mum.' Cyrus had put the knife back and was now examining a longer blade, with a slightly curved edge. It was glowing dimly like phosphorescence under water.

'Why?'

Cyrus smiled broadly, testing the edge of the knife against his thumb then pulling it quickly away with a wince. 'You're going to like this. Remember that prophecy you told me about years ago? The thing about the White Light? Remember when the rumours started flying around that she'd been found and you told me not to believe it because there was no way it could ever be true?'

Margaret's eyes had widened. 'Yes,' she nodded, her gaze flying back to Evie.

'Well, wait for it, it is true! Evie here is the White Light.'

The crossbow thudded into her lap as Margaret's mouth fell open. 'She's ... you're ... you're ... the White Light? You're sure?' She was looking Evie up and down, incredulous. 'The White Light was said to be the child of two warriors. There were no children born to Hunters. I would have known about it.'

'No one knew about it,' Lucas said in the voice he usually used to calm horses and dogs and occasionally her. 'Evie only found out about it herself a month ago.'

'How? Who told you this?' Margaret snapped, ignoring Lucas and focusing on Evie.

'Victor,' she answered. 'He was my trainer.'

Another swallow of fear. 'Victor? You know Victor?'

Evie narrowed her eyes at the woman. She could hear her heart beating rapidly now, the pulse of it uneven. 'Yes,' she finally answered, 'I know him.'

'He's been training her the last month, introducing her to the ways of the Hunter,' Cyrus said with a trace of sarcasm in his voice that riled her. What was he implying? She was trained. She knew what she was doing. Cyrus hadn't even seen any of her moves yet. She could take him. And his ego into the bargain.

'Who are your parents?' Margaret asked.

'James and Megan Hunter.'

Margaret's eyes grew almost as round and large as Issa's. 'James and Meg?' she exclaimed. 'Are you sure?'

'You knew them?' Evie asked, feeling her own heart starting to hammer in response.

'God, yes! Of course I know them. They ... But good Lord, I never knew they had a child.' She stopped abruptly, her gaze falling to the floor. 'What were they thinking?' she asked softly, almost to herself. Then her head shot up. 'What happened to them? Where are they?'

'Victor killed them.' Evie felt the wrench in her stomach as she said it out loud. 'I was just a baby. I don't remember them.'

Margaret stared at her, ashen faced. She shook her head, a trace of pity in her eyes. 'If I'd have known ... Cyrus, stop messing with that! It's not yours,' she snapped. 'Come and sit down.'

Cyrus dropped the knife he was playing with back into the cabinet and came and slumped in one of the two chairs placed in front of the desk, sucking the edge of his thumb which Evie saw was bleeding where he'd cut it on the knife. Margaret walked around and sat down on the other side of the desk.

'Tell me everything you know,' she said, putting her elbows on the table and clasping her hands in front of her as if she was praying. She nodded at the free chair and indicated that Evie should sit. Evie sat, glancing nervously at Lucas as she did. He moved to stand just behind her, resting a hand on the back of her chair.

'Well,' Evie began, 'we were hoping you'd be able to tell us everything you know.'

Margaret leant forward. 'How did Victor keep you hidden for so long? How did he keep it quiet?'

'I don't know,' Evie said. 'He wasn't exactly big on truth – it kind of had to be prised out of him. My whole life I never had a clue about any of this. I mean I knew I had been adopted when I was a baby. I knew that, but I never knew a thing about my real parents. I just assumed they didn't want me, they'd abandoned me, so I never bothered looking for them. And then, about a month ago, Victor showed up – he just breezed into the diner I was working in and – everything changed.' She closed her eyes briefly, remembering how he'd ordered a soya decaf latte and tipped her twenty dollars before offering her a job. A pretend job as it turned out – just a cover so he could train her. She realised she'd stopped talking. 'The same night the Brotherhood showed up and ...' She took a huge, heaving breath and felt the gentle pressure of Lucas's hand on her shoulder, 'Anyway, the long and the short of it is that Victor told me that I wasn't who I thought I was at all. That I was actually a Hunter.'

'You look so like them. I'm amazed I didn't see it.'

'I'm sorry?' Evie said, looking up at Margaret.

Margaret was smiling at her sadly. 'You look like your father, but you have your mother's smile. And her eyes.'

'That's what Jocelyn said too.'

Margaret blinked. 'Jocelyn? You know Jocelyn?'

'Yes.'

She shook her head in disbelief, 'She's still alive then?'

'Yes,' Evie said. 'She stayed in Riverview the whole time, watching out for me.' Evie frowned at herself. She didn't want to get into details about Jocelyn. That wound was still raw. Jocelyn had known all along that Victor had killed her parents but hadn't thought to tell her. Instead she'd let her think that Victor was a good guy and not the lying psychopathic nut-job that he actually was. There wasn't a rule about how forgiveness worked in situations like that. Jocelyn had looked out for her, had spent a life in tweed, playing bridge and knitting, all to ensure that she was kept safe. But after everything that had happened ... No, Evie thought, smiling grimly, forgiveness was still a long way off.

She realised Margaret was talking. 'Jocelyn and your mother were always close. Like sisters. We were brought together to train. There was your mum and dad, Jocelyn, Earl, Victor and me. Six of us. We were all teenagers at the time – about your age. I was the youngest. I was barely fifteen when we first met. They liked to start us young back then. The man who was training us ...' She broke off and Evie spotted the tremor in her shoulders that made its way into her voice. 'His name was David – he was our mentor – like Victor was to you. Victor was David's protégé even then.' Again Evie picked up the edge to her voice when she mentioned David's name. 'Victor was always following him around – a sycophantic lapdog. The two of them were desperate to figure out the prophecy, what it meant, who it was talking about.'

Margaret took a breath before continuing, 'We were living up in the Bay area, in an old school building. We spent the days training, the nights hunting. Back then there weren't so many unhumans.'

'How did you even get recruited?' Evie asked.

'Oh, I was born into it,' Margaret said, giving her a quick smile. 'My parents had been Hunters. All our parents were, apart from Victor's. He wasn't pure Hunter like the rest of us. They died when I was fifteen in a big battle with the Brotherhood.' Her eyes flew to Lucas briefly. 'And then it was my turn. In the old days being a Hunter was a family profession. An honour,' she added, answering Evie's frown, 'like generations of families going to the same college or all becoming doctors. I broke a twenty-five-generation trend by escaping.'

Evie pounced. 'Why? Why did you escape?'

She smiled again softly. 'The same reason your parents tried to, Evie. I was trying to protect my son, my unborn son.'

Evie glanced at Cyrus who was leaning back in his chair, one ankle crossed over the other knee. He blew air out of his mouth loudly.

'How old are you?' Margaret asked.

'Seventeen,' Evie answered, turning back to her.

'That's how old I was when I ran. I was pregnant. Can you even imagine what it was like? First discovering that I was pregnant? Then knowing that if I had a child I'd be bringing them into the world to be this? A Hunter?' she practically spat the last word.

Evie gulped. She couldn't imagine getting pregnant at seventeen. But she could imagine the fear of bringing a child into this world to become a Hunter because she'd already spent hours thinking about it back in Riverview, before vowing she would never do anything so stupid or selfish. She shook her head.

'No. Me neither,' Margaret said, 'so I ran. I wanted more for my child. I wanted to protect him. It's funny – you won't know what it's like to be a mother – but there is nothing you wouldn't do to protect your child. *Nothing*. Your parents helped me get away. They were the only ones I trusted – the only ones who knew why I was running. I wouldn't have been able to escape without them. I ran, first to

Europe and then, finally, when I thought it was safe, we came back here.'

'Victor told me you were dead. He told me he'd killed you for trying to escape.'

Margaret shrugged. 'Let me guess, was he threatening you at the time?'

Evie nodded.

Margaret began again. 'When Cyrus was about eight I let him stick a pin in a map of the world to decide where we'd go next. He chose here. By then I thought it would be safe. I hadn't heard from Victor or any other Hunter in years. I thought I had left all that behind. I had a new life, a new name.' She snorted air out through her nose. 'But then Cyrus chose this life.'

Cyrus groaned loudly next to her, his head banging the back of the seat.

Margaret ignored him. 'Cyrus doesn't seem to realise what I risked to get him away, to protect him from all this. To him it's just a game. I'm just some silly woman worrying about nothing.'

'Mum, would you just drop it already?' Cyrus huffed loudly.

'Drop it?' Margaret shouted. 'You could be anything you wanted to be, Cyrus, and yet you choose this? After everything I did. After everything I risked for you.'

'Seriously? Here? Can't we save this for therapy?'

Evie interrupted. 'I'm sorry, Mrs ...?'

Margaret turned to look at her. 'Locke,' she said. 'I changed my name. I'm Margaret Locke. I've not been Margaret Hunter for twenty years.'

'Mrs Locke,' Evie continued, trying to shake the thought that she was related in some way to this woman, 'we thought you might be able to help us. We need to find out more about the prophecy.'

'We need to know what we're supposed to do to make it happen, sooner rather than later,' Lucas added.

Margaret's gaze flew to Lucas. 'We? You mean her?'

'No. I mean *we*,' he replied pleasantly.

Margaret's mouth pursed. 'I don't know what you're supposed to do.'

Evie felt every particle of energy in her body dissolve. That was not the answer she'd been hoping for. Everything hinged on this – on this woman being able to help them. If she couldn't, what were they going to do?

'We only know one part of the prophecy,' Lucas pressed. 'We know the Sybll broke it into fragments but we thought maybe you might know where we could find the rest of it?'

Margaret's face seemed to freeze for a moment. Evie could feel the older woman's nervousness like a pungent waft of air. 'No,' Margaret said finally, holding Lucas's gaze.

'But what about all the books you've got? All the research you've been doing for the last twenty years?' Cyrus interrupted.

'What research?' Lucas asked. Evie heard the note of panic in his voice too.

Margaret gave a faint shrug. 'It's just family tree stuff. Genealogy. I was interested in discovering the roots to the Hunter family.'

'Why?' Evie asked, finding her voice.

'It doesn't interest you to know where you come from?'

'But you ran away from it,' Evie said, shaking her head, not understanding.

'Well,' Margaret answered, 'I wanted to know what I was running from.'

'There's a family tree. I saw it – in the same book the prophecy was in,' Evie said quietly, thinking of the convoluted diagram in the back of the book Victor had given her. It had detailed every Hunter that had ever been, right down to her. That's where she'd first heard of Margaret – her name had been scratched through.

'So you know then that you're the last one?' Margaret said, 'You're the last full-blood Hunter. Your parents were from the old line. Most of us were. David our trainer, Jocelyn and Victor too. But I doubt either of them had children.'

'Hang on, does that mean we're related?'

Evie turned her head. Cyrus was pointing his bloodied thumb at her with an expression of undisguised horror on his face.

'Only distantly,' Margaret said, shaking her head. 'Third cousins removed or something.'

Cyrus exhaled loudly. 'OK, that's good. I can work with that.' He grinned at Evie, 'Had me worried for a moment there.'

Evie couldn't see Lucas but she could guess at the look he was giving Cyrus. Margaret too was glaring at him. He seemed oblivious to it all, however.

'The generations thinned through the years,' Margaret continued. 'The concept of sending your children off to do battle in the name of a higher good disintegrated after the First and Second World Wars. People were questioning the sense of bringing children into the world just to have them sacrifice themselves in a war without end.'

'But you had me. You got pregnant,' Cyrus pointed out.

'Look,' Margaret snapped, staring at Evie, 'there's nothing I can tell you about the prophecy. I'm sorry. I wish there was. There's nothing I'd like more than for this to end. You've no idea how long I've waited. But,' she said, her eyes coming to rest on Lucas, 'you need a Sybll to tell you more. They're the ones the prophecy came from in the first place.'

'We've tried that,' Lucas answered. 'They don't know anything. Or at least nothing they're willing to share. But maybe ...'

Evie whipped around in her seat to look up at Lucas, a question forming on her lips. *Maybe what?*

'Maybe I can try again. Grace might know something,' he explained with a faint shrug of his shoulders. 'She was in the Brotherhood.'

'You were in the Brotherhood?' Margaret exclaimed, staring at Lucas horror-struck.

'Yes,' Lucas answered, his tone flat.

'You broke your oath?' she whispered, her eyes wide.

Lucas nodded. 'Yes.'

Margaret drew in a long breath. 'Can you find this Grace?' she finally asked, an unmistakably eager tone in her voice.

'I don't know. I'm not sure she wants to be found,' Lucas answered.

Evie was out of her chair, sending it flying. Lucas caught it in his left hand as it tumbled and righted it. 'She's a Sybll. If she doesn't want to be found, Lucas, you won't find her. You can't go. It's pointless, and ... and I won't let you.'

Margaret had stood too, both hands resting on the desk in front of her. 'It might be the only chance you have of finding out more,' she said.

'Evie,' Lucas said softly, 'she's right. We're hitting brick walls. We have to find a way forward. If anyone knows anything it will be Grace. And she helped me once before. I think, if I can find her, she'll help again. But she won't come near a group of Hunters.' He paused. 'I should have gone with Issa, but I didn't want to leave you then.'

'Well, why can you leave me *now*?' Evie couldn't help the shriek in her voice.

He smiled softly at her, his thumb briefly coming to rest on her wrist against her pulse, as if he could bring it under control just by his touch. 'Because now I won't be leaving you alone.' He jerked his head in Cyrus's direction, and she saw the shadow of a grimace pass across his face at the idea of leaving her with him. 'I'll come back, I promise,' he added.

'I'm coming with you,' Evie announced, trying to get around the chair that was blocking her path. There was no way he was going to turn invisible and get out of that door. No way. It wasn't happening.

'No,' he said, moving to stand in her way, his hand coming around her waist.

She opened her mouth to protest, aware that Cyrus and his mother were both staring at them, but she didn't care. Lucas wasn't going anywhere. Or, at least, not without her.

'You should stay here. He's right. You have to stay here.' It was Margaret talking. Evie turned and glared at her.

'If you come it'll be more dangerous for me, Evie,' Lucas said quietly, pulling her towards him and holding her by the arms. 'On my own I can hide. I can be invisible.'

Evie tried to think of another argument but before she could Cyrus appeared at her side. 'I'll take care of her, don't worry,' he said to Lucas with a grin.

Evie's stomach immediately tensed. Lucas raised his eyes slowly from Evie's face to meet Cyrus's stare. 'If you let anything happen to her,' he said in a voice that sounded like it could draw blood, 'if she even so much as scrapes her knee or gets a paper cut, I will kill you.'

'We'll see about that,' Cyrus answered. 'But don't worry, I won't let any unhumans near her.'

'So what are you waiting for?' Margaret spoke up, breaking the tension. 'No time like the present.'

'Evie,' Lucas pulled her back around to face him.

'Lucas,' she whispered, pressing her forehead against his shoulder. How was she supposed to let him go?

Cyrus made a loud groaning sound behind her.

'Don't do anything crazy. Promise me?' Lucas whispered into her ear.

'What if ...?' she began.

He cut her off, raising her chin with his hand and staring into her eyes. 'No. No *what ifs*. I'm going to be fine. I promise. I'll see you soon.'

She swallowed, but her throat had constricted and it felt like she was choking. 'OK,' she finally whispered.

'I love you,' Lucas said.

A big snorting exhalation from Cyrus.

'OK, OK, you'd best be going.' Margaret had walked around the table and was standing by the door, one hand on the handle, her body pressed against the bookshelf, as far away from Lucas as she could physically get.

'Here, I want you to take this,' Lucas said, pressing something into Evie's hand.

She looked down. 'No. No way,' she said, shoving her hands behind her back. 'That's yours. You might need it.'

He pressed his shadow blade towards her. 'I want you to have it.'

She shook her head more firmly.

'Just until I get back,' he pleaded. 'Please. I'd feel better knowing you had it.'

She took a deep breath and then slid her fingers around the hilt. It was so light it could have been a mote of dust she was holding in her palm. She felt that if she let it go it would float away or disappear – just like its owner.

'Bye,' Lucas said, his fingers slipping from hers. He paused briefly to press his lips against hers and then he was gone, leaving just the faintest pressure, a pulse against her lips, that was echoed by her heartbeat.

She stared at the open doorway he'd disappeared through and at Margaret, who was staring at her with a mixture of incredulity and what strangely seemed like fear. And then she looked at Cyrus, who was grinning at her like a fool.

'Cupcake?' he asked, pushing the door firmly shut with his foot.

24

Evie was counting the notches on the bedpost, trying not to think about what they represented – just trying to keep her head occupied with anything other than thoughts of Lucas. Because each time he flashed into her mind, in the space between numbers, it was as if someone was stabbing her in the heart with a pitchfork. And if it took until she'd counted to infinity to keep that pain at bay, then that's what she would do. But at fifty-six she stopped counting and rolled over, pressing her face into the pillow, taking a deep shuddering breath in. Infinity was hopeless.

There was just the faintest smell of him – the smoke from the fire last night, a trace of warm leather and cool air that made her think of late summer dusks. She felt her stomach contract, seeding an ache that spread quickly into her limbs, lighting fires in her joints. Why had she let him go? She hadn't argued enough. If she'd managed to hold onto him then maybe he wouldn't have left. She kicked her foot against the bedpost and heard a crack as the wood splintered.

She sat up and examined the deep rent that had opened up in the post holding up the bunk above her. Then she looked at her foot. She was getting stronger. She'd thought that was just a tap. She wondered idly what damage she could do if she really put some force behind it. It surprised her. When Jocelyn and Victor had talked about her making her first kill and the changes that would happen as a result she'd assumed they were talking metaphorically. That murdering something, even if that thing was already as cold and dead as a Thirster, would take something from you – a large chunk of your humanity say – leaving you more able to kill the next time. Like eating ice cream when you're on a diet. After that first tortured, guilt-ridden mouthful the rest of the tub went down pretty easily.

She flopped back onto the bed and resumed counting, trying to empty her mind of sex and death. The twin obsessions of adolescence. She was such a cliché.

'Do you want to eat?'

She turned her head. Cyrus was hovering in the doorway, arms casually folded.

'No,' she answered, turning back to stare at the bedpost, hoping he'd take the hint and leave.

He didn't. He strolled into the room and over to the bed, resting his hands on the bunk above and leaning so he was looking down on her. 'OK, so you don't want to eat. How about fight? Do you want to fight?'

'With you?'

He fought a smile. 'I was thinking we could go and find ourselves some nice unsuspecting unhumans for you to vent some of that frustration out on. Or,' he said with a grin, 'you can work it out on me. I could help you relax a little. You know, maybe a nice massage – a bath, some candles – fill the gaps that Lucas left behind.' His eyes trailed down her body as he spoke, landing on the notches on the bedpost. She watched the grin fade and a frown take its place as he noticed the crack she'd made.

She sat up quickly. 'Don't you think that's a bit dumb?'

'What?' he asked, his attention flying back to her. 'Getting you to relax? No, I think you could really use it.'

'No, I mean going out looking for trouble right now, when half the universe is searching for me.'

'Don't over-dramatise. It's not half the universe. Just seven realms. Six really, because the Sybll won't be looking for you. They'll already have seen you and generally speaking they stay out of things. 'And,' he sighed, 'what else are we going to do? You won't eat. You don't want me to take you to bed and show you what you're missing. So the alternative is just sitting here twiddling our thumbs waiting for lover boy to come back and, you know,' he shook his head grimly, 'the odds of that happening are rapidly dwindling.'

Evie swung her legs over the side of the bed and shoved Cyrus aside as she stood.

He took two laughing steps backwards, holding up his hands. 'Hey – I'm just saying. So, given the lack of other options I think we should do some of our own investigating. Find out what's happening in the realms. Maybe we can catch ourselves a newbie virgin to this realm and help him pop his cherry. What do you say? Come on,' he wheedled. 'What was all that crap you were spouting about the prophecy being marked? That means it's definitely going to come true, right? Which means you're invincible. You said it yourself. So what's the problem?' Evie heard him approaching softly, then felt his breath against her neck. 'Scared I'll show you up in a fight?' he whispered in her ear.

She whipped around, reeling from his closeness. 'OK, I'll get dressed,' she said, feeling both mad and flustered.

She watched him as he left the room, wearing a smug smile, and then she went over to the door and slammed it shut, pushing a chair in front of it, pre-empting his undoubted return in a few seconds' time with the excuse that he'd got lost on the way to the bathroom.

Lucas had stashed the bag with the clothes that Issa had brought inside the closet. Evie pulled out the selection and started sorting through the pile. She hated to admit it, but Issa had actually done a really good job. The clothes both fitted her and were things she'd buy herself – as opposed to jeans that should come with a thrombosis warning and underwear worn as outerwear. Gone, she realised, were the days of freebie designer handouts. Still, what was the point of wearing thousand-dollar couture to go out hunting in when what was needed was utilitarian black to hide the bloodstains? And, voilà, in the bag she found a pair of black jeans and a long-sleeved dark-grey T-shirt. Even the underwear came in her size and was black. She slipped on the grey Converse Issa had provided. They worked better than heels too. At least she could run in them.

'Thank you, Issa,' she whispered.

Frankly, she was more than a little freaked out by the fact Lucas had dated a Sybll, but even more freaked out that that same Sybll had foreseen her need for a toothbrush and black underwear. What else had Issa seen? That was what was really bugging her. She knew that Issa hadn't just come around to drop off some clothes and toiletries. She'd come to tell Lucas something. And the fact he hadn't told her what, meant that it was something bad.

The door rattled, catching on the chair she'd put in front of it. She heard Cyrus grunt.

'I'm getting dressed,' she yelled.

'Just thought I'd hurry you up,' he called from behind the door.

She didn't answer. She was glancing in the mirror hanging on the back of the door. With her amped-up eyesight she could see the pulse of an artery in her neck fluttering and each tiny crack in her lips, which were bruised dark-red and chapped.

She squashed the bag up with a sigh and rammed it back into the closet, then she pulled the chair out of the way and left the room to go start a fight with some unhumans. And maybe with Cyrus too, just for the hell of it.

Cyrus was in the kitchen, standing against the counter with a butcher's knife in his hand. He was running it up and down a stone block, causing blue sparks to rain down on him. He looked up when she walked in and flashed her a smile which she knew was meant to have some kind of dazzling effect over her. But all it managed to induce in her was annoyance.

She glanced around, looking for Vero and Ash. She hadn't seen them or heard anything all day. Was it just going to be her and Cyrus out on the prowl tonight? She kind of hoped not. Though being in close proximity to Vero and Ash wasn't high on her list of priorities either.

Finally, Cyrus finished sharpening and pushed the blade into a sheath, the shining eyes and unstoppable grin giving away the excitement he was feeling.

'You like it, don't you?' Evie asked, frowning at him. 'I mean, going out killing them? Why else would you do it?'

He gave her a confused, faintly amused smile. 'I do it because *a* – it's fun, and *b* – err ...' He blew air out of his mouth and shook his head. 'No, that's it.'

'Why's everything a joke to you?'

'Why's everything so serious to you?'

She could feel her nostrils flaring. Together with the rolling eyeballs, she was starting to feel like a hostile horse whenever she was around him. So unattractive. She tried to wrestle back some control of her facial expressions.

'Listen, Evie,' Cyrus said, 'people would be thanking me if they knew I've been keeping the streets clear of bloodsucking Thirsters and things that go burn in the night. I think they'd be thanking me profusely.' He walked over to a hook on the wall by the door and pulled off a leather belt with pouches and straps attached to it, then looped it over his head. Very guerrilla Boy Scout, Evie thought as she watched him attach the knife to it.

'Well, I'm surprised you aren't going around advertising the fact,' she said. 'Your ego sure could use a boost.'

He laughed off the comment. 'None of them belong here. But there's too many of them for us to kill. So we focus on the worst ones – the ones who go around killing people or, you know, just sucking their blood for a good time: the Mixen, Scorpio, Thirsters and Shadow Warriors. We tend to let the Shifters go. And the Sybll.'

'Because you couldn't catch one if you tried.'

Cyrus stepped closer, his eyes a bright aquamarine colour under the spotlights in the kitchen. She couldn't help but stare at the brown slash in his iris. It was interesting, like a crack in a stone revealing quartz or diamonds inside, though she wasn't sure that what lay beneath Cyrus's shallow exterior was quite so dazzling or priceless.

'It's the final reckoning that counts,' Cyrus said, distracting her from his eyes. 'When you die – did you do more harm than good? Did you die with honour?'

She swallowed and he turned on his heel. He went over to the kitchen counter again and started rummaging through the drawers.

'How did you and Lucas get together anyway?' he asked, looking up at her. 'Match dot com? No, let me guess – unhuman hook-up dot com?'

'Ha ha,' she answered. 'No. He was sent to spy on me, then to kill me.'

Cyrus snorted through his nose. 'Wow, what a cliché. He came to kill you and fell in love with you instead.' He threw her a cringe face. 'This could be a film script for a movie with one of those sparkly vampires in.' He kept shaking his head and laughing and she felt her teeth grinding in response. 'How romantic,' he went on. 'Stupid, but romantic. I'll give him that. So you fell for the Shadow Warrior?'

Evie didn't answer. She just continued to glare.

Cyrus carried on undaunted. 'OK, I'll grant you he's not bad-looking – not that I swing that way mind. He has the whole haunted-angst face that you girls seem to dig so much, but how'd you fall in love with him?' He paused, resting his hands on the counter. 'Are you sure you are in love? Because, you know, sometimes the feeling we get around unhumans – that whole palpitation, faster heartbeat, clammy hands – that has been known to be confused with feelings of lust and, er, love. It happened to me once. I thought I liked this Shapeshifter chick.' He shrugged. 'Turns out I just wanted to kill her.'

Evie exhaled loudly, trying to keep hold of the small piece of calm still left inside her. 'No, it's not just my instincts firing whenever he's around.' She smiled tightly. 'Trust me, I didn't feel this way about the Scorpio I put a knife through.'

Cyrus pulled a face, 'OK. But I really want to know what you see in him because, between you and me, I'm not seeing a whole lot of sparkling personality.'

'You haven't even spoken to him.'

He laughed. 'And you spend your time together speaking, do you? Not locking lips and other demon body parts? What are those like by the way?'

The nostril flare again. She couldn't control it. 'I am not about to explain our relationship. Least of all to someone as shallow and obsessed with sex as you.'

'Hey, I'm not shallow,' Cyrus answered, scowling.

'He saved me.'

He raised an eyebrow. 'As in bibles and dunking in the river?'

'No. He saved my life. More than once.'

Cyrus walked around the counter, his head nodding knowledgeably. 'Oh, so it's some sort of survivor guilt thing you have going on. I get it. Adulate your rescuer. Knight-in-shining-armour syndrome. It all makes sense now. You know, I think there's psych treatment you can get for that.'

Evie closed her eyes and breathed out slowly. 'No,' she said, 'I don't mean it that way. He saved my life, yes, but only when I didn't want it saving. He brought me back. And I think he was the only person who could have brought me back – made me want to carry on.'

Cyrus had actually stopped talking. And stopped mocking. He was staring at her with a serious expression on his face, the half-smug, half-droll smile gone.

'I hate fate,' she continued. 'I hate what it's doing to me. I hate the fact I feel like I have no choice in any of this. Everything just seems to happen to me, whereas everyone else gets to choose. But I accept it because that same fate brought me Lucas.' She drew in a breath. 'Maybe that was the trade. And if I did have the choice – to go through all this again or just carry on being Evie Tremain – if I could choose to be or not be this thing in the prophecy – I think I'd choose it all again, just to get the chance to know him.'

Cyrus still didn't say anything. His eyebrows were raised so high they were almost meeting his hairline. No doubt he was struggling to get his head around the concept of love. It must have confused his brain cell.

'Does that explain it?' she asked.

He took a moment to answer. 'I guess. But love as you call it is just an infatuation. It doesn't last.' The mocking smile reappeared. 'Also, not clever to be infatuated with someone who's probably going to die.' He checked his watch. 'Is probably already dead, in fact.'

The anger lashed through her body. 'Are we done here?' she asked, turning on her heel and heading for the door.

She heard his footsteps follow after her. 'Yeah, sure. Who wants to talk about love anyway when we have demons to kill?' He brushed past her and reached to open a locked closet by the side of the door. 'Weapon up,' he announced, throwing the doors wide.

The air emptied from Evie's lungs in one long exclamation. The view in front of her made Victor's collection of weapons seem like a kitchen utensil display for Barbie's dream house.

'What's your slaying item of choice?' Cyrus asked, indicating the rows of weapons with a flourish of his arm. 'Flamethrower? Grenade? Gun? Arrow? Saw blades?' He picked up a pair of hardwood sticks linked by a chain, 'Nunchuckers?'

Evie was struck dumb by the rows of weapons – some she didn't even know the names of.

'Or do you prefer to just beat them to death?' Cyrus asked. He reached inside and took hold of two Zippo lighters, shoving one into his back pocket and throwing her the second. Next he grabbed hold of a small bottle of lighter fluid and pushed it into one of the pockets on his utility belt. Finally, his fingers wavered over the nunchuckers and something that looked like a club with spikes in it, which had probably last seen action during a Viking invasion over a thousand years ago.

'Want to try this?' he asked, handing it to her.

She shook her head. 'I don't need a weapon.'

He nodded with respect. 'Oh, so I was right about the beating to death? Nice.' He put the club thing back in the closet.

'I'm already armed,' she said in answer, holding Lucas's blade up.

'Can I see it?' Cyrus asked, reaching a greedy hand towards it.

She passed it to him slowly. Cyrus took it, weighing it carefully in his palms. His face was childlike, filled with Christmas-morning-sized awe. He was practically cradling the thing like a premature baby.

'Cuts through Thirster skin like it's paper. Hell, this could cut through diamonds, never mind Thirster hide,' he said in reverentially lowered tones. Then he looked up sharply at her. 'This blade – this is a very special thing. It comes from the realms. You know that?'

She gave him a look. Of course she knew that. 'It belonged to Lucas's father,' she said, holding out her hand for it. 'He gave it to him, just before he died.'

Cyrus took one last, loving look at it, running his thumb along the flat, knowing that if he did the same along the edge he'd lose the whole digit. Evie took it carefully, sheathing it in the case that Lucas had left behind.

Cyrus had turned back to the closet and was rummaging for more weapons. Evie took a breath. 'Who's your father?' she asked.

Cyrus turned around with a bemused smile on his face. 'Wow, straight to the point, aren't you? What's it to you anyway? Are you worried my mum might have done the deed with another Hunter? Say, your dad? Is that what you're worrying about? That we're related? Because we can get a blood test if that's the only thing holding you back. Third cousins once removed works for me though.'

She bit her lip. 'Listen, let's get something straight right now,' she said, holding his gaze firmly. 'I will never – not in a million years, not until hell freezes over, not until your ego shrinks to the size of the Buddha's, not until the day I die – ever sleep with you. Or kiss you. Or even like you. Are we clear now? Just answer yes or no.'

Cyrus licked his lips, then walked past her, 'We'll see.'

Her mouth fell open as she stared at his back. 'God, do you ever stop?'

'Nope,' he answered with his back still to her, 'just ask Marcy.'

'Darcy! Her name was Darcy! Oh my God. I am going to kill you. I am seriously going to kill you.'

He turned around, smirking. 'You could try. But I think you'll find it's easier to kill an unhuman – a Shadow Warrior even – than it is to kill me.'

She drew in a deep breath and then another. 'So, who is he then?' she demanded, determined not to let him throw her off track again.

'Who?' Cyrus asked.

'Your father.'

He sighed loudly. 'I don't know who my father is. My mum told me it was someone outside the Hunters. Some random guy she met one night. Shocking, right? Under age and illegal in the state of

California. Tut tut, mum. But hell, at least she chose someone with superlative genes.'

Evie frowned.

'Why the face?' Cyrus asked. 'Were you hoping that I might be another pure-blood like you? Sorry to disappoint. But your dad was already with your mum by then and I think you'll find Victor's black and I'm not, so no need to do a DNA test there. I'm sorry. I bet you were thinking that would get you off the hook, but no. Hook.' He drew the shape of a hook in the air and then pointed at her. 'You. Still on it.'

They were standing like that, Cyrus pointing at her, when Vero and Ash walked in. Evie blinked. She hadn't felt them or heard them approaching. She was too easily distracted these days. She needed to focus.

'Hey Ash', Cyrus said, 'these are for you.' He threw the nunchuckers towards him. They cut through the air making a whirring noise. Ash caught them in his left hand and tucked them into his pocket.

'Vero, how are you doing?' Cyrus asked.

Vero glared at him, her dark eyes liquid poison. 'I'm fine,' she said through gritted teeth. 'What have you got for me tonight?'

'Well, tonight, Vero,' Cyrus answered, ignoring her glare, 'I thought maybe you'd want to vent some of your anger on a Thirster or six, so I have thoughtfully coated these arrow tips in Mixen acid for you to use with your crossbow and I am packing a litre and a half of lighter fluid with which we can have ourselves a nice flame-grilled Thirster barbecue.'

A cold smile appeared on Vero's face as she leant forward to inspect the arrows, which were lined up on the kitchen counter in a plastic container of sorts. Acid-proof obviously, Evie figured. Vero was wearing a black lace dress accessorised with several studded leather cuffs. A black onyx necklace made up the ensemble. So far she'd avoided looking in Evie's direction, which suited Evie just fine. Vero looked so like Risper that it was unsettling to stare at her for long.

'You sure you want to do this, Vero?' Ash suddenly asked.

She spun around to face him. 'Am I sure I want to go out and kill some bloodsucking piece of ...'

He held up both hands in a defensive gesture. 'OK, point taken.'

'See how we're all driven by revenge, Evie?' Cyrus butted in.

She turned to look at him. He was slinging a crossbow over one shoulder. 'It's quite the motivator. Ash getting revenge for his friend. Vero for her sister.' He let out a satisfied sigh. 'Revenge makes the world go round.'

'I thought that was supposed to be love,' Evie replied dully.

'No, you heard wrong. It's revenge. It's what keeps us going when we've given up on love.'

'What do *you* have to revenge?' she asked angrily.

He frowned for a moment and then he looked up at her as if he'd just had a revelation. 'Good point. Nothing I guess. Not yet anyway. Maybe I'm just getting revenge now for a future wrong, in case I can't get it later.'

'Sound reasoning.'

'Where are we going?' Ash asked, opening the grille to the elevator.

'The Tipping Point's closed for the foreseeable future while the under-realm gangsters in charge try to find more doormen. Apparently the last two were total failures.' Cyrus pressed Evie and Vero ahead of him into the elevator. 'I thought we could hang out near to the way through. Pick on some unsuspecting newbie.'

'Where is the way through?' Evie asked, turning around to face him.

A broad smile crossed Cyrus's face. 'Ahhh, you'll see. It's too good.'

They stocked the Prius's trunk with all their weapons and climbed silently into the car, Vero and Ash sliding into the back before Evie could get in. She weighed up the options and decided that lying in the trunk next to the crossbow and poison-tipped arrows was preferable to sitting next to Cyrus in the front. But he was holding the door open for her expectantly. She eyed the trunk longingly before climbing with an audible groan into the passenger seat.

Cyrus jumped into the driver's seat beside her and rammed the car into reverse, spinning them out of the warehouse and onto the street. Evie glanced down at his wrist, seeing the tattoo on the inside of his forearm clearly for the first time. It was an owl. She smiled in amusement. An owl? That was deeply hardcore.

'What's the tattoo for?' she asked, trying to suppress the smirk.

He glanced quickly at her before his eyes flew back to the road. 'The owl's a silent hunter. It hunts by night and it sees everything.'

'Why'd you not just get a tattoo of a Sybll then?' she asked.

He turned to look at her and she gripped the dashboard as they weaved dangerously into oncoming traffic. Cyrus righted the car's trajectory, shaking his head. 'Among most cultures, the owl is considered a bad omen, portending death,' he said, after a moment's pause. 'And I am portending the death of many unhumans tonight.'

The smile disappeared from Evie's face.

'Bring it on,' she heard Ash mutter from behind her.

25

Cyrus took a sudden turn and drew the car into a parking lot next to a burger drive-thru. Evie glanced out of the window in confusion and then looked back at Cyrus.

'What are we doing here? Is this where the way through is?'

'No,' he grinned back at her, 'it's where the Double Cheese & Bacon burger and chocolate milkshake are. Want something?'

'No, thank you,' she said, shooting him a look which she hoped conveyed both disdain and boredom.

'You need to eat something,' he said.

'That's not food. That's reclaimed cow testicles.'

Cyrus threw open his door, 'Cows don't have testicles. Someone needs a biology lesson.' He got out and slammed the door shut. Vero jumped out after him, enclosing Evie in the gloom of the car with a silent, brooding Ash for company.

Evie cleared her throat, trying to break the silence that had descended. Cyrus had taken the keys, so she couldn't switch on the radio. 'Is he always like this?' she asked.

'Like what?' Ash answered, sounding uninterested.

'So annoying.'

'Most girls seem to like it.'

Evie undid her seat belt and twisted in her seat. The bright lights from inside the burger place were shining through onto the back seat, making Ash's face gleam. His expression was stony as a rock face.

'How long have you known him?' Evie asked, determined to put a crack in it.

'Two years,' Ash answered, staring out of the window.

Evie did a quick mental calculation. 'How many do you need to kill before you've got your revenge?'

Ash's dark eyes flew to her, narrowing enough to make her shrink back against the dashboard. 'Every single one of them,' he said without any emotion.

A few seconds passed. Evie tapped her fingers against the headrest. She thought about turning back in her seat and just sinking into uncomfortable silence but for some unfathomable reason she didn't want to turn her back on him. 'You're a martial artist?' she asked instead.

'Let Wei,' he answered, his focus still on something way more interesting outside the car. 'Burmese kick-boxing.'

She studied his profile. His nose looked like it had been broken a few times and he had a jagged scar running across his forehead up into his hair, which was thick and dark and cut short. 'Where'd you learn that?' she asked.

He turned to face her. 'My father.'

'Must come in useful.'

He didn't answer. He stared at her blankly for a few seconds and then went back to looking out of the window. Evie thought about getting out of the car and going to see about that burger. Eating reconstituted cow parts seemed preferable suddenly to trying to make conversation with the Dark Knight here.

She decided to give it one last shot. 'So, have you thought about what you're going to do when this is all over?' she asked. She cringed even as she said it, realising that she sounded like a school guidance counsellor talking to the kid who's flunking out and has a snowball's chance in hell of getting a job cleaning toilets, let alone of getting into college.

'I don't think that far ahead,' Ash answered. 'The Buddha teaches right mindfulness. Staying alert to the present. If you miss the moment, you miss life.'

Evie choked on a laugh before quickly swallowing it down in the face of Ash's unamused expression and the sight of his biceps. 'You're Buddhist?' she asked.

Ash's eyes narrowed to thin slits, his mouth pursing into a tight knot, as though daring her to say just one more word.

'Didn't the Buddha teach non-violence?' Evie asked quickly. 'I'm pretty certain he said something about killing equalling bad karma. You might come back in your next life as a snail or something.'

'They're not people,' Ash fired back. 'They're not human. They're not even animals. They're monsters. Killing them creates good karma.'

Evie fell back on her haunches, the small of her back banging against the dashboard. Ash stared at her through the square hole of the headrest. She eyed him warily, mulling over her response. She knew he was daring her to answer him back. The words were swirling and gathering in her head but before she could get them out he spoke again. 'It wasn't humans who killed my friend,' he said. 'It wasn't humans who killed Vero's sister.'

Evie pressed her lips together and clamped them shut. He was talking about Thirsters. But just because one type of unhuman happened to like murdering people that didn't make them all monsters. That was like saying because some humans committed murder everyone on the planet deserved to die. And, OK, she couldn't care less about wiping out all the Thirsters in the realms because it wasn't like any of the ones she'd met so far were the vegan, meditating kind, and maybe she wouldn't be shedding tears over any Mixen or Scorpio that got killed either. But what about Lucas? And Jamieson? They weren't monsters. She had a moment's pause as she considered which side of the divide she'd place Flic, before she shook her head. It wasn't so easy to just dump them all into the same category and pull a metaphorical switch.

'It wasn't far from here, you know,' Ash said, interrupting her internal rationalisations. 'We'd been to a party. Got talking to these two girls. I thought they were some emo kids. Next thing my friend's making out with one, except he's not making out with her – she's eating him. You hear me?'

'I'm sorry,' Evie whispered.

'That night I found out that it takes a lot to kill a Thirster. I wasn't armed. Just had these.' He indicated his hands and his legs. 'I got away but that was about it. The next night I went back with a handmade flamethrower and a stake. I found them. Found out stakes don't work, neither does garlic or holy water. But flames do. I killed them. It got easier after the first one. You know? I was stronger, faster. That was unexpected but useful. I kept going out every night. Discovered the acid skin ones and the ones with the tails. Killed a few of them too. One night I met Cyrus doing the same.'

And you've never looked back. Evie filled in the blank.

'And you had no idea you were – um – one of us?' she asked instead. 'A Hunter I mean? Before you met Cyrus?'

Ash laughed a bitter laugh. 'No. Freaky co-incidence. right?'

She shook her head. 'I don't believe in co-incidence anymore.'

The door on Evie's side suddenly flew open, making her jump. Cyrus thrust a greasy brown-paper bag in her face. 'Here you are – one bacon double cheese and large fries. Got you full-fat Coke too, figured you're not one of those girls who needs to watch her weight.'

She took the bag gingerly between her fingers before it could spill in her lap and twisted back around so she was facing forwards.

Cyrus walked around the car and got in beside her. He paused to put his chocolate milkshake in the cup holder and to take a bite out of his burger, then he turned the key in the ignition and spun them out of the lot and back onto the street. They only drove a couple of blocks before he hung another right and pulled into a deserted lot opposite a fried-chicken joint.

'Are we doing a fast-food crawl or something?' Evie asked.

'Nope. We're staking out that building over there.' Cyrus nodded with his chin towards a building on the corner that looked vaguely familiar. It stood about five stories high and looked like it had been modelled on a Renaissance palazzo. It had a brown-brick façade with lots of square windows, which were all dark at this time of night. The ground floor was a row of shop fronts and on the corner, beneath a high stone arch, stood the main door.

'I know that building,' Evie said, squinting and trying to place it.

'It's the Bradbury building,' Cyrus answered. 'It's famous, not just to unhumans. They've used it in a lot of movies. It's also home to the internal affairs department of the LA Police Department. As well as to Subway, Kinko's and ...' he paused, noticing the takeaway bag sitting on her lap unopened. 'Are you not eating that?'

She shook her head.

'Such waste,' he tutted, finishing his burger and screwing up the wrapper before helping himself to hers.

'The way through is in that building?' Evie asked, unable to keep the disbelief out of her voice.

'Yeah, in the basement. They built right on top without even realising it was there. The unhumans were guarding it then, and are still guarding it now.'

'But how do people come in and out? Unhumans I mean? Without being seen?'

'There's a fancy-dress shop in the basement.'

'Ha ha.'

'No, I'm being serious. It's a cover. A pretty damn good one.'

'Not that the virgins ever know how to dress.'

Evie twisted to look at Vero who was leaning forward, her hands gripping Cyrus's headrest as she stared out of the window, watching the building.

'We should just blast in there,' Ash suddenly announced.

Vero spun around. 'Don't be stupid, Ash.'

He shrugged and she huffed in response and turned back to the window. Evie thought about taking her knife and cutting the tension between them.

'Have you ever?' Evie asked. 'Been in and seen it, that is?'

'No, of course we haven't,' Vero spat. 'Not even an army of Hunters could get close.'

Evie paused to recover from the scorn she'd just been slapped with. 'Why not?'

'They guard this place like they're guarding the Ark of the Covenant,' Cyrus answered. 'At least two Shadow Warriors, a handful of Thirsters, one or two Scorpio and several Mixen are down there at any one time.'

'Let me get this straight,' Evie snorted. 'You're saying that, right now, just hanging out in the basement of the Bradbury building, there's a band of unhumans guarding the way through? And the LA Police Department is right above them?'

'Yeah,' Cyrus answered, slurping a mouthful of milkshake.

'We could take them,' Ash said quietly from behind.

Evie felt the panic numbing her, then realised that it was just the Coke wedged between her thighs.

'What's the point? We don't know how to shut the thing anyway,' Cyrus muttered.

'You just don't want it shut, Cyrus,' Ash cut in.

'That's not true.'

'Why wouldn't he want it shut?' Evie asked, looking over her shoulder at Ash and then back at Cyrus. 'Why don't you want it shut?'

'What's he going to do for fun when there are no unhumans to slay?' Vero answered, a bitter edge to her voice.

'Um, get a job maybe? Live a normal life?' Even as she said it Evie felt the strand of hope she'd been desperately clinging to snap under the weight of her desperation.

'OK, people, enough about me,' Cyrus said. 'Tonight is not about fulfilling any prophecy or getting eaten. Tonight we're just going to have a therapeutic killing spree.'

The brown bag sitting on Evie's lap went flying, Coke drenching the dashboard and Cyrus's leg. He turned and glared at her.

'I thought we were going to find someone to question,' Evie spluttered.

'Yes, that's what I said,' Cyrus answered, grabbing a paper towel and trying to mop up the mess.

'No you didn't.'

'There's movement.' Vero's whisper cut through their argument. 'What are they?'

Evie turned her head at the same time as Cyrus. A hush descended in the car as they watched two people leave the building. One was in a full-length gold-coloured ball gown complete with a white fur wrap. The unhuman she was with was wearing a black tuxedo.

'Shapeshifters I think,' Cyrus said after a few seconds. 'Let's leave them.'

Evie felt her shoulders drop a fraction of an inch. 'Why are they dressed like that?' she asked.

'They don't know what to wear to blend in, so they take their cue from whatever glossy magazines they have lying around. Most of the time they shift into z-list celebrities.'

'Two more,' Ash called from the back.

Evie leant forward. Two people were standing on the top of the steps by the door. One was wearing a luminous-yellow minidress and metallic silver boots that made Evie's eyes water and the other was wearing a sailor suit. What kind of a fancy-dress shop was this place?

'Mixen,' she heard Vero whisper behind her.

'God, they're so obvious,' Cyrus said, sucking the last of his milkshake up through his straw. 'Isn't there some corrective foundation they could use?'

'Want to go for them?' Vero asked.

'Tempting. If only to stop them walking the streets in those outfits. Ash, what do you think?' Cyrus asked.

'Wait – behind them – look,' Ash answered.

Three more people had left the building, their heads jerking left and right as they took in the darkened street. One threw back the hood of the sweater she was wearing and Evie inhaled loud enough to make Cyrus turn and smirk. The girl had long dark hair, but it was the paleness of her skin and the red rims of her eyes that made Evie's stomach flip over.

Thirsters. The other two were wearing caps, their faces buried in shadow but their hands were in view; blue veined and white skinned. Evie's own hands had started to turn clammy. She wiped them on the seat.

'Thirsters,' Vero said.

'OK,' Cyrus said softly, 'we have a target.'

'Wait,' Evie said, grasping his arm. 'What if someone sees?' she asked. It was late but there were still people – humans – out walking around.

'We'll call it performance art and I'll hold out my hat for small change,' Cyrus answered.

26

By the time Evie had fumbled with the door and climbed out, the others were already by the trunk loading up with weapons. She hurried around to them.

'What's the plan?' she asked, watching Cyrus pass the crossbow to Vero, who took it and then, with delicate fingers sheathed in some gloves, prised three arrows out of their plastic shield and lined them up in the ridges of the bow. Ash stood behind her, flexing his shoulders.

'What's the plan, Vero?' Cyrus asked, slamming the trunk shut.

Vero barely raised her focus from the bow. 'Ash will take them down, I'll fire these through them and, Cyrus, you can light the match.'

Evie held onto the car to steady herself.

'Sound OK?' Cyrus said, glancing at her. 'You can sit this one out if you want.'

'What about questioning them? I thought we were going to question them?'

'Oh, yeah, good point. I'll hold fire on the fire while you ask the questions.'

He didn't wait for her to agree. He strode across the lot, sticking to the areas of ground where the light didn't reach. The unhumans over on the other side of the street hadn't noticed them. They were stopping at every shopfront to stare.

'First time through, you can tell,' Ash said under his breath. 'And not just by the fashion.'

'How?' Evie asked.

'They're moving too fast – haven't learnt to slow their pace to look more human.'

'How do you know so much about them?' Evie asked.

Cyrus grinned at her over his shoulder. 'We sometimes have Q & A sessions with obliging unhumans.'

'Q & A sessions? You mean you beat them up until they tell you what you want to know?'

Cyrus shrugged. 'Something like that.'

'OK, let's move before they hit the subway,' Ash interrupted. 'Ready V?'

'Oh yeah,' Vero answered, unslinging the crossbow and sliding like vapour into the shadows running up the side of the street.

Evie turned back to Ash but he was already gone. The street was deserted. Cyrus took hold of her arm and pulled her quickly across the road. They were about a hundred metres behind the Thirsters, who were walking faster now – so fast Evie and Cyrus had to jog to keep up.

'Where are we ...?' Evie started to ask, but Cyrus put a finger to his lips and yanked her towards a fire escape at the side of a building. She started climbing,

Cyrus hot on her heels, his eyes level with her butt – a deliberate move on his part, she thought. She climbed faster until she was able to swing her leg over a low wall and pull herself onto the flat roof of the building. Cyrus jumped the wall in the next instant and took her hand, pulling her at a sprint to the far side of the roof. She noticed how much faster she could run now. They'd covered fifty metres in less than two seconds. Ducking down, they peered over the edge. They'd overtaken the Thirsters, who were now just drawing parallel beneath them.

Cyrus pointed silently across the street. There, tucked into the shadows between two parked cars, crouched down on one knee with the crossbow resting on her shoulder, was Vero.

Cyrus nudged Evie's arm, directing her attention to another person walking along the sidewalk, heading straight towards the Thirsters. It was Ash. He'd circled around the Thirsters to come at them from the front. Evie wondered at how fast he must have run to outpace them all and double back like that, but then her attention swung back to the scene below.

Ash had drawn up in front of the three Thirsters. Evie leant further out over the parapet so she could see, but from this height she couldn't hear the question that stopped the Thirsters in their tracks. She heard a cackling laugh in response though and her hands tightened instinctively around the hilt of

Lucas's blade. She hadn't even realised she had drawn it from its sheath, and the sight of it gleaming in the moonlight was somehow reassuring. Her body was vibrating with adrenaline. She was sure she must be shaking the foundations of the building. Cyrus must have felt it too because his hand closed around her forearm, stilling her. He shook his head slightly, warning her to not make a sound or a move.

The thunking sound came next. It was a sound so shockingly familiar and so horrific that Evie almost screamed. She clamped her balled fist to her mouth and stared. The three Thirsters had been shot simultaneously by Vero. Two had been hit in the chest and one in the neck.

The one who'd been hit through the neck had been carried several metres and was impaled against the wall, her feet dangling several feet off the ground.

The second was lying spreadeagled on the sidewalk, shrieking loud enough to rattle the metal fire escape. Ash cut the scream off with a kick to the solar plexus.

The third Thirster was collapsed on the ground, his mouth opening and shutting repeatedly, like a fish gasping for water, as he tried to pull the arrow shaft out from between his ribs.

Cyrus stood up swiftly, swung a leg over the parapet and disappeared. Evie watched him slide effortlessly down the drainpipe and drop to the ground below. He looked up at Evie and beckoned her to follow.

Evie sheathed her knife, climbed over the parapet and shimmied down, her hands burning against the plastic as she picked up speed. Cyrus caught her as she landed, pulling her out of the way of one of the Thirsters who lunged across the sidewalk, fingers grasping for her foot.

'So you want to ask some questions? Go ahead,' Cyrus said, pulling out the bottle of lighter fluid.

Evie stepped carefully around the two on the ground and headed towards the one dangling from the wall.

'You might want to hurry it up,' Cyrus said calmly. 'We have incoming pedestrians at twelve o'clock.'

Evie glanced up. Bearing down on them, about two hundred metres away, were two humans. Crap. She turned back to the Thirster pinned to the wall.

'Um, what do you know about the White Light?' she asked.

The Thirster's eyes grew round and her mouth opened into a gaping hole, exposing black gums and dripping yellow fangs. She shut her mouth and tried again but no sound came out except for a gurgling hiss. Some bloody spittle landed on Evie's shoes and she stepped backwards.

'I think you might want to try asking one that doesn't have an arrow through its neck,' Vero suggested. She was holding the crossbow vertical, pointing it downwards at the Thirster writhing on the ground by her feet.

Evie crouched down a safe distance away from the girl on the ground and tried again, struggling to be heard over the hissing. 'What do you know about the White Light?' she asked.

A thin smile split the Thirster's lips, a trail of blood trickled out of the corner of her mouth and she paused to lick it. 'The White Light is going to die,' the Thirster hissed, wincing as Vero's booted foot kicked the arrow shaft poking out of her chest. 'There's an army coming – an army coming here to find it and destroy it. To destroy all the Hunters.'

Evie fell back on her haunches, the breath caught in her lungs, her head spinning. An army? As in battalions of unhumans, with weapons and some unhuman general in charge of them, coming here? To find *her*?

Cyrus was suddenly next to her, kneeling, his hands pressing the Thirster to the ground. 'How many in this army?' he demanded.

'Five thousand. More. You won't be able to stop them.' The Thirster laughed, her head lolling back on the sidewalk.

'When are they coming?' Cyrus asked, his knee ramming her chest and knocking the arrow shaft, forcing her eyes to fly open and a scream to explode from her mouth.

'Two days, maybe sooner,' she grimaced, her teeth breaking through the stretched skin of her lips, making a fresh stream of blood flow down her chin. 'This realm no longer belongs to you. Once the Hunters are all finished there'll be no one left to stop us.'

'Well,' Cyrus said, dropping his face until it was just a centimetre above hers. 'Newsflash. We're not Hunters. We're something else entirely. And this army you think is going to take us is not even going to make it through because the Gateway is going to be closed for business.'

He flicked something over in his hand and Evie saw liquid cascading over the Thirster's face into her open mouth and dousing her clothes. The Thirster struggled, choking and coughing. Cyrus jumped to his feet, shaking the remains of the lighter fluid over the other two Thirsters. Cyrus stepped backwards, flicking open his Zippo lighter. 'Thanks for the chat. Peace out,' he said, smiling grimly. Then he dropped the lighter.

Evie scrambled backwards as the blue flames licked towards her. The Thirsters ignited into balls of squealing flames, their screams cut off almost instantly, the flames dying down as the bodies burnt to nothing. Thick black smoke started billowing around them.

Evie felt a hand on her arm and then, without warning, she found herself being dragged along, the stench of burning flesh and acrid smoke scoring her throat.

They were suddenly back at the car and the others were flinging their weapons into the trunk, but Evie stood on the sidewalk staring back at the smoking piles of ash. The humans they'd seen walking towards them had stopped to gape, their feet kicking at the remains. One had drawn out a cell phone.

'Come on, get in,' Cyrus yelled. Evie turned. The car was revving and Cyrus had flung open the passenger door.

She glanced back at the humans standing over the smouldering remains and then climbed in beside Cyrus. An army was coming in just two days, she thought numbly – an army of unhumans. They were coming for her. And they'd go through whoever stood in their way. Issa had never mentioned an army. Why hadn't she said something? She must have seen it coming. Evie stared out of the windshield unseeing, not registering the flashing blue and red lights that flew past them, thinking only of Lucas. Maybe Issa had told him. Maybe that's what she'd come to tell him the other day. It made sense. As did Lucas lying to her about it. He wouldn't have wanted to worry her.

Epic fail on that score.

Cyrus pulled into the warehouse's parking garage and killed the engine. No one had said a word since they'd set fire to the Thirsters. Cyrus hadn't cracked a single joke. Even now his face was set in a seriously dark expression that she'd never seen him wear before. It kind of made her miss his normal mocking one. Evie's stomach constricted, her ribs too, squeezing her heart in a tight embrace. Where was Lucas? She scanned the empty space of the warehouse, hoping that her instincts might be wrong and that he was there waiting for her to return.

She sucked in a breath. Someone was here. She could sense it. But it wasn't Lucas. Then she saw her, sitting on the ground by the elevator. The others turned their heads as the person got up and started walking quickly towards the car, dusting herself off as she went.

'What's your mum doing here?' Ash asked.

Margaret stopped in front of the car, hands on her hips. Evie opened her door and followed the others out.

'Where have you been?' Margaret demanded. 'I've been waiting for you.'

27

Lucas had stopped beside Cyrus's car outside the coffee shop, debating. To take it, or not to take it? It was tempting. Just imagining Cyrus's face if he found his car gone made him smile, but then he'd thought about Evie having to take public transport and had decided instead to jack the BMW two cars down. He didn't want to have to take public transport either.

It wasn't until he hit the freeway that Lucas realised he had been driving on automatic pilot and that he was heading towards the Mission. He almost pulled off at the next exit and doubled back, but then he figured it wasn't such a bad idea to head to the Mission. Grace might be more likely to come to a place she was familiar with. And if he was being honest, he had a desire to see the place one last time.

It was a four- to five-hour drive. He made it in three. He calculated how long he should wait and decided that if Grace wasn't there by midnight he'd leave. Whatever happened he'd be back with Evie before dawn broke.

The Mission was an old church and friary, built over two hundred years ago. It looked abandoned from the outside. It looked abandoned on the inside too, the hallways echoing mournfully, slanted squares of moonlight dousing the floors. Lucas paced the rooms, staying invisible, moving silently, wandering aimlessly. He didn't expect to find anything or anybody. His senses were alert but the only sounds were coming from a couple of bats nesting in the roof and a few spiders spinning webs on the ceiling of the old chapel.

The weapons room had been emptied and the training room was bare. Except for a few holes in the wall and the crater in the floor where Shula had shoved Joshua's head through the boards one time, it was unrecognisable. He remembered the hours they'd spent in that room with Tristan forcing them to run scenarios over and over, testing them, getting them to trust each other. Maybe that's where it had all gone wrong. Trying to forge trust between species – the fundamental flaw in a Brotherhood that included Thirsters, Mixen and Scorpio.

Lucas wandered back down the stairs and into Tristan's study. It had been ransacked. Books were lying splayed on the floor with their pages torn out. His desk had been wiped clear – everything tipped up and papers scattered. Tristan's chair lay on its side as if in the first throes of rigor mortis. Lucas half expected to see crime scene tape and a chalk outline around it. He wondered who the Elders had sent for Tristan, and whether Tristan had tried to resist. He was a Shadow Warrior, so he could have faded and tried to evade them that way, but no doubt the Elders had sent a Shadow Warrior to fetch him. Lucas drew in a deep breath, pressing his hands to the doorway to steady himself. Tristan was probably dead already.

They were all dead. Joshua, Shula, Caleb. Even Neena. He whispered their names out loud. It was hard to believe they were gone when their presence in the building was so strong. Eerie sounds were pushing their way indistinct and muted through the walls – Shula's dirty cackle sounding far away, then rising to the rafters and scaring the bats into flight; a sudden swish to Lucas's right that made him twist around expecting to see Caleb stalking past; from beneath him the clang of the cellar doors bursting open, and then, just as he startled backwards into the hallway wondering whether any of it was real or if he was hearing things, he felt a flutter of wings brush his ear.

Neena.

He called her name and tried to grasp at the shadow that flew past, his heart hammering wildly in his chest. He watched the shape settle in the rafters. It was just a bat. Lucas stared at it, holding his breath, praying for it to shimmer.

'I'm sorry,' he whispered when it flew away. He sank down onto the bottom step in the great hallway. Coming back here had been a mistake. He closed his eyes. The past had gone. There was only the now. And there was no time for ghosts.

His head shot up. There – again, a footstep on gravel. He was on his feet instantly and merging with the shadows cast by the stairwell. A few seconds later Grace appeared in the open doorway before him dressed in a long, dark coat, her pale hair illuminated by the moon that had risen above the trees behind her. He stepped out from the shadows.

'Lucas,' she said, taking him in with a coolly appraising stare.

He scanned the woods behind her, checking that she was alone. 'Grace,' he answered when he'd confirmed she was.

'You wanted to see me.'

'Yes.'

She glanced at the dark and empty hallway behind him, as if she had no intention of crossing over the threshold of the building. Her arms were wrapped around her body defensively. It made him wonder what she'd seen him do. 'You know,' she said, 'you didn't need to choose here.'

He nodded. 'I realise. I just needed to see this place again.'

Grace raised an eyebrow. 'Why? To make sure they were all dead?'

He flinched, then took a stride towards her, seeing her head fly up in surprise at the speed at which he had moved. 'You knew it was going to happen, didn't you?' he shouted. 'You knew they were going to die and yet you let them go anyway?'

Grace took a step back away from the onslaught, but Lucas carried on. 'You could have stopped them! You could have warned Neena at the very least. Why? Why didn't you ...?' His voice caught and he paused, pressing his lips together to try to stop his voice from shaking with all the pent-up rage.

'I didn't see it all, Lucas,' Grace answered calmly. 'It all changed so quickly. If you hadn't gone back that night, then it would be done by now. And, likewise, if Evie had killed you then the prophecy would have come true already. But you did go back. And she didn't kill you. And that changed everything. Well,' she paused, 'not everything. But it's brought us to where we are now.' She sighed with what could have been boredom or could have been sadness. 'And Neena dying – I didn't see that coming at all. She made the choice so quickly. As soon as I saw it, it was done.' She shook her head and her hair flew like a curtain caught in a gust of wind. 'It's all so pointless though.'

Lucas frowned at her, something sliding into place with a certainty that stopped his breath. 'You've always known about the prophecy being marked, haven't you?' he asked quietly.

She held his gaze. 'Yes,' she said with a shade of defiance in her voice. 'That's why I tried to stop you, Lucas. Don't you see? Nothing you have done in the past or will do now or in the future will make any difference. It just brings you closer to death.'

He contemplated her for a few moments. The moon had disappeared behind some clouds and without any light to illuminate her all he could make out were the two enormous pools of her eyes, like sunken cavities in her skull. 'So everybody keeps telling me. I guess I still choose to believe we can be masters of our own destiny.'

'Your fate needn't be the same as Evie's,' Grace answered, her voice cracking like a shot against the walls.

'What do you mean?' he asked, feeling the shudder prickle up his spine.

Grace's expression hardened, her chin lifting defiantly, almost in challenge. Suddenly everything became clear to Lucas. 'You know the rest of the prophecy, don't you?' he whispered in a hoarse voice.

Grace paused for a second and then nodded. 'Yes. I know it. The Sybll have always known it. We just broke it into pieces and hid those pieces from the rest of the realms because it was the only sensible thing to do.'

For several seconds they stood in the gloom of the doorway staring at each other in silence. Lucas frozen, and Grace's eyes fixed on him, trying to foresee what his next move was going to be. *So Issa knew too*, Lucas thought to himself. She had known all along and had lied to him. Why? He couldn't understand. He found his voice, forcing the question out. 'What does it say, Grace? What does the prophecy say?'

Grace studied him. She gathered herself before she spoke, drawing back her shoulders. 'A sacrifice is called for,' she said. 'A life to close it. The White Light's life. She has to walk through the Gateway.'

For what felt like whole days Lucas stood there, the air growing still around him, his body frozen in place. Then he shook his head and said simply, 'No.'

Grace's expression shifted, pity welling in her eyes. Rage exploded out of him in response. 'Why didn't you tell me – back then – why didn't you warn me?' he yelled, lunging for her, but she had foreseen his move and darted backwards out of his reach.

'Because, Lucas,' she said softly, 'you can't change anything. All these decisions that you are making are pointless, like throwing a paper towel onto a forest fire in an attempt to put it out. No matter what happens to delay it, nothing changes the final outcome. You can't stop this from happening. The way through will close. And the White Light will be the one to close it. She will die. And the only difference will be whether this realm, and everyone in it, gets destroyed along with her or not.'

'What are you talking about?' Lucas asked, stunned.

'There's an army massing on the other side of the way through. Unless the Gateway closes in the next forty-eight hours you may as well forget about having anywhere to run to. They will try to kill Evie before she can fulfil the prophecy. The prophecy is marked but the Elders refuse to believe it. So they will try and they will fail, just as the Brotherhood have tried and failed several times already, and you will die for no reason. As will countless more innocent people.' She paused and took a step forward towards him, her fingers gripping his wrist. 'You have the power to change their fates as well as your own, Lucas.'

He ripped his arm free from her grasp and tore past her without another word, jumping the steps and hitting the driveway at a sprint.

Grace's voice, soft as snowfall, pulled him up short. 'She's not there,' she said.

Lucas reeled around and was back in front of Grace in the next second, holding her by the arms. 'Where is she?' he demanded.

Grace smiled and her smile, though sad, seemed tinged also with victory. 'She's with Margaret. The Hunter,' she said finally. 'She's taking Evie to Victor. They're on their way right now to Riverview.'

Lucas let go of Grace's shoulders as if she'd burnt him. 'Why? Why is Margaret taking Evie to Victor?' he asked.

'Because Margaret knows. She knows the rest of the prophecy too. All that research she's been doing over the years, it was always to find the prophecy. She's going to give it to Victor when she delivers Evie to him. She wants the way through to be closed.

That's all she's ever wanted. She sent you off to find me so you'd be out of the way.' She paused, looking at him pityingly. 'Do you see how it's all falling into place, Lucas?'

Lucas shook his head, trying to understand, then he let go of Grace and ran to the car. He needed to leave. He needed to get to Evie before ...

'You won't ever be in time to save her,' Grace called out after him. 'Do you understand?'

He climbed in the car and shoved the key into the ignition.

'You just keep delaying things,' he heard Grace whisper, her words cutting across the revving of the engine, 'but it's all going to end soon anyway.'

28

Evie stared at the clock on the dashboard watching the neon display blink like the countdown timer on a bomb. It was close to midnight. Her foot was tapping the floor and Margaret kept glancing down at it every few seconds and frowning. But Evie couldn't stop the bouncing, or stop her fingers from twisting knots into her T-shirt. She was worried that Lucas wouldn't know where she had gone. She didn't trust Vero and Ash to tell him if ... no, she shook her head, *when* he got back. She should have written him a note but Margaret hadn't given her time to even scrabble for pen and paper. And Lucas didn't have a phone on him. In fact she wasn't even sure he owned a phone.

But it wasn't just concern about Lucas that was making the adrenaline short-circuit her body. Ever since Margaret had shoved her backwards into the Prius and snatched the keys from Cyrus, Evie had been feeling as if she'd tumbled over the edge. And it wasn't Margaret's driving and it wasn't the fact they were heading back to Riverview. No. She took a deep breath and glanced sideways at Margaret – it was something else entirely that had sent her into a freefall spin.

Cyrus's mum had barely said a word to her since they'd got in the car. Her hands were gripping the steering wheel as if she was sat in the front seat of a rollercoaster car without a seat belt on, and she was leaning forward over the dashboard, her nose nearly pressed to the windshield, as if by sitting that way she could exert some extra forward motion on the car to make it go faster.

She didn't trust Margaret. That's what this weird, knotted feeling in her stomach was. It was the same feeling she'd had around Lucas when she first met him – something pricking at her, her senses screaming that she shouldn't trust him. Back then she'd known instinctively that Lucas had been hiding something from her. It just turned out that the effect he had on other parts of her body overrode her gut suspicion and all her instincts. This time, though, she recognised what her gut was telling her and she wasn't going to ignore it. Margaret was keeping something from them. Something Evie didn't think was going to be a pleasant surprise. She pressed her hand to the hilt of Lucas's blade and felt it dig into her spine. Her foot instantly stopped tapping.

Cyrus leant forward suddenly between the two front seats. 'Mum, do you want me to drive?' he asked for the fourth time. 'We might get there sometime before the army of unhumans invades that way.'

'No,' Margaret answered tersely. 'The way you drive we'll get pulled over by the police.'

Cyrus huffed and flopped noisily against the back seat. 'Why aren't we taking your car anyway? I just got this valeted and now I'm going to have to do it all over again.'

'My car got stolen earlier today,' Margaret answered, 'and, Cyrus, unless we make it to Riverview the least of your problems is going to be getting your car valeted.'

'Fine,' Cyrus sighed, 'no need to remind me. But tell me once again why we're driving halfway across the state of California for a book that Evie says contains nothing we don't already know?'

'I think it may have some hidden clue in it as to the location of the rest of the prophecy. I told you this already,' Margaret snapped, not taking her eyes off the road. 'I remember reading something once.' She trailed off.

'And you're remembering this fact only now?' Cyrus asked, taking the words right out of Evie's mouth. 'You didn't think to remember this earlier, back when it was first mentioned and before you sent the hybrid demon off to hunt down the missing part?'

Margaret didn't say a word. Evie stared at her, feeling the nausea in the pit of her stomach growing, but Margaret just kept driving with a fixed expression on her face. Her face in profile was striking. She had Cyrus's square jaw and wide-spaced eyes, and the same short hair, a shade darker than her son's, though Evie had a sneaking suspicion Cyrus lightened his because those streaks were far too symmetrically spaced to be the work of the sun. Margaret swallowed, her jaw starting to pulse mechanically as she felt Evie's scrutiny. Evie turned away and stared out of the window instead, trying to imagine what Lucas might make of the situation – what he'd do.

'And you didn't think to take this book with you when you skipped town?' Cyrus went on. 'You didn't think *maybe this will come in handy some day. I think I might keep a hold of this?*'

Margaret glared at him in the rear-view mirror. 'No, I was too busy running for my life – for yours – to think of taking anything.'

Cyrus's eyebrows shot up. 'Except for a few priceless antique weapons?'

Evie twisted once more to look at Margaret, whose grip on the steering wheel had tightened so that the bones of her knuckles were practically shearing through the skin. So, she'd run off with some of the Hunters' ancient weapons. Was that how she'd financed her time on the run? Was that how Cyrus lived his playboy lifestyle and wasn't forced to work a day job at Starbucks? She wished she'd had the presence of mind to think of doing the same when she had run.

'That ruby-hilted knife – remember the one, mum? You got a good price for that on eBay last year.'

'Not here, Cyrus,' Margaret snapped.

Evie bit back the smile.

'OK, so the plan is to what? Get to Evie's house, break in, find this book and then what? Hope to whichever divinity is on our side that the answer's in it?'

'It *is* in it,' Margaret hissed, glancing up to read the interstate signs, then swerving hard across two lanes of traffic.

Cyrus contemplated his mother with narrowed eyes. 'Well, I sure as hell hope you're right about this book, because though there is no questioning my skill, I'm not that confident of my chances of emerging unharmed against an army of five thousand unhumans. And if the answer isn't there then ...'

Margaret cut him off. 'We'll close the Gateway before they can come through. OK? Stop panicking.'

Cyrus bolted upright, affronted, 'I'm not panicking. I don't panic. *Ever*. I'm just cautiously expressing my concern.'

Evie stayed quiet. Cyrus might not be panicking but she sure as hell was. They had just passed the first sign for Riverview and her heart rate had rocketed. She unlocked her fingers from her T-shirt and started flexing and unflexing them, trying to remember the way Lucas used to stroke her palm to get her to relax, then trying to take deep breaths when that failed. She repeated silently the words that Lucas had whispered to her: *It was all going to be fine.* In a few hours they'd be back together, they'd have the book, they'd know what they needed to do and this whole nightmare would be over.

She sank down into her seat as they turned onto Main Street, though she didn't expect to see any traffic or people about. This was a country town: people went to bed with the sun; there was nothing whatsoever in the way of nightlife. She glanced warily out of the window anyway. Last time she'd been here, which felt like centuries ago rather than just a few days, she and Lucas had left a pile of dead unhumans behind and Victor trussed up like a stuffed pork loin in his own store. But gazing out on the deserted street, painted eerily chiaroscuro under the streetlights and reminding her of a Hopper painting, it was hard to imagine that a demon massacre had occurred right here.

They cruised past Joe's diner and Evie stared in the dark windows remembering the night she'd served Victor – the same night the Brotherhood had showed up to get her and she'd been outed by Victor as a Hunter. It felt strange to think that once upon a time she'd been a waitress. Now she was a demon slayer slash walking prophecy. How was that for a career move?

She turned her head quickly to look at the boutique on the other side of the road which Victor had set up as a cover. Though he'd employed her as a shop assistant, in reality he'd been training her to fight. The stock room had functioned as a weapons training room. The mannequins Evie had dressed in couture were still in the window, plastic limbs splayed in surprise as if they couldn't believe the sign hanging on the door announcing that the shop was closing down. Evie wondered if the weapons were still laid out in the back room or if Victor had taken them.

Margaret paused at the next intersection, looking at her for directions. Evie pointed her left. They drove for a few minutes, passing her ex-boyfriend Tom's house. His bedroom light was still on. She tried to picture him. Was he talking on the phone to Kaitlyn Rivers like he'd once done with her – in hushed whispers under the covers so that his mother couldn't hear? Was he safe? Would the Elders send anyone to hurt him? Or threaten him? The knots twisted in her gut. How was she supposed to protect everyone she'd ever been close to? She kept staring at the house over her shoulder, checking the shadows, trying to sense if anything lurked in them, until she noticed Cyrus narrowing his eyes at her in suspicion.

'So,' she said, turning back to Margaret before Cyrus could ask anything or start jibing her. He already knew enough of her business. 'Um, Mrs

Locke, you've been researching the Hunter family all this time?'

'Mmm,' Margaret murmured in response, keeping her attention fixed on the road.

'What were you trying to find out exactly?' she asked innocently.

Margaret licked her lips and swallowed. 'I was trying to find out how this all began. Why the Gateway first appeared, I wanted to find out more about the Hunter family.'

'And did you? Find out anything, I mean?'

'Yes,' she answered. 'I found out plenty.'

Evie waited for her to continue but she didn't. 'And?' Evie finally had to ask.

'And I'll tell you later,' Margaret snapped. 'Which way now?'

'Keep going straight,' Evie said, thrown by the older woman's tone, 'then take a left at the end of the road. My house is the last one on the right.' Evie leant forwards, her heart now in her mouth, gazing at her neighbours' familiar houses. She'd taken Margaret a slightly roundabout route, so she had to drive past Jocelyn's place. The porch light was on, though the rest of the house was buried in darkness. Was Jocelyn holding up her end of the bargain? Was she looking after her mum?

Half a mile further on, they came to Evie's house. Margaret cut the engine and cruised to a silent stop at the edge of the road, pulling onto the grass verge.

Evie stared at the old Victorian house. The lights were all out, even the porch light, which her mother normally left on to welcome visitors. Evie scanned the windows upstairs – her own bedroom under the eaves, her mother's at the far end. The curtains were drawn in both rooms. The house didn't look welcoming. For the first time in Evie's life it looked threatening.

29

Evie eased open the door and stepped out into the night, the first leaves of fall crackling under her feet. A thin wedge of moon lit the driveway, though beneath the cover of trees at the edge of the plot total blackness lay. She hesitated for a moment, trying to gauge her surroundings, at once so familiar but at the same time now alien. She scanned the area. She couldn't feel any unhumans. Her heart was beating fast, the blood pounding in her temples, and her hearing was so acutely tuned that she could hear the mournful hoots of an owl down by the river and some rustling in the long grass in the orchard behind the house. But her senses weren't pricking, so she knew it wasn't an unhuman or even a human. It was just an animal.

'Do you remember where you left the book?' Cyrus asked. He had appeared beside her, his hand casually brushing her lower back.

'Yes,' she answered, looking up at the darkened windows, 'it's upstairs in my bedroom, under the mattress.'

'That's original.'

She started walking up the drive, the crunch of the gravel sounding as loud as buckshot. Cyrus hurried to keep up. Margaret seemed to be staying in the car, which was fine by Evie.

'Is your mum home?' Cyrus asked under his breath.

Evie frowned up at the darkened windows, her pace slowing. 'She should be,' she whispered back. But now he'd asked the question she realised that was what was bothering her. Her mum's car wasn't there. There was only Evie's old truck, parked by the side of the house.

'If she's there, don't wake her up, OK? Let's just get the book and leave,' Cyrus murmured.

Evie turned to him, her eyes narrowing to slits. She needed to see her mum. Cyrus could shove his advice where the sun didn't shine. 'I need to warn her ...' she started.

'What are you going to tell her?' Cyrus hissed through the darkness. '*Run, the apocolypse is coming?* This is not the moment for reunions, hysterics and explanations to family,' he said, taking hold of her by the elbow. 'Call her later and tell her you need her help. Tell her you need her to come and get you because you've been abandoned by lover boy in Alaska or somewhere else a thousand miles from here. That'll get her out of town. Well away from any trouble that comes looking for you.'

Evie snatched her arm free and scowled at Cyrus in the darkness, watching the old oak tree slash angry shadows across his face. She bit her tongue and strode off down the driveway. He had a point. Turning up in the middle of the night with Cyrus in tow, when she'd only skipped town three nights ago with Lucas, wasn't exactly going to be an easy one to explain to her mother. But no way was she ever going to admit to Cyrus that he was right.

On the front porch she pulled up short, her hands hovering at her sides. Cyrus bounded up the steps and drew up alongside her. 'What is it?' he asked. 'I don't feel anything. There's no one here.'

Exactly, she thought to herself. Where was her mother? She turned the door handle. It was locked. Her stomach clenched in panic. The front door was never locked. She turned and started heading around to the back door, Cyrus jogging to keep pace with her. On the back porch Lobo's bed lay empty. The panic trebled.

'What? What is it?' Cyrus asked, a note of worry creeping into his voice when he saw the expression on her face.

'Lobo,' Evie said, pointing at the dog's empty bed and water bowl. 'The dog's gone.' She reached for the back door. It fell open.

Cyrus stepped quickly past her into the kitchen, flicking the light switch as he went. A howl sent him jumping backwards. Evie pushed past him, dropping to her knees, holding her arms out wide as Lobo leapt towards her, pressing his muzzle into her shoulder.

She grabbed hold of him by the scruff of the neck and buried her face in his fur.

'Lobo,' she whispered, 'good boy, where's mum?'

The husky dog whined and pawed the ground. Evie sat back on her haunches, her fingers carefully stroking the back of Lobo's neck where Shula had acid-burnt him. The skin beneath the fur seemed to be healing.

'There's a note.'

Evie looked up. Cyrus was reaching for a sheet of paper lying on the kitchen table. She was on her feet in the next second, snatching it out of his hands.

Evie, in case you choose tonight to come home, I'm at Joe's. I'll be home in the morning. Mum x

Evie stared at the note. What the hell? Joe? And her mum? She reread the note. Joe? Evie's old boss, Joe? She blinked a few times trying to clear her head and the visions now occupying it. Since when had her mum been sleeping over at Joe's? Was this a recent occurrence?

Cyrus put his hand on her shoulder, 'So your mum's getting some, huh?' he asked.

Evie crumbled the note into a ball and spun around, her cheeks blazing but words choking in her throat.

'Look, call her later,' Cyrus said, his smile fading. 'Send her and this Joe guy on a mission to get you from Alaska.' He grabbed her by the elbow once more. 'Come on, we need to find this book.'

Evie yanked her arm out of his grip and walked through into the hallway. She ran up the stairs, Cyrus following right behind. She opened the door to her bedroom slowly and stepped inside, switching on the light. Her mum had tidied her room. She almost didn't recognise it. The closet doors were visible for once, not buried under an avalanche of clothes. All her books had been piled on her desk neatly alongside a half-written paper. She felt a momentary stab of guilt as she realised that school was due to start back in a few days – about the same time that the army of unhumans was due to come by looking for her. How was that for timing? But at least she would have an excuse as to why she hadn't finished the paper.

She felt Cyrus nudge her and dropped to her knees in front of her bed, sticking her hands under the mattress and rummaging. She spread her arms wide, sweeping the bed slats. Then, when she found nothing, she dropped to the ground and peered beneath the bed to see if the book had fallen to the floor.

'Did you find it?' Cyrus asked impatiently.

She wriggled out from under the bed. 'It's not there,' she said, jumping to her feet.

Cyrus pulled the mattress off the bed and upended it against the wall.

'Hey,' she yelled, but her voice died away in the face of the dust and the obvious lack of book.

'Damn it,' Cyrus shouted, taking the words out of her mouth. 'Are you sure it was there? You didn't hide it in your underwear drawer or somewhere else?'

Evie shook her head, at the same time turning to the dresser and pulling the drawers open. She started rifling desperately through her clothes. 'No, no, it's not here. I put it under the mattress. I know I did. If it's not here, then someone's taken it.' Had her mum moved it when she tidied the room? That had to be the only explanation. She turned to the desk and knocked over the pile of books stacked there, looking for the familiar leather-bound cover among them – but nothing. Cyrus had moved to the dresser and was rooting through her underwear drawer. She shoved him roughly aside and his cry of protest almost drowned out the squeak of floorboards.

The two of them spun towards the door. The bottom stair creaked again as someone shifted their weight. Evie's senses went into overdrive. It was a Hunter. That feeling she had whenever she was near Cyrus or any of the others was getting more obvious to her now. It wasn't exactly the magnetic attraction that Cyrus had claimed it was; it was more like someone was pulling an invisible string attached to her sternum. There was a tug that made her want to draw nearer, to find out who was tugging at her.

'It's just my mum,' Cyrus said, pushing Evie aside and starting to tip the contents of her drawers onto the floor.

Evie stayed staring at the door, her hand instinctively reaching behind her, her fingers closing around the hilt of Lucas's blade. The door opened and she drew the knife with a speed that caused blue sparks to shower over her and make Cyrus swear and leap around.

A man stood towering in the doorway. Evie took one glance at him before bringing the blade up with a snarl.

'Looking for something?' Victor asked.

30

Evie stared at him – at the familiar purple cravat he was wearing and at the smug smile on his broad face. She saw him glance at the blade she was holding in front of her and hesitate for a moment on the brink of the doorway. He was clutching the book they were looking for in his right hand, holding it against his chest as though it was a bible and he was about to preach the word.

Evie's feet were rooted to the spot. She did a quick calculation. Victor was armed. There was a knife sheathed on his belt and he was probably carrying a gun too, despite his preference for the medieval. His frame entirely filled the doorway, eclipsing the light from the hall. There'd be no way around him. She weighed the knife in her hand. On the upside he made a big target. She could try throwing it and hope it hit home. But she remembered when she'd thrown a knife at him once before he'd actually caught the damn thing in midair and she didn't want to risk losing the blade – given it wasn't hers to begin with. Her only option then was to get past him somehow and to run.

'Who the hell are you?' Cyrus demanded, stepping suddenly in front of her and squaring up to Victor.

'Victor,' Evie said hoarsely. 'It's Victor.'

'Victor?' Cyrus asked, tipping his head to one side, taking in the bulk of the man in front of him. Evie caught the flash of metal in his hand and knew Cyrus had pulled his knife from his belt.

'Cyrus!' Margaret's voice came as a warning yell. She appeared behind Victor's shoulder and Evie watched in dawning horror as Victor shifted slightly to let her pass into the room. Her eyes darted between them both. What was going on? Hadn't Margaret been running from Victor? Hadn't he been trying to kill her? So what was she doing now treating him like he wasn't standing right there in the room next to her, clutching the book they'd driven halfway across the state to find?

'So this is why you ran?' Victor asked, his eyes flashing to Margaret before returning to Cyrus. He studied him for several seconds. 'He looks a lot like his father, don't you think?' he asked, raising his eyebrows in a smirk.

Cyrus's head flew up. 'What's he talking about?' he asked through a clenched jaw.

Evie stared at Margaret. What was going on? But Margaret was glaring at Victor, her face turning pale.

'Where's Lucas?' Victor asked.

'He's not here. I got him out of the picture,' Margaret answered.

'What?' Evie heard herself ask. She closed her eyes and then opened them again, shaking her head at Margaret in disbelief. 'You planned this? You knew Victor would be here?'

'What's going on?' Cyrus asked, sounding every bit as confused as she was.

Victor reached out an arm. 'Evie, come with me,' he demanded.

She burst out laughing and took a step backwards, thrusting the blade out before her. 'No,' she said. 'Are you kidding me? I'm not going anywhere with you. I wish I'd let Lucas kill you. I wish I'd killed you myself.'

Faster than Evie had anticipated, Victor lunged, his fingers closing around her left wrist. She pulled backwards, her right hand swiping with the blade, slashing the top of his arm. The Shadow Blade sliced easily through his suit, drawing blood. Victor instantly let her go, staring at his arm in surprise as the blood started to drip to the carpet. He tugged at his silk cravat, pulling it free from his neck before wrapping it around his arm, the whole time keeping his eyes trained on her. Evie's own gaze fell instantly to the thin red line against the front of his throat that had been hidden up until now. That was the scar from where Lucas had pressed his knife to Victor's throat. As she stared at it, and Victor was momentarily distracted with tying a tourniquet, she took two small steps sideways, closing the space between her and the now-empty doorway.

'She's not going with you,' Cyrus said, raising his voice. 'She's not going anywhere until you tell me what's going on.'

'Cyrus, it's for the best,' whispered Margaret.

Cyrus shook his head. 'For *whose* best?' he asked. 'No one's going anywhere, least of all Evie, until you tell me what's going on. Why did you bring us back here? I'm guessing it wasn't for the book, was it?'

Margaret shook her head. 'No,' she admitted.

'There's nothing about the prophecy in it, is there?' Cyrus grimaced.

'Give it to me,' Victor demanded, turning to Margaret now and holding out his hand.

'Give him what, Mum?' Cyrus shouted.

Margaret glanced at Cyrus. 'This,' she said, pulling something out of her back pocket. She held it up. It was a piece of torn, crumpled, yellowing paper.

Evie stared at it, her heart starting to leap in broken rhythms.

'What? What is it?' Cyrus asked, shooting them both confused looks.

'It's the prophecy,' Evie answered him, her eyes tracking back to the piece of paper in Margaret's hand. 'That's what you've been researching, isn't it?' she asked, her gaze flying now to Margaret's face. Evie wanted to snatch the piece of paper from Margaret's hand, but she was rooted to the spot, a feeling of terror inching through her body.

'Give it to me!' Victor shouted, snatching the piece of paper out of Margaret's hand.

'What does it say?' Cyrus demanded.

A slow smile seeped across Victor's face as he read whatever was written on it. He glanced up quickly at Cyrus then began reading out loud, his eyes flaming.

Of two who remain a child will be born,
A purebred warrior, the fated White Light
Standing alone in the eventual fight
Severing the realms and closing the way

Passing through the light and into the dark
Memories will rise, shadows fade on this day

Confronting an army drawn from the realms,
The sun, the giver of life and the light
Together will stand and together fight
One sacrificing all to close the way

Passing through the light and into the dark
Memories will fade, shadows fall on this day

He stopped, raising his eyes from the page and fixing Evie with a look that burnt the breath clean out of her body.

'That's it?' Cyrus burst out. 'That bad pretence at poetry is what we've been running around looking for? *Sacrificing all?* What the hell does that mean?' He looked at his mother and Victor for an answer. The two of them stood staring at Evie; Margaret with an expression of pity, possibly guilt, on her face, and Victor wearing the smug smile that his name suggested.

Evie took a trembling step backwards. Her breathing was coming fast and shallow now, and sweat had started prickling along her spine. She wasn't getting enough oxygen. Her lips were starting to tingle. Her feet felt leaden.

'To fulfil the prophecy Evie has to walk through the Gateway. Through the light and into the dark – that's what it means.' Victor answered Cyrus without taking his eyes off Evie. And before Evie could move or talk or process anything further, Victor made a move, taking a blindingly fast leap towards her. She held up her hands automatically to deflect him but Cyrus was quicker, sidestepping between the two of them, blocking Victor.

'Sacrificing all ...' Cyrus mumbled to the ground. Then he looked up sharply, staring over his shoulder at Evie as if she was a ghost. 'You mean that ...' he stammered, 'that Evie has to die. To close it?'

There was just the word *die*. It was all she heard and then sounds became muffled as if she was entombed in a coffin, listening to voices seep through the soil at her graveside. Victor's face grew blurry and indistinct. Evie was only half-aware of Cyrus turning to her in slow motion, his mouth stretching, forming words she couldn't make out. Blocking all the noise, cancelling out the yelling was the sound of the river rushing loudly outside the window as if it had suddenly changed course and was raining down on the house. But then she realised with a start that it wasn't the river at all – it was the sound of her own blood pounding in her ears. As if on cue, her senses spun like a tuning dial and noise rushed back in, in full stereo. The blurred faces in the room flew sharply into focus.

'... this all along?' Cyrus was yelling at his mum. 'When we came to see you? You knew what Evie would have to do?'

Margaret nodded, 'Yes.'

He shook his head, 'You didn't say anything ...'

'Of course she didn't say anything, Cyrus ...' Victor interrupted.

'It's why you brought me here though, isn't it?' Evie spoke up, addressing Margaret. Her voice sounded normal, without even a trace of anger or surprise in it, and she was amazed at that. It shouldn't sound normal given the voice inside her head was screaming hysterically. 'It's why you called Victor to meet us – even though you hate him.'

Margaret fixed her with a defiant stare, throwing her shoulders back and tipping her chin up. 'Yes,' she answered.

'I don't get it,' Cyrus shouted. 'Can someone enlighten me? Why bring him into this?' He jerked his knife in Victor's direction.

'He'll see that it's done,' Evie whispered.

'How did you even find him?' Cyrus asked, turning to Margaret.

'I looked up Jocelyn's number after Evie told me she lived in Riverview,' Margaret answered. 'I convinced her to help me find Victor.'

'Did Jocelyn know?' Evie demanded, feeling a sudden spurt of anger. 'Did she know all along about the prophecy too? About this suicide mission?'

'No, of course she didn't,' Victor laughed. 'Even I didn't know the full meaning until now. I only suspected.'

Evie turned to look at him. There was that smug smile again. She wanted to swipe it off his face. Her fingers, which had loosened on the knife, suddenly tightened, gripping the hilt with force. She raised it to chest height and saw the fleeting look of surprise pass across Victor's face before the smirk returned. Evie's head was still whirling, trying to process everything, the word *die* beating like a drum against the inside of her skull.

'Evie,' Victor said, gently this time, as though he'd guessed her next move, 'There's nothing you can do. It's the prophecy.'

'She can't die. That's insane,' Cyrus burst out. 'There has to be another way. Why would walking through the Gateway kill her anyway? It doesn't hurt unhumans.'

Victor shrugged, his eyes glinting. Now he had the prophecy in his hands he didn't care about the hows or the whys, just about seeing it was done.

Evie felt like pointing out to Cyrus that even if she could walk through it she'd walk headlong into an army of unhumans all primed to kill her. Either way she lost. But she couldn't bring herself to open her mouth. A part of her welled up in sympathy for Cyrus; she could feel his confusion thick as fog, even as her own cleared away and the truth lay gleaming in front of her. She glanced at Margaret, who was still blocking the doorway, and almost smiled at the woman. There was no way out even if she found her way past these Hunters. There was no way back to Lucas and there was no choice. There never had been. Lucas had been wrong to believe there was. She took a step towards Victor.

'What are you doing?' Cyrus demanded, staring at her wide-eyed, as he blocked her way. 'You're just going to go with him?'

She did smile then – genuinely, sadly – feeling a rift tear along her heart as she let the knife fall to her side.

31

There were four. Lucas counted each of their heartbeats. Four Hunters inside the house. He could sense Evie the strongest, feel her presence fighting his reason, pulling him nearer when he needed to bide his time out here in the shadows, far enough away so the others couldn't feel him. Cyrus's car was parked at the end of the driveway so he was assuming that he was in the house too, along with Victor and Margaret. Victor's car was parked further up the street.

He'd slashed the tyres of both cars with the knife he'd found hidden in his old room back at the Mission. And now he was hovering at the start of the drive, crouching in the shadows of an elm tree, his eyes fixed on Evie's room, the one buried under the eaves. The curtains were drawn but the light was on and he could make out a dark shape moving back and forth in front of the light. Lucas drew his knife and closed his eyes, trying to concentrate his hearing.

Nothing. Even blocking the sounds from the orchard and the river in the distance, he still couldn't hear any voices coming from the house. He faded and slid silently through the trees on the edge of the plot, circling the house to see if he could hear anything from the back. The lights were on in the kitchen, the back door slightly ajar.

He weighed his options. Victor and Cyrus were both strong and well trained, and Margaret's instincts were still good – she'd obviously honed them over the years, had never let her guard down. He didn't doubt they were all armed as well. He ran his hand through his hair and swore under his breath, trying to figure out his next move. Grace's words were running through his head – *you won't ever be in time to save her*, she'd said. Issa believed the same. It was why she'd lied to him about the prophecy. Because she had known that he would do anything in his power to stop it from coming true. Maybe they were right and it was futile – he looked up at the silent façade of the house – but that wasn't going to stop him from trying.

And then he heard her – heard Evie cry out – except there was no echo and no raised voices in reply. He realised in the next instant that he hadn't heard her cry out at all – he'd *felt* her – felt her distress as clearly as if it was his own, sharp as a needle, bright as day. That was all it took.

He was black lightning – invisible – striking across the orchard, flying up the veranda steps and in through the back door in under two seconds. He was up the stairs in the next second, not giving them a moment to react, if they had even felt him at all.

Margaret was standing in the way, Evie just visible behind her. And behind her stood Victor. Cyrus was standing open-mouthed in the centre of the room between Victor and Evie, his arms spread wide. Lucas gauged all this in the time it took for his heart to beat just once. In the next heartbeat he had slid invisibly beneath Margaret's outstretched arm, reaching Evie in the same moment. She half turned, her mouth falling open in shock and confusion, sensing him even before the others had registered he was there.

'Down,' he whispered, his lips brushing her ear.

Her eyes widened in understanding and she dropped to her knees, the back of her head banging his waist just as the blade left his hand. Victor let out a bellow as he saw the blade go whirling past Evie's head and finally his senses allowed him to see. He reacted fast, twisting sideways, but not fast enough, and the blade sank into the flesh of his shoulder.

Victor roared in anger, collapsing to his knees, his face contorting in pain as the blood started to spurt.

Lucas didn't pause. He bent, bringing his arm across Evie's chest and hauling her to her feet. He felt her stagger slightly against him and he clutched her tighter, dragging her backwards towards the doorway where Margaret stood blocking their way.

Lucas materialised, sliding the knife out of Evie's limp hand and into his own. He levelled it at

Margaret, registering the shock that drained the blood from her face as she realised what was happening. She backed away silently, out into the hall with her hands up.

Lucas edged past her, his arm still locked around Evie and headed to the top of the stairs.

'Don't let her get away!' he heard Margaret scream, and suddenly Cyrus was there at the top of the stairs, reaching for Evie, grabbing hold of her by the arm and trying to pull her towards him.

'Let her go,' Lucas said, holding Evie tighter and baring his teeth at Cyrus, aware the whole time that Evie wasn't putting up a fight. Her body stayed limp in his arms.

Cyrus snarled at Lucas, his eyes flashing with anger, but then his expression shifted as he looked at Evie and without warning he let go, stepping backwards and blocking Margaret who was now standing at the top of the stairs screaming at them to stop.

Lucas didn't give Cyrus a chance to reconsider. He dived down the stairs, pulling Evie after him, and threw himself against the front door, hearing the wood splinter over the noise of Margaret's screams. He dragged Evie down the steps of the veranda and started sprinting up the driveway, feeling the slackness of her hand in his and the drag as her feet kicked up the gravel. He skidded to a stop in front of the car, having to catch Evie around the waist to bring her to a halt.

He opened the car door and ushered her in, before climbing in beside her and spinning them up onto the verge and down the road in a cloud of dust. He drove without looking back and without looking at Evie, though his hand held onto hers tightly. Ten miles down the road he finally pulled off onto a dirt track and killed the engine.

He turned to face her in the gloom of the car. After several seconds Evie slowly lifted her eyes to meet his. Her face was bleached white as a Thirster's, her eyes unblinking and huge – dead-looking. Her bottom lip was shaking slightly. She swallowed once and took a deep breath.

'You know about the prophecy. You know what I have to do, don't you?' she asked in a voice he didn't recognise.

Lucas stared at her, feeling her words like a sound wave lashing him, knocking him back into his seat. She knew. Margaret had told her the whole prophecy. He hadn't been in time to save her from that. That's why she seemed so lost, so far from him. He kept staring at her, unable to tear his eyes away, unable to answer her either. Her shoulders were slumped. She looked as defeated as she had that time he'd seen her on the veranda of her house with Tom, the moment he'd realised his true feelings for her were as far from hate as it was possible to get.

'You know, don't you?' she said again, this time a tremor of impatience in her voice. 'Was it Grace? Did she tell you? Or Issa? Were you hiding it from me all this time?'

'No,' Lucas answered, his eyes dark as storm clouds, 'Issa didn't tell me. Grace did, earlier tonight. But it doesn't matter what she told me, none of it matters, you're not walking through the Gateway.' He brought his hand to rest against her cheek. It felt cold, even her breath against his fingertips felt icy. He turned the key in the ignition and racked the heat up full, letting it blast them, then he put his arm around her shoulders and pulled her against his chest. She fought him at first, her shoulders tensing, her fists coiled in her lap before his lips against her forehead undid something in her resolve and she collapsed against him, shaking. Her fingers gripped his shoulders and she took two deep breaths, each one ending in a shudder that rocked her whole body. Lucas stroked her heaving back, smoothed her hair, pulled her closer, trying to make the shivering stop. Eventually she fell still in his arms, her breathing calm.

'It'll be OK,' he whispered.

Evie pulled back and stared at him. 'Lucas,' she said, speaking slowly and clearly as if he was deaf, 'I'm going to die.'

He twisted away from her, pulling his hands free and gripping the wheel tightly. 'Don't say that.'

'You know it's true. There's nothing you or I can do about it, Lucas.'

'Yes there is!' He rounded on her, his voice a snarl. She shrank back in her seat and he immediately regretted his tone. 'There is, Evie,' he said more softly. 'We changed a prophecy once. We'll do it again.'

She shook her head, confused. 'When? What prophecy?'

'Grace once told me that I was going to die. In the beginning, she told me if I went back to Riverview I was going to die. But I didn't. We get to choose, Evie. We get to choose who we are and what path we take.'

He frowned hard and pressed his lips together. He wanted to smash his fists into the dashboard, pummel the steering wheel, kick his foot through the floor of the car.

It was Evie who moved this time, covering his hands with her own, pulling him gently around to face her. 'OK, OK, Lucas,' she said. 'If you think we can change it, let's try.'

He studied her, the breath catching in his throat. She was smiling tentatively at him though her eyes were still guarded and wary. Did she mean it? Was she really willing to try? The last time she'd been this defeated it had taken anger and betrayal to force her back into fighting mode. She leant forward and pressed her lips against his, and he closed his eyes and breathed her in – felt her skin, still cool beneath his hands. Maybe, he thought to himself as she pulled away and he caught the way her eyes lingered on his lips – maybe she didn't need anger and betrayal anymore to motivate her, maybe he was enough.

'OK,' he finally agreed. 'We'll figure a way around this. We'll find another way to close it. And no one is going to get hurt, I promise.'

Evie turned to stare through the windshield. 'We should go to Flic's,' she said.

'Flic's?' he asked, confused.

She nodded quickly and shrugged. 'We need to go somewhere. And we need help. We can't do this alone.'

'But Flic's?' he said, frowning at her. 'I'm not sure that's such a good idea.' Flic had made it very clear she didn't ever want to see him again and she also despised Evie. What help was his sister going to offer them? Other than showing them the way to the Gateway and shoving Evie through it?

'It's not safe going back to LA,' Lucas said.

'Victor'll expect us to head east or north,' Evie continued, speaking quickly, 'not back to LA.'

Lucas studied her. He didn't know what to do. He wanted to protect Evie and the only way he could see of doing that was by getting them as far away as possible from all this, to hide her away from danger. Lucas slammed his palm against the wheel. Goddamn these choices. For an instant his father flashed into his mind, an image of him saying goodbye, telling Flic and him that running away never achieved anything – that spending your life looking over your shoulder was no way of living. If he wanted to change the future then he needed to choose the harder path.

With a silent curse, he threw the car into drive once more and pressed his foot to the floor.

32

They drove through the night. Evie sank back into her seat watching the white stripes of the road slide under the car, feeling fury at every one that disappeared behind them and at every blink of the clock, which wasn't counting time anymore but was instead counting down the minutes and seconds she had left with Lucas – that she had left to live.

She'd told Lucas what he wanted to hear, not what she believed. They couldn't change the prophecy any more than she could change how she felt about him – this half human, half Shadow Warrior who'd saved her yet again. Saved her from what though? He couldn't save her from her fate, even though he seemed determined to keep trying, determined to keep fighting the inevitable. There was no such thing as choice.

She felt like she'd known the truth all along. The disquiet in the car with Margaret made sense now. The problem – the complicated question that had had them puzzling over it for days – now had a solution. And a fairly simple one at that. And, really, why was she even surprised? When Victor had revealed to her she was a Hunter and explained what that entailed she'd realised pretty fast that her life expectancy had shrunk. She'd always known that everything was going to end badly eventually. Or maybe not badly, but definitely sooner than she would have liked.

She stared at Lucas out of the corner of her eye, the muscles of his arms rigid as he spun the wheel, his expression a rigid mask of suffering, a muscle pulsing angrily in his jaw. She wanted to reach over and brush his hair back from his forehead, stroke away the worry lines creasing his brow. She didn't want to make him feel this much pain. More than anything she wanted to pull his face towards her and feel his lips against hers. She felt so much love and so much longing for him in that instant that it made her clutch her arms around her body in an effort to contain it all. If she had to die, she was doing it alone. Lucas would live. She wasn't going to drag him any further into this fight. If they kept running from it he would die. She drew a deep, jagged breath. That was the deal she would make. Her life for Lucas's. It made it easier to think of it in that way.

Lucas parked outside Flic's apartment block and, taking Evie's hand, led her back to the apartment. Evie walked in silence, distracted, occupied with planning. Lucas had no idea what was going through her mind. If he even suspected, he'd no doubt force her back into the car and drive non-stop until they hit the Atlantic and even then he'd probably try to keep going.

They stood as they had started – dishevelled, exhausted, on the run from Hunters and with nowhere else to turn. Only the clothing had changed. No more blood-spattered ball gowns. And this time Lucas didn't lean nonchalantly against the doorpost with a roguish smile on his face. He stood side by side with her, his fingers laced tightly through her own, as though he was scared to let her go, his smile replaced with a tight-lipped glower.

Flic opened the door wearing only a T-shirt. This time she looked genuinely surprised to see them. Her eyes were a burnished gold colour – she wasn't wearing her contacts, which meant that she hadn't been expecting them and that therefore Issa wasn't around.

'What are you doing here?' Flic hissed, her eyes darting down the corridor behind them. 'Goddamn it, Lucas.' She ushered them inside, then bolted the door quickly behind them.

'We know how the way through has to close,' Lucas said once she'd turned back to face them.

'Well, why aren't you out there closing it then?' Flic shouted. 'It's what you wanted, isn't it? And don't tell me you've come here for help because you can ...'

'No,' Lucas interrupted, silencing her with a look. 'The prophecy says that the White Light has to ...' He paused, unable to finish the sentence, then drew a breath and began again, 'to close the way through, to seal it and sever the realms – it says she has to walk through the Gateway.'

Flic blinked at him. 'Well, that doesn't sound so hard. What's the big deal?'

'Apparently a sacrifice is called for,' Evie explained. She watched Flic's eyes grow round as she finally figured it out.

'Did Margaret show you the prophecy?' Lucas suddenly demanded, pulling Evie around to face him, his fingers pressing into her shoulder blades. 'Do you remember the exact words?'

'Um,' Evie said, going blank. She shook her head, trying to shake the memories back into place, but she was distracted and confused by the look on Lucas's face – by the fear clouding his eyes. She'd never seen him look so afraid. Or so lost. Not even when facing down the Brotherhood.

'Maybe they have it wrong,' Lucas burst out. 'Maybe it's not talking about you at all. Who knows for certain? I mean, it doesn't mention you by name.'

'The giver of life. It said something about the giver of life. That's me. *Evie* – it's what my name means. It's talking about me.'

'I think we established a while ago the prophecy is talking about Evie,' Flic said, shooting looks between them both. 'So let me get this straight. This guy Victor and all the other Hunters – rogue and official – all know about Evie having to walk through the Gateway to close it?'

Evie nodded. Lucas stayed silent.

A knot of tension pulsed in Flic's jaw. She pressed her lips hard together and winced. 'So, am I right in saying that now you have every Hunter as well as every unhuman in the realms after you?'

Neither Lucas nor Evie said a word.

Flic crossed her arms over her chest and glared at them both. 'And you decided to come here?'

33

Lucas watched Evie go down the passageway. She was moving too slowly. Everything was moving too slowly, as if each second was being stretched on a rack. She disappeared into the bathroom and he turned impatiently back to the door, dimly aware that Flic was standing there watching him, her eyes narrowed with fury.

'Why did you come here?' she asked.

'I thought Issa might be able to help us. I need to figure out how to keep Evie safe.'

Flic rolled her eyes. 'Issa isn't here.'

What had he been thinking coming here? How in all the realms had he let Evie convince him? He should have headed east immediately. Now they'd have to backtrack. He wasn't thinking straight. Hell, he wasn't thinking in any direction – he needed to get it together.

'Can I borrow your car?' he asked Flic.

Flic stared at him, her eyes growing wide. 'How are you going to outrun an army of unhumans in an old Ford Cortina?'

Lucas swore. And once more Grace was in his head – *you won't ever be in time to save her*. He wanted to smash his fist into the wall, yell, throw something ... Instead he started pacing, anxiously eyeing the bathroom door, feeling Flic's gaze tracking his every move, as grating as claws raking against his skin.

'Why are you doing this?' Flic hissed. 'Yesterday you were all about shutting the way through, you couldn't stop going on about it needing to happen, and now little Miss Hunter's changed your mind. She just needs to click her little fingers and you jump to attention, blade at the ready.'

He didn't have time for this. 'I still want it shut, Flic. It's the right thing, just not this way. There *has* to be another way.'

Flic rolled her eyes. 'There isn't time, Lucas, for you to figure out that there isn't.'

'If it was Jamieson?' he said, struggling to keep his voice low. 'Is that what you would do? Would you just give up on him? Or would you fight until your last breath to try and save him?'

Flic stared right back at him. 'What do you think I'm doing, Lucas?' she asked. 'I'm trying to save him *and* you.'

His shoulders slumped.

'If she doesn't do it,' Flic said, taking a step towards him, 'have you thought what will happen to the rest of us? To this realm? Not just to Evie but to every damn human? There's an army coming through, Lucas, or did you forget? They're not going to make nice with the humans. I hear the revelation law has been suspended. It's going to be a bloodbath.'

'Shhh,' Lucas said, raising his hands and shushing her, 'Evie doesn't know the rumour about an army.'

'She doesn't know?' Flic shrieked. 'You didn't think to tell her that this whole realm's going to be turned upside down while an army of unhumans searches for her?'

'No, she doesn't need to know.'

'Yes, she does,' Flic spat. 'It's not a rumour, Lucas. She could stop it from happening.'

'The Hunters can stop it. The Elders couldn't even recruit enough unhumans to the Brotherhood. This army will be a handful of Thirsters who've been dragged from their realm – they'll be easily taken out. The Hunters can deal with them. That's their job.'

Flic stayed silent, glowering at him, her jaw set.

'I'm sorry, Flic,' he said, shrugging. 'I know you don't understand and I'm not asking you to. There's a reason I can't just accept this.' He bowed his head, staring at the ground. 'And it's not just about loving her, it's something else – it's as if my life is marked in the same way as hers. Something's making me fight for her, something bigger than me. I just don't know what or why yet. I can't give up on her – it's like asking me to stop breathing.'

He looked up and saw Flic was blinking rapidly, fighting the tears. He'd never seen Flic cry. Not even when their parents had died. He resisted the urge he had to reach out a hand and place it on her shoulder, knowing she'd only swipe it away if he tried. For a brief instant he saw their mother in the expression on her face. Their mother who had lived in perpetual fear and worry for her two unhuman children. It had etched lines into her face even when she was not much older than they were now. He saw it clearly for the first time from Flic's perspective. He was all the family she had left and he was choosing Evie, a Hunter, over her. And, though he hated himself for it, he couldn't choose differently.

Lucas was talking to Flic, who looked like she was on the verge of tears. For a moment Evie froze, watching them. Then Flic looked over Lucas's shoulder right at Evie, her eyes burning yellow fire. Evie pulled her shoulders back, took a deep breath and continued towards them. Lucas had turned too now, was looking at her as if she was about to break. Did it look that obvious?

'Lucas,' Evie said in a rush, pulling herself together, 'I think I just dropped my mum's wedding ring down the drain.'

His gaze dropped straight away to her hand. Then he nodded once. 'I'll get it, don't worry,' he said, heading towards the bathroom.

The second he vanished into the bathroom Evie turned to Flic. 'I need your help,' she whispered, darting a glance over her shoulder, making sure Lucas was well out of hearing range.

Flic turned on her heel and strode into the kitchen. Evie followed after her, finding her standing up against the kitchen counter with her back turned.

'Flic?' Evie said.

Flic looked over her shoulder. 'I'm not going to help you,' she snarled.

'You don't even know what I'm going to ask,' Evie said, closing the kitchen door.

Flic whipped around and flew across the room, backing Evie against the wall. 'You say you love my brother? Well, if you loved him you wouldn't be doing this! He's going to die if he keeps trying to protect you ...'

'No, he's not,' Evie answered calmly.

'Yes he is. Issa saw it!'

'She saw what?' Evie asked, reaching a hand to steady herself against the counter.

'Lucas dying,' Flic spat, 'trying to protect you. You don't need to be a Sybll with big eyes to see that. Or that thousands of other people will die too, unless you close the way through.'

Evie stared at her, speechless. Trying to fill her lungs was like trying to suck air through a crushed straw.

'Lucas isn't telling you the whole story,' Flic hissed, eyeing the door and lowering her voice. 'There's an army – an army of unhumans coming through here – to this realm ...'

'I know,' Evie cut in.

Flic stared at her, startled, 'You know?'

'Yes,' Evie nodded. She took a quick, unsteady step towards Flic, putting her hand on Flic's arm, more to steady herself than to make Flic listen. 'I'm not going to let him die. I swear to you. I'm going to finish this. And keep Lucas safe. But I can't do it on my own. I need you to do something. That's why I made him come here, rather than letting him head east.'

Flic glowered at her, her yellow eyes pulsing hatred. Evie pushed down the anger that bubbled in response and started talking, watching Flic's scowl slowly transform into a frown as she explained what she was planning on doing. She finished in a hurried whisper, hearing Lucas's soft tread heading towards them. 'Will you help me?' she begged.

Flic studied her. Her face had lost the disgusted look. Her eyes were wide. The hatred had muted into something less vicious. She nodded once.

'I couldn't find the ring.'

They both turned. Lucas had appeared in the doorway. He shook his head at Evie. 'I'm sorry.'

Her stomach clenched. 'It doesn't matter,' she answered, forcing a smile, her insides jittery all of a sudden. She saw the pain on his face and guilt cut a swathe through her.

'Lucas,' Flic said, sliding between them, 'I think you two should stay.'

Lucas opened his mouth to argue, clearly puzzled by her change of heart.

Flic cut him off before he could say anything. 'A few hours isn't going to hurt. I'm going to go and find Issa. I'll make her help you. And I'll get you a car too. You guys stay here, get some rest, eat something. I'll be back soon.'

Lucas's dark-ringed eyes narrowed at Flic, one brow arched in suspicion. He wasn't buying it. Not two minutes ago she'd been practically throwing them out of the door. His gaze flew to Evie, the suspicion growing in the light of her nervous shuffle.

He shook his head. 'No, we need to go right now,' he answered, reaching for Evie's hand. 'If Issa wanted to be here, she would be here.'

'No, Flic's right,' Evie spoke up, snatching her hand out of his grasp. 'I think we should stay. We've not slept in almost twenty-four hours. We need to rest.' She slumped her shoulders and gave him a pleading look, 'Please? I'm exhausted. I can't fight if I'm tired.'

His eyes were storm-laden and shifting as he paused awhile, scrutinising her as if he could read her mind. She forced herself to stand still and hold his gaze.

'Listen,' Flic said, clearing her throat behind them. 'You're my brother. I might never see you again. I can't stop you from doing this, but I can try to help you.'

Evie registered the look of guilt that flooded Lucas's face. 'If there's any chance that you can change things,' Flic pressed on, 'then I want to help.' She put a hand on Lucas's shoulder. 'Promise me you won't leave until I get back.'

Lucas frowned, then finally exhaled loudly, his teeth clenched. 'Fine. OK. We won't go anywhere until you get back. But hurry,' he growled.

Flic brushed past them, shooting Evie a warning look that made her shudder. She disappeared and a minute or so later they heard the apartment door slamming.

Evie stood beside Lucas, her pulse quickening, listening to the hush descend and feeling Lucas's tension like an undertow pulling her down. 'So,' she said, trying to smile, aware it probably looked like she was grimacing.

He brought his hand up and stroked a strand of hair out of her eyes. She dropped her gaze, knowing full well he'd see through the deceit in her eyes as easily as if she'd spoken it. Just as he was about to say something she took his hand and silently led him to the room they'd stayed in before.

He stood in front of the bed, then abruptly pulled his hand from hers and walked back towards the door. 'I'm going to stay up and keep watch. You sleep,' he said. She could sense the motion inside him – the effort it was taking for him to stand still, to stay in this place.

'I don't want to sleep,' she said, feeling suddenly afraid. She stuffed her hands deep into her pockets and looked down at her feet.

Lucas turned to her in the doorway. 'You just said you wanted to rest. I don't ...' He stopped abruptly.

Evie took a tentative step towards him, her stomach falling away. 'Hold me,' she whispered.

He hesitated, registering what she'd said. She watched the worry fade from his eyes and in its place a silent question form. But it was fleeting, there one moment and gone the next, the question apparently answered without needing to be voiced. He moved quickly, surprising her – was in front of her in just one stride, pulling her hard against his chest, kissing her in the next instant, cutting off her breath. One hand was pressed against her waist, the other holding the back of her head so she couldn't have pulled away from his lips even if she'd wanted to. Her hip bone jarred against his and she pushed closer, her fingers looping through the waistband of his jeans, pulling him towards her until his stomach was flat against hers.

She heard the low moan escape as she caught his bottom lip between her teeth and bit down softly. His hold of her tightened and for the sweetest, most perfect of moments she forgot everything – everything she had committed to be and everything she had committed to do – she felt so completely safe and so sheltered, as if his promises were all true and he could hold all the darkness at bay so that nothing could ever come near her or hurt her.

She pulled away from him for the brief seconds it took to tear her T-shirt off over her head with trembling fingers. She heard him take a breath as he glanced down, and he murmured something she couldn't hear as he fell to his knees in front of her. His lips brushed the cool skin of her stomach leaving a burning shiver in their wake. He pressed his cheek against the hollow shadow of her hip and it felt to Evie as if he was trying to fade into her, become part of her, and she closed her eyes and wished with every fibre of her being that he could.

When she opened her eyes he was looking up at her, uncertainty and desire and hope mingling in his expression, and she dropped to her knees level with him, taking his face between her hands, feeling the softness of his skin beneath the stubble along his jaw. He leant forwards and kissed her and she let her hands fall away so she could pull his T-shirt off. He hesitated and then raised his arms to let her tug it over his head, keeping his eyes steady on her the whole time. His skin was gleaming, almost too painful to look at, to have to memorise. Her fingertips wanted to trace him, etch him onto her own skin. She wanted to touch and taste every part of him, and knowing there wasn't enough time made her heart sing with pain.

'Evie,' Lucas said in a voice that made her startle. 'Evie,' he repeated, taking a deep, unsteady breath, 'are you sure?'

She blew the hair out of her eyes. 'I might be about to die. You think I want to wait any longer?'

It was the wrong thing to say. His expression instantly darkened, the fire that had been burning in his eyes extinguished at once. His hands fell away from her waist but before he could pull away completely she darted forward and kissed him full on the lips. She felt him resist for half a second, before his hands circled her waist once again. He kissed her back, more insistently this time, forcing all other thoughts out of her mind as the sensations in her body took over. Her skin was fire, pulsing with current, but her mind was empty. She felt light and free as air. It was Lucas who pulled back this time, just an inch, one arm still wrapped tight around her waist, his other hand coming to rest just over her heart.

'I love you,' he said looking her in the eye. 'I will always love you.'

'I know,' Evie answered, looping her arm gently around his neck and pulling him towards her.

35

She wasn't sleeping. She was lying across him and he was slowly stroking a hand up her spine feeling the trail of goosebumps he was leaving in his wake. Her own fingers were tracing the line of the scar that Caleb's tail had given him across his collarbone and chest. Then with lighter fingertips she started stroking the finer, almost invisible scars across his upper body – old wounds from knives, that he'd sustained as a kid, and later, training with Tristan and the others. Evie paused after a time and moved her hand until it was resting just over his heart.

She couldn't know what she was doing to him by just lying here.

But then she was gone, wriggling out of his arms and leaping out of the bed. He tried to stop her, rolling on his side and reaching a hand out to catch her, but she had already run to the window. She stood there, gleaming in the amber glow of the streetlight, her long dark hair trailing in tangled knots down her back.

'What are you doing?' he asked, sitting bolt upright, his attention on the surroundings, on the outside, focusing his hearing right down and scanning his senses for anything he'd missed. He hadn't picked anything up. Was it possible that Evie was out-sensing him now?

But she turned to him and smiled. 'The sun's about to come up,' she said. 'I want to see it.'

He shook his head and smiled. 'What about sleeping?'

She gave him a rueful, slightly bashful smile, letting her hair fall over her face as she turned to the window once more.

He stood up and pulled on his jeans, noticing Evie swivel away from the window to watch him. He grinned at her and crossed over to where she was standing, pulling on his T-shirt as he went, and then he bent to kiss her bare shoulder. 'I'm just going to make some coffee,' he said. 'Get dressed.'

Out in the hallway he leant against the wall and took a deep breath. Flic wasn't back. She'd left over an hour ago. If Issa wanted to be found Flic would have found her by now. And if she didn't want to be found then there was no way in all the realms that Flic would be able to find her. A Sybll was always ten steps ahead. He shouldn't have let Evie and Flic waylay him. That excuse about needing to sleep had been just that – an excuse. They hadn't exactly slept. Though, thinking about it, given the choice between sleep and doing what they'd just done, he'd happily forgo sleep for the rest of his life.

The panic that had subsided for the last hour while he'd been otherwise distracted was back now, in full force. Stronger even than before. Every time he took a breath he could feel it catching in his chest, causing another shot of adrenaline to flood his system. He was fighting every instinct in his body as well as the voice in his head, which was currently screaming at him to get Evie, get the hell out of the apartment and run. To where, though, he still didn't know. He knew he should be standing and fighting. He was the one who was causing all this to happen. He was the one challenging fate. Instead of fleeing he should be trying to figure out another way of closing the way through and of stopping this army. But first he needed to get Evie some place safe. Some place far away. He drew in a sharp breath, an idea forming in his mind – a house in the middle of nowhere. The house he grew up in. His grandmother's house – a million miles from anywhere, nowheresville, Iowa. No one would find her there.

36

'What are you doing?' Evie asked, watching Lucas tear through the apartment. She dragged her feet, following him into the kitchen, and stood there, watching him pull out the drawers and start rifling through them.

'I'm looking for a pen,' he said without looking up. 'I need to write Flic a note.'

'Why?'

Lucas was now bent over the counter, a pen in one hand, a scrap of paper in the other. 'Because we're leaving right now,' he said, 'before it's too late.'

'I'm hungry. I want sushi,' Evie announced.

Lucas looked up, pen poised. 'You want sushi. Right now? At six in the morning?'

She nodded. 'Yes. Then I want to go back to bed.' She took a nervous step forward, hoping he couldn't hear the way her heart was pounding. 'With you.'

Lucas put the pen down slowly and turned towards her. His grey eyes were ablaze, the tiny yellow strikes at the centre even more noticeable than usual. 'Evie,' he said, 'those sound like the wishes of someone who's only got a day to live.'

'Why?' she asked, smiling. 'Does everyone with just one day to live choose to go to bed with you and eat some raw fish?'

His expression darkened, his scowl becoming more pronounced. 'Evie, why are you talking like this?'

She gave him a weak smile and a half shrug in response. 'What else is there to do?'

He stared at her, uncomprehending. 'I should never have let you convince me to bring you here in the first place,' he finally said, swearing under his breath. He returned his attention to the piece of paper in front of him.

She watched him. She was shaking, she realised. Her whole body was shaking. It wasn't enough time. Her eyes skipped to the clock on the wall before darting jealously back to Lucas. It wasn't anywhere near enough time. And she didn't know where to start, which part of him to focus on first.

More than anything she wanted to cross the arm's-length distance between them and fold herself against his chest. But she knew if she touched him she would have second thoughts about what she was about to do. She was having to clamp her lips shut to stop all the words that were just there on the tip of her tongue from tumbling out. All she could do was stand there in silence, staring at the curve of his back as he bent over his note, the hilt of the shadow blade that she'd returned to him visible at his waist. She studied his profile, trying to imprint it onto her memory so she could take it with her.

His head was bowed, shadows falling over the paper as his hand moved furiously across it scrawling the note for Flic. She felt her stomach tighten at the memory of those same hands moving with a similar urgency across her body just a few minutes ago. His forehead was creased into a frown, his dark hair, unkempt as usual, was falling almost into his eyes. His mouth was unsmiling. She wanted to trace her fingers over the curve of his lips and watch a smile break there one more time.

She drew in a massive gulp of air, a shiver running up her spine and around her shoulder blades, spreading to the tips of her fingers. Her head flew up as her hearing funnelled. They were back. She could hear Flic's footsteps tripping lightly, jogging along the hallway outside.

Evie turned back to Lucas, who didn't seem to have picked up on Flic's imminent arrival. Before she could stop herself she had taken a step towards him. She put a hand on his shoulder, feeling the ripple of muscles as he turned. He dropped the pen and took hold of her instantly, his arms circling her waist and drawing her closer. She reached up on tiptoes and kissed him, a sob rising in her chest, sticking in her throat.

With a monumental effort she drew back. 'Thank you,' she murmured, staring into the darkening grey of his eyes, 'for everything you've done.'

Lucas cocked his head to one side, frowning. 'We're still in this together,' he said. 'I'm not leaving you.'

'I know. But thank you. I know what you're giving up for me.'

'Evie ...' he began, her name a sigh falling from his lips.

She swallowed. 'I'll never forget it. I love you.'

'It's going to be OK,' Lucas said.

She smiled at him, as brightly as she could, hoping to reassure him. How many times he'd said that. Did he think if he kept saying it he could lull her into believing it? It didn't matter. She loved him anyway for saying it.

The door opened just then and Evie skittered backwards out of Lucas's arms as Flic strode into the kitchen. Lucas's hand went straight to the counter, flattening over the note he'd written.

'That was pointless,' Flic announced as she planted herself in the centre of the room.

'Of course it was,' Lucas said quietly, scrunching the note up in his hand. 'If Issa wanted to be found she'd be found already. She'd be here.'

'What were you doing?' Flic asked, her eyes darting suspiciously to the crumpled note on the counter.

'Nothing,' Lucas lied. 'Listen, we have to go.'

Flic shot a nervous glance in Evie's direction.

Evie gave a start, adrenaline kicking in sluggishly, 'Um, I just need a few minutes first.'

'What?' Lucas asked, rounding on her, clearly frustrated.

'I want to write a letter to my mum,' Evie stammered, her cheeks burning.

He raised his eyebrows in disbelief. 'You can call her later,' he said.

Evie shook her head, backing away, 'No, it's important, Lucas. What if something happens to us? What if I never get the chance?'

'You will,' he said, but for the first time she saw a shade of doubt momentarily darken his eyes.

'What if I don't?' she said, trying to keep her voice steady. 'I need to do this. I only need a minute.' She caught Flic's grim-faced stare. 'Maybe two,' she added quickly. 'Then we can go. We'll get out of LA. Get somewhere safe.'

Lucas frowned, pushing his hair out of his eyes, 'OK, hurry though,' he said. He turned to the clock on the wall, his foot already tapping. Evie took a step backwards. She knew she was supposed to leave at this point but she simply couldn't tear her eyes off him. She just wanted one more second. And then just one more, each extra second being spent trading with herself for just one more. And then Flic stepped in front of her, blocking her view and Evie stumbled backwards towards the door, half-blinded by tears.

She fumbled for the door handle to the bedroom and in a haze of blurry vision crossed straight to the window, throwing up the sash and letting in a blast of wind. The tiny, feathered bird that had been sitting patiently on the windowsill looking in flew straight past her head, its wings beating against her ear.

In front of her face the bird stopped and started shimmering wildly – a prism caught in a blast of sunlight – and in the next second Jamieson was standing in front of her just as she had asked Flic to arrange.

'Hey,' Jamieson said, forcing a smile.

'Hey,' Evie answered automatically.

'You ready?' he asked.

She felt a moment of panic, as if she was about to drop through the trapdoor of a gallows. The rope felt tight around her neck, was already burning her skin. 'Wait,' she said, turning in a dazed circle, trying to think straight. She was clutching at thoughts as though they were being carried away on a fast-moving current, and no matter how she tried to grasp for them they kept spinning just out of reach. She spied Lucas's car keys lying on the desk. She picked them up, weighing them in her hand. Then she looked up at Jamieson. 'OK, I'm ready. No.' She stopped, hearing Lucas's voice and freezing with the heart-stopping realisation that that was the last time she would ever hear it again.

'Evie ...' Jamieson's hand was a gentle pressure on her arm.

She looked down. And then nodded to herself. 'OK,' she said, taking another deep breath and crossing quickly to the window. She swung a leg up onto the ledge and pulled herself onto the sill. Then she suddenly remembered something. She dug quickly into the pocket of her jeans. 'Here, take this,' she said, pulling out her mother's wedding ring and thrusting it at Jamieson. 'When he figures it out, give him this. Please. Tell him I wanted him to have it. And tell him ...' She broke off, closing her eyes. She wanted to finish her sentence but she couldn't. There was too much to say and not enough time. She looked down at the ground, two storeys beneath her. Never enough time.

'It's OK,' Jamieson said softly. 'He knows.'

She glanced back at him and nodded. His hand closed over her own.

'Evie?' he said.

'Yeah?'

He gave her a smile that faded almost instantly to nothing. 'Good luck.'

37

Something wasn't right. Something had changed – in the atmosphere, in him. Something had shifted, almost imperceptibly, but shifted nonetheless. Where he always felt her heartbeat like a murmur in his own chest, there was stillness. Yet he could still feel her, smell her faintly, her scent hanging in the air of the kitchen, on his skin.

He pushed past Flic and headed for the bedroom, his hearing tuned acutely. Flic was shouting something after him, trying to grab for him. Lucas shook her off, moving faster now, sensing something was definitely wrong.

He threw open the door to the bedroom. But Evie was there, sitting at the desk, facing away from him. She didn't turn when he came in, though her hand stopped moving across the paper.

He walked towards her feeling the rush of relief speed through his body. The window was open and a stiff breeze was stirring the papers on the desk and making the loose photographs on the wall flap. Evie was still wearing his dark-grey V-neck sweater. It was too big and had fallen down over one shoulder revealing a narrow slat of pale collarbone, which he felt an overwhelming urge to slide his fingers along.

He reached out his hand and felt her tense. Her skin felt warm to the touch.

'You ready?' he asked.

'Um, give me another minute,' Evie mumbled, still not looking up at him, her hand moving to cover the paper she was writing on.

Her heart was beating strangely, faster than normal. Lucas stepped back and looked around the room. Flic was hovering nervously in the door, clearly wanting them to leave. After half a minute he turned to Evie, anxiety getting the better of him. 'Are you ready to go? I promise we'll stop for sushi.'

Evie glanced up at him, looking confused. 'Sushi?'

He frowned. 'Did you finish your letter?' he asked, moving in a flash to her side. He cast a glance down and caught a glimpse of the paper before Evie quickly flipped it over. It was covered in doodles.

'Hey, you didn't write anything,' he said, reaching for the sheet of paper.

Evie leapt up from her seat. 'I changed my mind,' she said, brushing past him. 'Let's go.' She took his hand and started pulling him towards the door. Her hand felt warmer than normal, but her touch was empty. There was no familiar jolt of heat jumping between them.

Lucas let her pull him into the hallway.

'Wait,' he said.

Evie hesitated, her eyes darting over her shoulder to Flic who was now standing in the kitchen doorway. 'What?' she asked nervously, avoiding his gaze.

'Come here,' he said with a soft smile. She let him pull her towards him, though he noted the reticence. He looked into her eyes, the familiar dark blue of them. She was far more wary than she normally was around him, skittish almost. He lifted his hand slowly and stroked back a strand of hair, pushing it behind her right ear and smiling. He felt Evie tense at his touch, a small and totally strange frown line forming between her eyes. He took hold of her wrists and squeezed tight.

'Where's Evie?' he asked.

Evie pulled back, the look of surprise on her face quickly replaced by nervous indignation as her eyes flashed to Flic. 'What are you talking about?' she stuttered.

'Wrong ear,' he murmured. Shapeshifters were mirror images. Evie's bad ear was her left one, not her right.

In the next instant he'd let go of one of her wrists and had brought his father's blade to rest against the pale of her throat. A pale blue vein pulsed beneath the metal.

Evie's skin suddenly exploded into a wall of shimmer. He heard Flic shouting, felt her hands beating uselessly against his arm trying to get him to release his hold. Evie's wrist thickened in his grip and Jamieson appeared in her place. The blade pressed against his neck.

'I'm sorry,' Jamieson said through gritted teeth, his eyes nervously eyeing the thin blade.

'Where is she?' Lucas demanded, dropping the knife, but not letting Jamieson go.

'It was her idea,' Flic shouted, 'not ours. Don't blame him.' She pulled Jamieson out of Lucas's way, planting herself between them. Her arms were outstretched, one hand resting on Lucas's chest, as if that could hold him back.

'Where has she gone?' Lucas asked, staring from one to another.

Flic and Jamieson glanced at each other. Neither of them spoke.

Lucas seized hold of Flic by the arm. 'Has she gone to the way through?' he demanded, shaking her. 'Does she even know where it is? Tell me!'

Flic shook her head. 'I don't know.'

He squeezed her arm.

'Yes, I think so,' Flic yelled. 'She asked me to give her two hours alone with you and that ...' Flic stopped, biting her lip, shooting a look in Jamieson's direction.

'That what?' Lucas shouted, shaking her harder.

'Just said to tell you that she's sorry,' Flic sobbed. 'And that this was the way it had to be. And she's right!' She lowered her voice, 'This is the right thing to do. Don't you see that? Lucas – she's trying to save you.'

His hand fell to his side. 'Flic, what have you done?' he asked, his hand pressed to his side.

'I haven't done anything,' she answered.

'If anything happens to her because of this ...'

'It's going to happen to her anyway,' Flic yelled. 'She was doing you a favour. Trying to let one of you have a chance.'

Lucas blinked at her. *A chance? A chance at what?*

'She asked me to give you this,' Jamieson interrupted, holding something out to him.

Lucas saw at once what it was and reached out and took it slowly between his thumb and forefinger, staring at it, not quite believing. His heart, which had sunk into the depths of his stomach, was now caught in his throat.

He felt Flic's hand on his shoulder and he shrugged it off, resting his arms against the wall instead and pressing his forehead against his folded hands.

'It's over,' he heard Flic say.

He turned to face her.

'It's far from over,' he whispered hoarsely.

Flic stared at him in confusion, shaking her head, and then, when she saw what he intended to do, her face fell. Lucas moved past her towards the door.

'What kind of spell does she have over you?' he heard Flic shout to his back.

'I don't know,' he answered truthfully as he closed the door behind him.

38

Evie jumped three red lights, slowing down and hitting the brakes just before the fourth set. A police car rolled across the intersection and she noticed that her hands were shaking as they gripped the steering wheel. She was in the car that Lucas had stolen. She couldn't afford to be pulled over for a traffic violation. That was how serial killers got caught. And she couldn't afford to get arrested and sent to prison because she had somewhere to be right now. She laughed angrily. Waiting for a traffic light to change colour felt like an unjust and totally ridiculous use of the short amount of time she had left.

The light blinked to green and she floored the accelerator, her stomach kangaroo-jumping into her mouth. Her eyes flashed to the clock. It was nearly eight am. She wondered if her mum had made it home yet and got the answerphone message she'd left – garbled but she hoped not totally incoherent. If all went according to plan, her mum would be shortly on her way to a gas station in the furthest corner of New Mexico. She hated lying to her mum but it would get her out of Riverview for at the very least twenty-four hours while all this went down. She tried to picture her mum in Joe's green pickup; the two of them speeding across the state on a rescue mission.

Her mum would no doubt be tearing her hair out and Joe would be providing steady-voiced reassurance and calm. It was a good thing – her mum and Joe. Her mum would have someone to look after her when she finally got the news. She wouldn't be completely alone. That note was actually the one good thing she'd discovered by going home. The stuff about the prophecy – not so good.

She flew through another red light without seeing it, almost rear-ending the car in front. She ignored the cacophony of honking horns and swung the car left, navigating the narrow roads around the warehouse district until she pulled up outside Cyrus's building. The double doors to the parking bay were open and she swung in, leaving tyre marks across the concrete floor.

Her foot hit the brake as someone threw himself out of the way of her screeching wheels. Cyrus took a moment to lower the crossbow he was holding. He strode towards her as she climbed out of the car, his eyes scanning over her shoulder.

'Where's your shadow?' he asked gruffly.

She stared at him, unable to answer.

'What are you doing here?' Cyrus asked, a furrow appearing between his eyes, his tone changing. She didn't answer. He sucked in a breath and nodded in understanding. 'Does he know?' he asked.

Evie shook her head, swallowing to clear her throat. 'No. But he will soon, so we need to go now.

That's why I came. I need your help. I can't do this alone.'

'That's why you came back here?'

'Why try to fight the inevitable, right?' she answered, her voice shaking. 'I guess I just got tired of running. We can't let that army come through – too many people would die. One life versus many.' She shrugged, amazed at her nonchalance.

Cyrus pressed his lips together as if holding back a response. Eventually his eyes slid from her face and came to rest on something behind her.

'Why are you driving my mum's car?' he asked.

Evie turned and looked over her shoulder at the BMW. 'It's your mum's?'

'Yes.' He laughed under his breath.

'Lucas must have taken it outside the bookshop,' Evie said, looking over Cyrus's shoulder and noticing the red pickup truck behind him. 'But you stole mine, so I guess we're quits.'

'Your boyfriend slashed my tyres. You left us with little option other than trying to hitch our way in the middle of the night from nowhere, in the middle of Hicksville.'

Evie smiled despite herself.

'It's a piece of junk. You know that, right?' Cyrus said, slapping the side of her pickup.

'Well, you can keep that piece of junk if you want,' she answered. 'I'm not going to be needing it.'

He caught her eye and for a second held her gaze. She broke away first, clearing her throat. 'What happened to Victor?' she asked. 'He's not here, is he?' She wasn't sure she could deal with that.

'Oh no, we left him,' Cyrus answered tersely.

Evie's head flew up. 'You didn't kill him?'

'Didn't have a chance,' Cyrus answered. 'For a big man with an injury, he can move fast. I tried to follow him but my mum was freaking out. She wanted to get back here and pack our bags. She has some idea that we should run and hide.'

'Maybe you should,' Evie said.

'You'll never get into the Bradbury building on your own,' Cyrus said, not looking at her, but sorting through the weapons in the back of her pickup. 'You need us. That's why you came here anyway, isn't it? Vero and Ash are upstairs getting ready.'

'What were you planning on doing? Trying to hold off an entire army just the three of you?'

'Something like that,' Cyrus answered, grinning at her.

Evie shook her head in wonder at his staggering yet mildly impressive arrogance.

'OK, come on, let's get you prepared,' Cyrus said, walking past her, his shoulder banging hers. 'You're going to need to be armed. Remember the protection we spoke about,' he added, looking at her as he reached for the elevator grille, 'the unhumans that guard the Gateway?'

She nodded. 'Yes.'

'That's been doubled. The first wave of that army is already through.'

Evie stalled, feeling her heart dive to the bottom of her chest. 'For real?' she asked.

'Yes,' Cyrus answered, ushering her inside the elevator and pulling the grille shut behind them. 'Fifty-odd Thirsters, a handful of Scorpio and about twenty Mixen. We did a drive-by on the way back here to see what activity was coming through.'

Evie felt a new hit of adrenaline burn her stomach. How were they going to get though this?

'We took down twelve altogether,' Cyrus continued. 'Mainly Scorpio, some Thirsters and a couple of Mixen. That was just before sunrise – the rest will come through after dark.'

The elevator started to sway. For a moment Evie felt as if they were plummeting to the ground and were about to smash in a twisted heap of limbs and metal, but then she realised the elevator had just jolted to a stop.

'We have to move now,' Cyrus was saying, 'before nightfall, before even more come through and there are too many for us to fight.'

'How is this possible?' Evie asked.

'You're still asking that question?' Cyrus asked, looking at her sideways.

Evie's fingers clutched at the grille in front of her. She could feel Cyrus's eyes on her. His arm was stretched across her as if he was protecting her from something – or holding something back. Then she realised he was only reaching for the grille to pull it open. The owl on his inner arm was visible, peering at her, with eyes as all-seeing as a Sybll. A shiver travelled up her spine and she pressed her hand suddenly against Cyrus's arm, obliterating the tattoo with her palm.

39

Cyrus threw the elevator door back with a crash. He stepped out into the loft, ushering Evie in front of him. Margaret was standing beside the punchbag. When she saw Evie her mouth fell open. Then, faster than Evie could believe possible, the woman had crossed the space between them and was lunging for her.

'She's here? Oh my God. Don't let her get away again! Quick!' she yelled.

'I'm not going anywhere,' Evie said tersely, jerking away from Margaret's outstretched hands. Her gaze swept the loft. She noticed Vero and Ash sorting through a pile of weapons in the centre of the room, though they had both stopped what they were doing to stare at her in heavy-lidded silence.

'Mum,' Cyrus said, stepping between Evie and his mother, 'she came back. Evie came back to ask for help in closing the way through.' He stopped, then carried on, avoiding his mother's eye. 'We need to move fast before ...'

'Before I change my mind?' Evie said, giving him a wry look. 'Don't worry, I'm not going to.'

Cyrus gave her only the briefest glance before heading towards the others and throwing the crossbow on top of the pile of weapons. 'Ash, Vero, what weapons you going for?'

Ash tore his eyes away from Evie finally. 'UV lamps and grenades,' he answered, 'flamethrowers, crossbow, semi-automatics and swords.'

'We can't use the flamethrower,' Cyrus cut in. 'It's the Bradbury building. It's a historic landmark. The police are right above the Gateway. Let's at least try to be subtle.'

'How subtle is it going to be when five thousand Thirsters and Mixen and creatures with tails bust their way through in a few hours?'

'OK, point taken,' Cyrus said, chewing his bottom lip. 'Take the flamethrower, but use it only as a last resort. If we toast the place it's going to be difficult for Evie to get near the Gateway. She's not flame-retardant.' He crouched down and started loading a gun with bullets.

Evie gazed at the display of tangled weapons laid out before her, then looked up, sensing the others still staring at her. Vero looked instantly away but Ash continued to glare, warily, as though unsure of her next move. Which was ironic given that she was certain of it.

'Do any of you know what I'm supposed to do exactly when I do get near it?' she asked, trying to sound matter-of-fact.

'Walk through it, right? Isn't that what it said?' Vero answered, her head bent over the knives she was inspecting.

Evie frowned. Just walk? She'd been thinking about this ever since she'd heard the second half of the prophecy. She had no idea what the Gateway even looked like. *A break in the fabric of the universe*, Lucas had said – what did one of those look like? She was drawing a blank. Would it hurt? That was really the only question she was concerned about. Where would she go? Would she disappear? Would she stay conscious? Would it be like falling through space? Or would everything just – end?

'There's four of us against at least three dozen of them. Getting near this thing is going to be difficult,' Cyrus said, interrupting her train of thought. He stood up from his crouch and shoved a gun into his waistband.

'I'm coming too,' Margaret called from her position guarding the elevator door.

Cyrus wheeled around. 'What?' he yelled. 'A minute ago you were trying to get me to pack up and leave with you, and now you're suddenly coming with us?'

'Yes, Margaret nodded. 'I can still fight, Cyrus. I need to see that this is done.'

'Mum, no offence but you're, like, old. Way past it. You might put your back out or something. Do you even know how to load a gun? Were they even invented back in your day?' Cyrus asked.

'Cyrus,' Margaret snapped, striding towards them, 'I'm not *that* old.' Her hand closed around the gun shoved down the back of Cyrus's jeans. She yanked it out before he had a chance to stop her, then checked the safety catch was on before pushing it down the back of her own waistband.' And I'm not letting you all go in there by yourselves.'

She glanced at Evie once more, holding her gaze. She had the exact same blue-green eyes as Cyrus, yet without an ounce of humour or light in them.

'OK, whatever,' Cyrus sighed, turning away from his mother and picking up a sword instead. 'Right, here's the plan. Vero and mum, you take the Thirsters down. Think you can handle them? Should be easy enough with the UV lamps. I'll deal with the Shadow Warriors.'

'I see them better.' It was Ash who'd spoken.

'Well, they'll be the hardest to handle,' Cyrus replied. 'You'll need help.'

'You need to keep Lucas away from me.'

Cyrus turned instantly back to Evie. 'What?'

Evie cleared her throat, feeling how dry her mouth was. 'He'll come looking for me. He'll try to stop me. You can't let him near me.'

Cyrus studied her for a few seconds before nodding slowly. 'OK.'

'And promise me,' she said, taking a breath, 'swear you won't hurt him.' She glanced at all of them. 'Any of you. Swear it. Or I'm not doing this.' She looked at Margaret as she said it and the older woman pursed her narrow lips and muttered something. Evie waited.

'OK, OK,' Cyrus finally said. 'We get it. We won't hurt lover boy.'

'Lucas,' Evie said through gritted teeth, even though saying his name felt like someone was hammering rusty nails into her body. 'His name is Lucas.'

'OK. Lucas. We won't hurt him.' Cyrus said more quietly.

'Swear,' Evie snarled.

'I swear.'

She stared at all of them in turn. Vero's eyes dark and narrowed as a serpent's; Ash guarded, his shoulders rolled forwards, as though tensed and ready to spring; Margaret's mouth drawn into a white-lipped pout. 'All of you,' Evie repeated.

She waited until they'd all nodded, each in turn.

'Now arm her,' Cyrus said, striding away.

'What do you want?' Vero asked, looking up from where she was kneeling. Evie noticed that she wouldn't look at her directly. She was nervous, her fingers fumbling with the weapons she was sorting through.

Evie scanned the pile of weapons in front of her. She couldn't focus enough to select one, but then she noticed something glinting silver at the bottom of the pile. She bent and reached her hand beneath a sabre and a couple of machetes. 'I'll take this,' she said, pulling the circular-saw blade free. It had been Risper's weapon of choice. She smiled to herself, imagining what Risper would say if she could see her now. Vero looked up at her, a curious smile on her lips. Evie smiled back.

'That's all?' Ash asked.

She nodded.

'Evie,' Cyrus said from where he was stacking weapons inside the elevator, 'stay in the middle of us, wait until we've cleared a path and then ...' he looked away, tailing off.

'Yeah, I think I've got a handle on the rest, thanks, Cyrus,' Evie mumbled.

He was in front of her in the next instant, almost brushing his chest with hers, forcing her to look up at him. 'Are you sure you want to do this?' he asked with a softness in his voice she'd never heard before.

'Don't ask her that,' Margaret shrieked from across the room.

Evie shook her head. 'Look, please don't ask me again, OK? I've decided. I'm not going to flake out, or change my mind, or run any more. Just back off.' She pushed past him.

'OK. Chill, dude,' he called after her.

She couldn't help it. She spun around to face him. 'I *am* chill. I'm freaking ice. I just want everyone to stop looking at me like I'm an eggshell and I'm about to break. I'm *not* going to break.'

Cyrus gave the others a quick, nervous glance and then stepped towards her once more, his shoulders hunched. 'I'm just concerned,' he said in a low voice. A small frown of frustration passed across his face before quickly vanishing.

'And there I was thinking you never worried about anything but yourself,' Evie said, giving him an ironic smile. She couldn't believe she was trying to cheer him up by cracking jokes. It was ridiculous. Here she was in the final hours of life and she was spending it with a guy who notched his bedpost and thought way too much of himself, trying to cheer *him* up. Shouldn't it be the other way around? 'Let's just go,' she snapped, 'We don't have time to stand around. I just want it to be over already.'

No one said anything. She marched to the elevator and stood in front of Margaret, glaring at her until the older woman stepped silently out of the way. Evie turned and watched the others shoulder even more weapons, stealing anxious glances at her all the while.

'You're not going to ...?' she heard Vero murmur under her breath at Cyrus.

'Let her?' Ash whispered, covering the words with a cough.

Evie frowned. What were they talking about? But Cyrus put an end to the conversation by picking up a flamethrower and striding over towards her.

He didn't look at her. He just stepped into the elevator and held the door for the others. Evie kept her eyes closed. She could feel the energy pulsing off everyone – waves and waves of adrenaline and fear until it felt like she was going to drown in it. She almost clutched at Cyrus's arm to force him to open the door and let her out so she could take the stairs. The combating heartbeats of five amped-up Hunters were a cacophony of drums in her ears. She was the first out of the elevator when it reached the bottom, gasping for breath and trying not to let the others see. Margaret was hot on her heels though, clearly panicking that Evie was going to have second thoughts and run. Evie very nearly turned and pushed her away, but Margaret suddenly came to an abrupt stop beside her.

'Hey, that's my car,' she said, pointing. 'What's it doing here?'

'Lucas stole it,' Evie answered. 'I don't think he realised it was yours.'

'He stole my car?' Margaret screeched at her.

'What are you going to do? Call the police?' Evie asked, rolling her eyes.

'Mum, you got it back, OK?' Cyrus said, marching past her. 'Evie, do you have the keys?' he asked.

She nodded and threw them to him. They piled the weapons in the trunk and then squeezed in. Evie took the passenger seat before anyone could stop her, reaching for the seat belt out of habit as Cyrus put the car into drive.

Margaret, who was sitting behind her, reached forwards and pressed the lock down on Evie's door. Evie let go of the seat belt and twisted in her seat, about to yell something at Margaret, but her words were cut off as Cyrus slammed on the brakes and she was thrown against the dashboard. Evie jumped around in her seat, her hand reaching for the saw blade.

'Shit,' Cyrus yelled, staring straight ahead at the figure standing right in the middle of the warehouse. 'Who the hell is she?'

40

[Double Click To Add Text]

41

Evie was first out of the car. She stared at the girl, who had appeared out of nowhere and who was now standing in front of the car, motionless and frozen-faced as one of the mannequins in Victor's boutique.

'Who are you?' Cyrus asked, jumping out the car a second after Evie, the others quickly following suit.

Evie turned to him, catching a glimpse of something metallic in his hand. She held a hand up to still him. 'It's Issa,' she said.

'The Sybll from the Brotherhood?' Cyrus asked, levelling his gun at Issa's head.

'No,' Evie answered. She thought for one moment about telling Cyrus to drop his weapon, but then changed her mind. 'It's Lucas's ex.'

Cyrus darted a startled look in her direction. 'He dated a Sybll?'

Evie didn't answer. She stepped around her door and walked towards Issa. 'What are you doing here?' she asked. Issa was staring at her with eyes so large they resembled two pale-blue moons floating in an oval of winter-white sky. But more striking than that was the fact they were filled with more fear than Evie knew how to handle. 'What's happened?' she heard herself asking.

'Not what *has* happened,' Issa answered her. 'That's not why I'm here. It's what's *going* to happen if you don't listen to me.'

'Is it Lucas?' Evie asked, feeling her heart hammering wildly. 'Is that why you're here? Is something going to happen to him?'

'Yes,' Issa answered.

'But this was supposed to protect him,' Evie whispered, feeling the panic building inside her. 'I'm doing this to protect him.' She scanned the warehouse as if she could find an answer or a way out, hidden in one of its dusty corners. 'Does he know already that I've gone? That it was Jamieson and not me?' she asked, her eyes flying back to Issa.

'Did you really think that he'd not be able to see through a Shapeshifter?' Issa answered, her tone so snide that it made Evie wince.

'I tried, OK?' she said, feeling a dull anger start to stir. 'I didn't know what else to do.'

'Listen,' Cyrus cut in, suddenly in front of Issa, 'Are you going to tell us what you came here for because, if not, we need to be on our way. We have a date with destiny we really have to keep.'

'Your date with destiny is more like a date with death,' Issa shot back.

Cyrus opened and shut his mouth.

'As it stands,' Issa continued, 'you're planning to assault from the front of the building. If you do that none of you will make it through the door.'

Cyrus swore loudly.

Issa pointed at Vero who had come to stand just behind Cyrus's shoulder. 'You get killed by a Thirster,' she told her.

Vero's face paled.

'A Shadow Warrior is going to kill you,' Issa went on, turning and nodding at Ash, who was standing by the car door. 'Your mother,' she said, circling back to Cyrus, 'gets killed before she even gets out of the car.'

Evie heard Margaret gasp behind her.

'And Lucas?' Evie cut in. 'What happens to him? Is he going to get hurt?'

Issa didn't answer her. She didn't need to. The look on her face was answer enough.

'No,' Evie whispered, tears burning the back of her eyes.

'And it will be pointless,' Issa hissed. 'They'll all die for nothing. You won't close the way through. You won't even get near it.'

'But I thought it was a done deal?' Ash blurted. 'She's the White Light. She has to end it. Isn't that what's supposed to happen?'

Issa turned to him. 'Yes,' she said, 'but it's never been known for sure *when* she ends it exactly. It should have happened already.'

'Well, why hasn't it?' he asked, staring at Evie, confused.

'Because she fell in love with someone she shouldn't have.'

Evie glared at Issa. You don't get to choose, she thought angrily to herself. She didn't get to choose anything. She never had. Least of all falling in love with Lucas.

'It has to be tonight,' Margaret said desperately, pushing past Evie to confront Issa.

'Well, if you want it to be tonight you'd better listen to me,' Issa answered, shooting her a withering look.

'Why should we trust you?' Cyrus demanded.

'I thought Sybll stayed out of unhuman affairs?' Ash added.

'We can trust her. She's doing this to protect Lucas,' Evie said quietly. 'That's why she's here. To save him.'

Evie understood it completely. And a part of her – the part not hating Issa – was actually grateful.

Cyrus whistled through his teeth and shook his head. 'What is it about him? What is it that makes you females of all the species lose the plot so entirely?'

'Listen to her. We need to listen to her,' Evie said, ignoring him again.

'OK, OK, I'm listening,' Cyrus huffed.

'If you promise that you won't hurt him I'll tell you everything I see,' Issa answered.

'For God's sake!' Cyrus shouted, his head rolling back and groaning at the ceiling. 'Not you too. We already swore this.'

'I know,' Issa answered. 'Swear it again.'

'We swear we won't hurt Lucas,' Cyrus said in a bored, singsong voice.

'Now or in the future,' Issa said, narrowing her eyes. 'And believe me,' she added, 'I'll know if you even plan to, and I'll come and find you. And I'll pre-empt your every move.'

'I didn't think Sybll were violent,' Cyrus said pulling a face at her. 'You're sure undoing the stereotype, sweetheart.'

'Issa, please – tell us what we need to do,' Evie interrupted, hating how desperate she sounded, and hating too the way Issa turned to her – her owl-like eyes filled to overflowing with blame. Evie stalled, words dissolving on her lips. Wasn't she doing enough? What more was she supposed to do? Besides kill herself?

'Can you please start talking before the sun goes down and our problems get a whole load more fanged?' Cyrus asked, glancing at his watch. 'Do you think that might be possible?

Issa nodded. 'OK, yes, let's try,' she said.

'Try?' Evie said, feeling her frustration mounting. 'What do you mean, *try*?'

'I need you all to start rethinking your moves. We need to see how that changes things.'

'You mean you can't just tell us what to do?' Vero asked, frustration biting at the edge of her voice.

'Not completely, no. The visions change as you each decide to do things differently.'

'OK, so start,' Cyrus snapped. 'Do that weird eye thing that you Sybll do.'

Issa glared at him for a moment before taking a step forward. She gripped Cyrus's arm in one hand and Evie's in the other and closed her eyes. When she opened them a second later the blue irises were filmed with white.

'Lucas is going to be waiting on the north corner,' Issa said, her pupils starting to move rapidly under their milk-coloured blankets as if she was in a deep sleep.

'So we come from the south corner? The back entrance?' Ash asked, leaning forwards over the car bonnet.

'Yes,' Issa said, before pausing and then nodding her head slowly. 'OK, it's changing. You all make it out of the car alive.'

Evie heard Margaret sighing with relief behind her.

'Park by the fried-chicken place,' Issa went on, her eyes flickering wildly. 'But be careful. The two kids in uniform – they're not human. They're Scorpio.'

'I'll take them down,' Ash said quietly.

Issa nodded, 'Yes, you do.'

Evie stared at her and then at her long, pale fingers circling her wrist. How was she seeing all this? Was it playing out like a movie in her mind? Could she rewind and replay at will?

'Evie, stay close to Cyrus,' Issa said next, her head swivelling towards Evie and a frown wrinkling her brow. She hesitated, seeing something that Evie didn't want to imagine, something that caused a deep shudder to run up her body. 'Stay *behind* Cyrus,' she said more firmly.

Cyrus looked back over his shoulder at Evie. 'Are you hearing the lady?' he asked.

'Yes,' she murmured. 'Stay behind you. Understood.' She tried not to imagine why she needed to stay behind Cyrus. What the hell was going to be in front of him?

'OK, Cyrus, there's a Scorpio just inside the door,' Issa went on.

'Left or right?' Cyrus asked quickly.

'Your right.'

He nodded. 'Got it.'

Issa smiled, 'Yes, you get it.' The smile faded instantly. She flinched. 'Vero, that's your name isn't it? Watch your back. And take what's in front of you.'

Vero shuffled from foot to foot. 'OK,' she whispered, shooting Ash a questioning glance.

'Once you're inside, keep walking. Don't stop. Don't look back.' She paused for a second before continuing. 'There are three Thirsters in the lobby.' She looked at Vero, her eyes suddenly flashing back to blue, and gave her a bemused smile before her eyes blanked out once more. 'Stay together,' she said. 'It's important you all stay together. There are six Thirsters waiting downstairs guarding the door, and two Mixen, a Scorpio and, whoa ...' She broke off, her whole body jolting as though she'd been shot with a charge of electricity.

'What?' Evie and Cyrus shouted at the same time.

Issa squinted, turning her head rapidly left and right. 'It's chaos. I can't see clearly. Things keep shifting. There are Shadow Warriors. I can't see them. Ash, Ash is fighting them.' Issa suddenly threw her head sideways, wincing hard.

'What? What is it?' Vero shouted.

'Nothing, he'll be fine,' Issa answered, glancing at Evie in appraisal.

Evie squeezed her eyes shut and felt the ground swaying dangerously beneath her feet, only Issa's grip on her keeping her upright. 'After I – afterwards – what happens to Lucas? Does he get away?'

'I can't see,' Issa said quietly, her hands dropping finally to her sides. 'There are too many other choices in the way. *His* choices. And I'm losing my connection to Lucas.' Evie didn't miss the way Issa's nostrils flared in her direction. 'It's still unclear what his future holds.'

Evie felt all of a sudden like screaming – drowning everyone in her screams. All this then might be pointless. Lucas might die anyway. All the subterfuge and the lies – it might all have been for nothing. He might still die because of her.

'Evie,' Issa said quietly as if she could hear the screams going on inside Evie's head. 'You doing this at least gives him a chance at a future – a future he could never have with you. And I promise you, after today I'll stay with him. I'll warn him of anything coming. I'll keep him safe.'

Evie thought her head might explode with the rage that was pounding the inside of her skull.

'Well, I'm more concerned about *my* future and the future of every other human on the planet,' Cyrus butted in. 'If we do it your way, like you've said, does it stop this army of unhumans coming through?'

Issa nodded. 'Yes, I think so.'

'You *think* so?'

'Unless someone does something that changes it. What I've just told you is the future as it stands right now in this instant. For some reason I can't see what happens after Evie walks through.'

'Oh, for God's sake,' Cyrus growled. 'So if someone makes a last-minute and totally unexpected decision that you haven't seen yet – if someone changes their mind and dodges left instead of right, or if a butterfly somewhere in a rainforest in Brazil bats its wings, for instance ... If that happens, which undoubtedly it will, everything will change. Is that what you're saying? That it's probably not going to happen like you've seen it happen?'

'Yes,' Issa admitted after a few seconds' pause.

'Well, what good is that?' yelled Margaret, slamming a hand down on the car roof. 'What point is there in listening to any of this?' She turned away in disgust. 'What a waste of time. We should have left already. We could be on our way. The way through could already be closed.'

I could already be dead, Evie thought to herself.

'No. There's a point,' Cyrus interrupted, speaking in a firm voice. 'It's better than not knowing anything – than walking into this completely blind.' Suddenly he paused before reeling around. 'But let's shorten the odds even more in our favour. Get in the car,' he ordered Issa.

'What?' Issa stuttered.

'You're coming with us,' Cyrus announced. 'I want an RSS feed as we're fighting. I want to know second by second what's coming at us. That tips the odds in our favour.'

'I'm not allowed to interfere,' Issa said, taking a step backwards, her eyes widening. 'If they find out ...' she whispered.

'You just *did* interfere. By coming here you interfered. Who are you talking about anyway? The Elders? Why are you worried about them? It's not like they'll ever be able to catch up with you. And, besides, don't you want to make sure I don't change my mind about killing the Shadow Warrior?' He took a step towards her, his tone becoming low and menacing. 'Split-second decisions and all.'

Issa shut her mouth and stared at him, her eyes becoming milky-white once more as she tried to scan the future.

'You'll have more chance of saving Lucas if you come with us, right?' Cyrus pressed.

Her eyes faded back to blue. 'Yes,' she finally admitted, glowering at him.

Cyrus turned back to the car and walked around to the door, throwing it open for her. 'So get in,' he said.

42

‘Let me get this straight. Everything you told us just now might be complete and utter horseshit? Is that right?’ Cyrus asked as he crunched through the gears. His eyes were fixed on the rear-view mirror where Issa sat wedged uncomfortably beside Ash. Evie was this time squashed up against the car door beside Vero. Margaret had stolen the passenger seat. No concessions for the girl with the noose around her neck.

‘No,’ said Issa, obviously struggling to keep her tone even. ‘I keep telling you that’s the future as it stands, but if you’d let me concentrate I could keep you updated on any changes.’

‘But in the heat of battle how’s that even possible? Decisions get made in snap seconds, in the instants between seconds. But how would you know that? You’ve never been in a fight, right?’

Evie gripped the door handle as they swerved around a corner.

‘I know how these things work,’ Issa answered, staring right back at him in the mirror. ‘I’ve been seeing the future since before you were born.’

‘How old are you?’ Ash asked.

Issa sighed. ‘Eighty-three human years old.’

'That's older than my grandma,' Ash said, edging away from her. 'How old do you live to exactly?'

'Old,' Issa answered, lifting her chin and staring straight ahead.

'How old's Lucas?' Vero asked.

Evie started at the mention of his name.

'Twenty,' answered Issa. 'He ages like a human.'

'So if Lucas is twenty and you're like, eighty-three or whatever, doesn't that make you something of a cradle snatcher?' Cyrus asked, turning to look at Issa over his shoulder.

A car swooped out of a side road, almost careering into them. Cyrus spun the wheel, veering into oncoming traffic to avoid it. He righted them with a loud whoop, slinging Evie and the others into each other.

'You,' Margaret barked at Cyrus, 'keep your eyes on the road!' She turned to Issa, 'And you – keep your eyes on the future!'

Evie rested her forehead against the headrest in front of her and shut her eyes. She swallowed, feeling her throat constrict as if some clawed demon was squeezing her neck. *Keep your eyes on the future.* She couldn't keep her eyes on anything else – what little of it remained seemed to be slipping too fast through her fingers, vanishing as quickly and in more of a blur than the buildings they were speeding past.

She thought about her mother being woken up in a few hours' time by a knock on the door. She tried to picture her mum's reaction. She didn't need to imagine it. She'd been there when the neighbours had come to tell them about her dad's accident. It would look something like that. Her mum would collapse to the ground, and her cries would threaten to lift the roof, and the doctor would probably come and prescribe yet more sleeping pills, and her mum, dosed up on Valium, would sit tranqed-up in the church at her funeral, which probably wouldn't be that full given that Evie had spent the last few months not talking to anyone. Maybe Tom would come. Would Lucas?

She could hear Ash through the haze in her head, still quizzing Issa about her visions.

'How does it work?' he was asking. 'What do you see?"

Issa sighed heavily, 'It's like watching a film. And sometimes you get a bad copy and it's all fuzzy and the picture's unclear – that's because there are too many external factors coming into play and not everything has been decided.'

'So there is free will then? We do have choice?' Ash asked.

'Yes, of course we all have choice, except in a few cases. There are certain things that are just meant to happen, no matter what we do to try to change them – things like the marked prophecies. There's no point fighting it then – the destination will always be the same no matter what path we take to get there. But,' she said, 'most times we do get to choose the outcome. Like we just got to choose a different outcome for tonight. When you make a choice, you change the future. Only, most people don't make choices. They follow the path of least resistance. They take the easiest route – the one that doesn't require courage or thought.'

Evie opened her eyes and sat back. 'Lucas said that sometimes in life you have to choose one path over another. He said the hard path leads us past places we don't want to go.' Her voice cracked and she struggled to hold it together. 'But that path brings you to the exact place where you're supposed to be.'

'He always did believe that,' Issa said smiling, 'that we each had a purpose in life.'

'Philosophical discussions parked to one side for one moment,' Cyrus broke in impatiently, 'what's happening in about five minutes from now?'

Issa fell silent. Evie watched her eyes start swimming under their white coats.

Suddenly Issa started gasping for air as if she was drowning. Her eyes flashed open. 'Oh no,' she gasped, her fingers clawing at the seats.

Cyrus braked hard. 'Oh no, what? Oh no, it's going to rain? Oh no, you see five thousand Thirsters blocking the road up ahead? Oh no, we're all going to die? What's *oh no*?'

Issa shook her head hard, her eyes still blank. 'No,' she said despairingly. 'Why are they coming?'

'Who?' Ash asked, his knuckles white on the door handle as he scanned the block. 'Who's coming?'

Issa's eyes flashed to blue, she blinked and focused. 'Jamieson and Flic. They were supposed to be leaving. I told them to leave town.'

'Who are they?' Margaret and Cyrus asked in unison.

'Lucas's sister and her boyfriend,' Evie answered, not taking her eyes off Issa. 'What are they doing?' she demanded. 'They were supposed to keep Lucas away.'

'That's what they've come to do,' Issa snapped. 'They're following him to try to stop him.'

'What happens? Does their coming change anything?' Evie demanded.

Issa winced, pressing her temples between her hands. 'I can't see.'

'Don't tell me – *it's fuzzy*,' Cyrus said, throwing the car around another corner. 'Are you sure you wouldn't lose a fight?' he asked, his eyes flying to the rear-view mirror. 'Because I'm willing to try my luck.'

'Shhh, just give her time,' Vero growled.

Issa's eyes flashed open in the same instant. 'Someone has to stop them,' she said. 'We can't let them get near the building. It'll all go wrong. Lucas will be distracted.' She shook her head and Evie didn't have to ask what kind of *wrong* she was talking about.

'How do we stop them?' Cyrus asked, his eyes on the road ahead.

'I'll do it. I can stop them,' Issa said sitting forwards, grasping the back of his seat.

'And there you were saying you never interfered,' Cyrus grinned.

'Let me out,' Issa snapped. 'Let me out now. I need to head them off before they get too close.'

Cyrus studied her in the mirror, 'If you're lying to me, Issa, I will put your precog skills to the test. Do you understand?'

Issa nodded.

'If this doesn't play out like you said – then ...'

'Brake!' Issa suddenly shouted.

'What?' Cyrus asked, glancing up.

'Brake!' Issa yelled at the same time as Margaret.

Cyrus slammed his foot to the floor, sending Evie flying into the back of the passenger seat.

'Stop signs generally mean stop!' Margaret shouted as a truck thundered past in front of them.

Evie whipped around, feeling a sudden gust of wind. The far door was flung open and Issa was already gone.

43

Cyrus was holding her close, crushing her, or maybe it wasn't him crushing her, maybe it was fear squeezing the breath out of her body. She shouldn't have looked back. Hadn't Issa warned her not to? Because now all she could see in her mind's eye was the expression on Lucas's face – the despair, the anguish, the hurt at her betrayal. Damn it. Why had he followed her? Why couldn't he see this was the only way?

The door was just ahead of them, gaping like a toothless mouth. Evie could see the dimmed and hushed interior inside. And in the shadows just beyond the door she could sense something lingering. Cyrus too could feel it – he slowed his pace fractionally, sliding a short, flat sword out of its scabbard as he walked.

'Stay close,' he said to her, not taking his eyes off the door. She nodded as she felt his hand fall away. But there came a pull, as if her body was attached by invisible cords to something – no, not to something, to some*one* – and it was yanking her powerfully in the opposite direction. She faltered even as she tried to keep moving forwards and Cyrus's hand closed around her wrist. He pulled her close against his side, his fingers biting into her wrist, and shot her a warning look. Behind her Vero nudged her with what felt like the point of an arrow.

She threw off Cyrus's hand, rolled back her shoulders and marched forwards, crossing the darkened threshold into the Bradbury building. It was as if they were tourists come to ogle at the skylights and the historic interiors. As if they weren't fully armed and about to do battle with monsters and demons.

As soon as they were through the door, Cyrus swung fast to his right, pushing Evie with the full weight of his body behind him. He brought his right arm up at the same time in a wide arc. The Scorpio who'd sprung at them fell forwards, toppling towards them with a startled expression on his face, his sunglasses flying off his face. His red eyes blinked once in shock as Cyrus twisted the blade and, with a grunt, threw the Scorpio backwards. He slammed into the wall with a crunch and then vanished, leaving only a smear of blood where his head had smashed into the brick.

Without breaking stride, Cyrus sheathed the sword and pulled Evie towards the atrium. The others closed ranks around her, Vero and Ash walking backwards, their heels scuffing against Evie's.

A shout from Ash made Evie spin around just in time to see Vero drop to one knee and slash two swords in front of her chest in a wide, sweeping motion. Evie blinked. Through her lashes, caught in a strand of sunlight, she saw the faintest outline of a Shadow Warrior leap into focus. And just as quickly it vanished and something clattered to the ground, sending up a hail of blue sparks.

Vero sheathed both her swords across her back and reached forward to pick up the shadow blade that had fallen by her feet. She hefted it into her right hand, feeling its lightness, then grinned up at Ash. He grinned back at her as she stood and sheathed the weapon through the belt of her dress.

'Let's go,' Cyrus said, checking over his shoulder.

They swung into a well of light and Evie looked up, startled. They were standing beneath a central glass atrium. Sunlight was fracturing through it, refracting off the red brickwork around them and making it seem as if it was inlaid with quartz crystal. Slats of light were painting the floor and poking their rays through the twisted wrought-iron balustrades. A marble staircase swept up to the first floor and beyond. It was majestic and echoing and beautiful. And completely empty. Hadn't Issa said there would be Thirsters waiting?

'I thought this place was open to the public?' Margaret asked in a whisper.

'It is,' Cyrus answered, heading towards two elevators encased in iron cages. He pressed the call button.

'Well, where is everyone then?'

Evie glanced around. It was true. The place was emptier than a Thirster's grave.

'I think maybe they got eaten,' Ash said quietly.

Evie turned her head slowly, her senses overwhelmed by the stench that had just hit her. The elevator doors stood wide open, and for a moment Evie could only stare, unseeing, trying to piece together the image in front of her. It looked as if someone had dumped a heap of dirty clothing into the elevator, but then limbs began to materialise. Just by the door lay a hand – just a hand. No arm was attached. On one finger was a wedding band and Evie stared at it in shock.

She realised too, with ghost-like detachment, that the floor wasn't in fact painted gloss red either. It was a small lake of blood that was pooling at her feet. Evie kept staring at the two – or was it three? – bodies, all in police uniform, lying torn and dismembered inside the elevator. She wasn't really seeing them. She was seeing Risper. And Neena.

So many people dead. So many more who would die.

The others were equally horror struck. Vero was pressing her head into Ash's shoulder, Cyrus was staring dumbly, Margaret was clutching his arm to steady herself. Evie stepped quickly past them all and strode to the other elevator. Cyrus called after her, running to catch her up.

'Stay by my side,' he said through gritted teeth, seizing her by the hand.

She snatched her arm from his grip and reached to press the call button on the second elevator. The others joined them, watchful and on edge, their weapons at the ready, as the doors cranked open. This one was thankfully empty. Margaret was first in, a UV lamp clutched in each hand.

'Wait up,' Ash called, as Cyrus pulled Evie into the elevator behind him.

They hesitated, stepping gingerly back into the lobby. Ash was pointing across the atrium to where three Thirsters now stood toeing the line where shadow met bright sunlit floor. They were spitting like a pit of angry snakes, their fangs bared, eyes bursting with blooms of red. A hiss of steam erupted as one of them thrust his chest forwards into the light. He screamed and fell back.

'They're newly made,' Cyrus said. 'Check the fang marks in their necks. And they're blood-high.'

Blood-high? She'd never heard the expression but Evie could guess what it meant.

'They're trapped,' Ash murmured, glancing up at the blue sky and ribbons of sunlight cascading through the roof. 'We're lucky it's not cloudy today.'

'We're lucky they're not Originals,' Cyrus muttered, striding across the lobby towards them.

'That the best you can do?' he roared at them. 'What's the matter? Can't cross the line?' He stopped a tantalisingly few centimetres in front of them. One of the Thirsters thrust his hand forward, grabbing for him, pulling it back with a high-pitched scream as it brushed the rays of sunlight. 'Oooh, did that hurt?' Cyrus taunted. 'You big baby, don't you want to get your fangs into this?' He bent his head to the side, exposing his neck and a slickly pulsing artery. The middle Thirster threw back his head and howled. The others started snapping wildly at the scent.

'Cyrus!' Margaret yelled.

Ash brushed quickly past Evie, hefting a flamethrower up to his shoulder as he went.

'You can't use a flamethrower – this is a historic building, Ash,' Cyrus said, glancing at him.

'Well, what do you suggest?' Ash shot back.

The words were barely out of his mouth when one after the other the Thirsters went flying backwards, each letting out a scream as they thudded into the brickwork behind them.

'That. That works,' Cyrus said, turning to Vero who was throwing her crossbow to the ground.

She snatched the flamethrower out of Ash's limp grasp. 'Give me that,' she said.

Cyrus winced but closed his mouth and backed away as Vero sprayed the three bodies with a burst of flame. He jogged over to Evie, leading her to the elevator as slaughterhouse squeals erupted behind them. They stood watching in silence as Vero doused the bodies with flames, making figures of eight, until

Ash started tugging at her elbow and eventually pulled her away.

Cyrus pushed the button and Evie tipped her head back, feeling the last rays of light slide across her face and the cries from the Thirsters slowly dying, as they descended into darkness.

44

Cyrus dropped to one knee inside the elevator, and slid a second blade from his boot. 'Ash, you ready?' he asked, darting a quick glance at Ash who was standing, shoulders squared, head lowered, in the centre of the elevator. Ash nodded.

The elevator door cranked open and Ash was gone. In a blur Evie saw him move. The long sword he'd been wearing in a sheath over his back was somehow already in one hand and flashing wildly, clanging against invisible shadow blades, raining down purple and blue sparks.

Vero and Margaret were next out. The lamps in Margaret's hand alight, illuminating the large room they'd stepped into. Evie shrank back against the elevator wall as a barrage of screams and hissing deafened her, but Cyrus had her by the arm and was dragging her out and into the midst of it. Six or seven Thirsters were lying on the floor screaming as their bodies steamed and crackled. The stench of burning flesh filled her nostrils. A whoosh of flames roared past her ear and Evie pressed herself against Cyrus's back as Vero threw a wall of fire over their shoulders, scouring the ground with it. The screams crescendoed and a bank of black smoke filled the room.

Through the haze Evie could see shapes moving. Ash darted fast as an arrow, this way and that, sweat pouring from his body. Vero dropped the flamethrower in the next moment and was in the fight with him, her lithe body moving with the grace of a dancer, her shadow blade leaving neon traces in the smoke-filled air.

Cyrus was edging her through the billowing folds of smoke, through the fight that was raging around them, towards a far door. The smoke cleared for a moment and Evie let out a scream as she caught sight of a dark shadow lashing towards them. Cyrus flung his arm upwards to ward it off, his sword taking the blow. Through the smoke a Scorpio had come charging towards them. His tail was now hanging limply, scraping along the ground behind him where it had been sliced almost in two by Cyrus's blade.

Cyrus abruptly let her go, bellowing in pain as his sword clattered to the floor. From out of nowhere a Mixen had appeared and had wrapped his hands around Cyrus's arm. Evie didn't pause to think. She pulled the knife out of the battered leather sheath on Cyrus's waist and, as the Mixen brought his other hand up to Cyrus's neck, Evie twisted, spinning beneath Cyrus's arm, dropping to her knees and ramming the knife upwards with all her strength until she felt it slide slippery and quick between two ribs. A spatter of acid blood sprayed her hands and arms but she didn't feel it. She had rolled forwards, instinctively, out of the way of the Scorpio who was now coming at her. As she rolled, her hand closed around the hilt of Cyrus's sword lying discarded on the floor, and she brought it upwards as she jumped to her feet, spinning in a whirl. She felt the resistance of flesh soft as butter and then the freedom of the blade as it met air.

Both the Mixen and the Scorpio had vanished by the time she turned back to face Cyrus. His eyes were burning with pain and stretched wide with shock. Issa hadn't predicted that one. The smoke around them was clearing. Evie became aware of an alarm going off. It started off muted but got louder until it was slamming her eardrums, disorientating her, making her want to slide against the wall to get her balance.

She turned unsteadily in a circle, trying to make out the others. She saw Ash wiping sweat from his face, one arm slung over Vero's shoulder as she supported him. He had a long bloody streak across his chest and seemed to be limping, but they were both alive she thought, her heart pounding with relief. And there was Margaret too, resting the lamps on the ground, pointing them at the door ahead of them.

'You were supposed to stay behind me,' Cyrus said to her through gritted teeth.

She turned back around to face him. 'You're welcome,' she answered.

'I didn't know you could fight like that,' he said, frowning at her. 'Where'd you learn those moves?'

'Cheerleading,' she answered, handing him back his sword and brushing herself down.

She looked around the room. It was a hallway of sorts rather than a room. There were several wooden doors coming off it – what looked like storerooms. And, ahead of them, a thick metal door. Above it a sign read: Other Realm Costume Hire.

So this was the way through to the way through, Evie thought, taking it in.

'How do we get through that door?' Ash asked, hobbling to Cyrus's side.

'No idea,' Cyrus answered, holding his arm against his chest.

'Wait,' Evie suddenly hissed, cocking her head to the side. 'There are more.'

A rush of nausea hit her. Before any of them could ready themselves one of the doors to the side had flown wide open.

'Behind me,' Cyrus yelled.

Evie rolled her eyes but obeyed, falling in behind him as Cyrus charged at the two Mixen who were stampeding towards them. They were in swinging distance of his sword when they both faltered and fell. Evie caught sight of the cent-sized hole, like a bindi between the closest one's eyes, before he vanished. The other one was blown sideways by the force of the shot.

Evie turned. Margaret was holding a smoking gun in both hands. She walked steadily towards the one on the ground, who lay there gasping. The bullet hole was in her side. Her green skin was turning pale, slicked with sweat, her eyes darting wildly between them all.

Margaret stood over her with the gun poised.

'No!' Cyrus shouted, putting his hand on his mother's arm to stop her firing.

'Wait, I've a better idea. Help me move her,' he said.

He tore his shirt off and started ripping it to shreds, wrapping the strips around his hands. He handed the rest of his shirt to Margaret. She looked at it, confused, before she began following his lead. When they were done they bent and hauled the Mixen's body towards the metal door. She let out a low moan as they moved her, dark, foul-smelling liquid bubbling at her lips.

'What are you doing?' Ash asked, as they propped her against the metal door.

'He's getting us through the door,' Vero answered with a smile.

'Stand back,' Cyrus shouted, jogging back towards Evie. He pulled Evie under his arm, sheltering her against his side. 'And get ready.' He threw his arm back as if he was pitching a baseball and then let something fly.

The world exploded into a ball of furious light and scalding flame. The alarm became a faint trilling noise underneath the patter of concrete that began raining down on them. A hot splatter of something landed on Evie's forearm and she gritted her teeth to stop herself from yelling and covered her head with her arms as Cyrus curled his body around her, taking the brunt.

When he loosened his grip and she dared to look around, the Mixen was entirely gone. Where she'd been sitting propped up against the door there was now an enormous smoking hole. The door itself was a mangled piece of metal, jagged-edged and dripping molten metal to the ground. Evie looked down at her arm and saw the red marks on her skin, and then at Cyrus whose bare shoulders had taken the worst of the hit and were now scored with blistering red burns.

Cyrus had created an acid bomb out of a Mixen.

'Nice thinking,' Ash murmured, stepping forwards to examine the damage.

Light was streaming through as if the room was beneath the atrium upstairs, but it wasn't. She knew it wasn't. The roof was concrete. The light was coming not from the ceiling but from the Gateway itself. It was blinding, so dazzling that even the arm Evie threw up to shield her eyes couldn't stop the tears from streaming down her cheeks.

Cyrus edged slowly forwards, weighing the sword in his hand, towards the gap. A shadow fell then across the light, subduing it, and Evie dropped her arm as a shudder travelled up her spine.

'Holy shit,' Cyrus mumbled, stumbling backwards.

Evie's heart pounded in her chest as she took in the size of the person silhouetted against the light. Her head felt as though it was about to float clean off her shoulders and the adrenaline running wild through her body was setting her damaged nerves alight. She knew instantly that whatever it was that had appeared in the doorway was nothing she had encountered before. This was something entirely new – a new breed of unhuman altogether.

He was well over six and a half feet tall, with white-blonde hair that caught the light, and piercing blue eyes that roved the room before flicking over each of them in turn, until they finally came to rest on Evie. He cocked his head at her, as though she was a present – her clothes the bow, her body the box – and he was puzzling out how exactly he was going to unwrap her. Then he smiled and Evie caught sight of the razor-sharp, pointed incisors and finally understood what he was. He was one of the Originals – the unhumans that had, according to everyone, been wiped out a thousand years ago. Not so much with the wipe out, Evie thought as her eyes travelled the length of his body. This one looked pretty damn animated.

'The lamp,' Evie hissed sideways at Cyrus.

'I'm using the lamp,' Cyrus replied between gritted teeth.

Evie glanced down and saw that he was telling the truth. He was holding the lamp and aiming it at the Original but the usual flop to the ground and start-hissing thing wasn't happening. Nothing was happening. The man didn't even seem to have noticed the UV rays bouncing off his skin. All his attention remained fixed on Evie.

'What do we do?' Evie asked, her voice trembling. Why hadn't Issa warned them of this?

'We kill it,' Cyrus whispered back, but she detected the waver in his voice as he said it.

Evie's gaze darted to the floor for a weapon, something more substantial than a saw blade. The flamethrower lay on the ground just by the Original's foot. She glanced back up at him, weighing her options. If only she could distract him and make a dive for it she might be able to bring it up and blast him with flame. But would he even feel it? Would the flames just bounce off him, like the UV light was doing? Before she could figure out whether to take the risk or not, the Original took a quick stride forward. The flamethrower crunched like a sheet of aluminium foil beneath his foot. Evie stared in flaring panic at the flattened buckled metal and then lifted her eyes to the Original's face. He was still smiling at her. She took a faltering step backwards, her knees shaking.

'Vero,' Cyrus called out urgently under his breath.

An arrow went flying past Evie's ear and bounced off the Original's chest as if the shaft and the tip were made of rubber. The man caught the second arrow in his hand and tossed it to the side with a bored expression. But then his lips stretched back over his teeth, the dark rings of his irises flooded with blood, and he let out a roar which shook another layer of debris from the ceiling.

Evie's hand closed around the circular-saw blade she'd stuffed into her pocket. She pulled it free and clutched it to her chest. Chucking it would be like throwing confetti at him. She brought her elbow back anyway and took aim. But just as she was about to let it fly, the Original vanished into thin air, reappearing a split second later in front of Vero, his speed so unexpected that all of them stood blinking, including Vero, who didn't even have time to move a muscle. The Original's hand closed vice-like around her neck as he lifted her clean off the ground. A gargled croak burst from Vero's throat and her eyes bulged out of their sockets. Her toes scuffed the ground as the man dangled her in front of his face and snarled. Ash yelled, throwing himself at the Original, levelling a stream of roundhouse kicks to the chest and arms.

The Original flicked Ash away with his free hand as if he was deadheading a plant.

Evie threw the saw blade, watching as it struck the Original on the side of the head and bounced straight off. The Original turned to Evie and narrowed his eyes. She felt Cyrus back into her, trying to shield her. The Original tossed Vero to one side. She smashed into the wall with a thud and lay there unmoving. Out of the corner of her eye Evie saw Ash limp towards Vero's body, but then all her attention was drawn back to the Original. He was ambling towards her, studying her curiously. She stepped backwards, her foot crunching on the flattened flamethrower. What now?

Evie cast around once more for something – anything – she could use to distract him, just long enough for her to make it through the Gateway. And at just that moment she saw it – the hilt of it, poking out from beneath Vero's leg – the shadow blade she had picked up earlier. With a hurried glance at Cyrus who was now circling the Original, distracting him, Evie threw herself sideways, falling half on top of Vero, her hand closing around the hilt of the blade and dragging it free in the same instant.

'Hey!' she yelled from her position, crouched by Vero's side, 'it's me you're after! It's me you want!'

The Original stopped stalking Cyrus and turned his head towards her.

'Evie!' Cyrus yelled out in anger.

She ignored him. 'Come and get me you piece of …'

The Original was in front of her before she could finish her sentence, his knees level with her head. She glanced up at him and then with a scream leapt to her feet, bringing the blade up and driving it straight through his throat. It slid through his flesh as easily as a butter knife through frosting. There was an ear-splitting roar which cut off almost instantly and then a crash which shook the ground as his head hit the floor and rolled like a bowling ball across it, coming to a stop right by Ash's foot.

For a moment everyone stood in stunned silence, gaping at the head. Then Evie looked around. Ash had pulled Vero onto his lap and was trying to shake her awake, calling her name over and over. Eventually Vero stirred and groaned, opening her eyes and screaming loud as she saw the Original's wide, gaping mouth staring up at her. Margaret was standing in the corner, breathing heavily, tears rolling down her cheeks.

And Cyrus was in front of her. Gently, he took hold of her arm, which she realised only now was still raised, and lowered it to her side, then he eased the blade free from her rigid fingers. After staring at her for a few seconds until he was sure that she was OK, Cyrus walked over to the Original's head and dropped a lit match into its open mouth.

45

Evie was first through the gap in the wall. She stood there paralysed, staring at the blinding white light opposite. So this was the way through. It looked like a mirror reflecting the sun. The light was so fierce and white hot she couldn't look at it straight on, couldn't even make out the edges of it when she squinted. There was no way of telling what lay on the other side. Other than oblivion, that was. Which was probably a good thing all in all. If it had just been a doorway with five thousand blood-high unhumans visible on the other side she doubted she'd have been able to walk through it.

Her heart was suddenly beating a thousand times a minute, her breath short. Wasted. She shouldn't have to struggle for breath – not now, when every single gulp of air was a luxury, something she wanted to savour and suck deep. Her legs were shaking and she felt angry at their betrayal. She hadn't come this far to not be able to finish what she'd started.

The others were standing at the edge of the room, waiting, watching, and the resentment bubbled in her. She suddenly felt what it must be like to be a prisoner on death row, with everyone staring through the glass waiting for the switch to be pulled. Except she was expected to strap herself in and throw the switch all by herself. She hesitated for a moment, wondering if she should ask Cyrus to push her through – one good hard shove. But then she gritted her teeth. She needed to take her dignity with her, that much she knew. Was it going to hurt? That's what she couldn't help wondering. She drew comfort from the knowledge that it didn't seem to hurt any of the unhumans that came through. But then again, it didn't kill them either.

She was doing everything in her power not to think Lucas's name. Not to picture where he might be right this instant, above them somewhere. Had he managed to kill that Shadow Warrior on the roof? What if Issa had failed to see something? Evie tried telling herself that everything so far had gone exactly as Issa had foretold and surely that was a good sign. That had to mean that Lucas was fine. And, besides, she was sure she would feel it if he wasn't.

She stared at the way through and took another small step towards it. She thought about asking Cyrus for the shadow blade he'd taken from her. She hadn't figured she would need it – but what if? She almost laughed at herself.

She could sense the others getting restless behind her but none of them wanting to call it. Was she supposed to turn around and offer some last words of regret or forgiveness or farewell? No. The last thing she wanted to see before she died was Margaret's face. She wouldn't mind seeing Cyrus's – she might be able to draw some reserves of courage from seeing him. But Issa had said she should just walk and she shouldn't look back, so she stayed squinting straight ahead of her at the Gateway she was supposed to walk through. No, not supposed to, she corrected herself, that she *had* to walk through.

OK. She lowered her head. One step. Two steps. She could reach out and touch it. She lifted her hand. Her fingers grazed the edge of the light and she turned her head away, blinded by a spray of golden sparks. A tingling feeling shot up her arm as if she'd touched a live wire. She took a deep breath, filling her lungs full, and held it as if she was about to free dive a thousand metres. Then she closed her eyes.

'Evie!'

Her eyes flew open, the breath exploding out of her. She wasn't supposed to turn. She was supposed to keep walking. But a hand closed around her wrist and she was spun around.

Cyrus was holding her, gripping her hard now by the shoulders. He stared at her for a few seconds, his expression fierce, then without a word he placed his hands on either side of her face and pulled her towards him, bending his head at the last minute and kissing her on the lips.

He let her go just as suddenly as he'd kissed her, his hands falling to his sides. Evie gasped in a smoke-filled breath of air. Cyrus was watching her intensely, his breathing unsteady. 'Don't ever let anyone tell you chivalry is dead, OK?' he said hoarsely.

'What?' she asked, her own voice husky.

'I've led a charmed life,' Cyrus answered, a rueful sad smile playing on his lips.

Evie shook her head, still not understanding, and then she saw it. She saw it suddenly, in the flash of fear that glanced across Cyrus's eyes even as he grinned at her and turned away.

Evie raised her hand, grabbing for his arm, but he was too fast. Her palm grazed the Scorpio scar on his back, and then he was gone. Cyrus had stepped through the Gateway instead of her – and all that remained of him was a black fading outline standing out against the curtain of light in front of her. And then there was nothing left of him at all, not even the memory of his shadow. He was simply gone. Evie was staring at a brick wall. The light had vanished. The room was empty. The way through had closed.

Margaret's howls spun in her head and Vero's cries split the air and darkness threatened to swallow her whole.

46

Lucas caught her as she fell, crashing to his knees, holding her. Nothing else registered – the noise, the screams, sirens and alarms were all just white noise. The only thing that he registered was that Evie was alive. That he was holding her in his arms, touching her. That it was all over. And she was still here.

'Evie,' he whispered her name, burying his face in her hair, feeling her breath shallow and warm against his neck. 'Evie,' he said again, taking her face in his hands. She opened her eyes slowly and the whole world rushed into them – the blue dark as indigo. He felt the scream inside her head, tearing through her, could hear it echoing in his own skull.

'Lucas.' She whispered his name as if she didn't quite believe it was him kneeling in front of her, holding her. As though she was scared that she was dreaming. Her hand hovered just above his skin, almost too afraid to touch him.

He clasped hold of her fingers and she let out a gasp, then fell against him, holding him tight. After a few seconds she glanced up at him. Tears were sliding down her face.

'How ... how did ... what happened? I thought I was supposed to be the one to close it?' she asked.

Lucas couldn't give her an answer. He just shook his head. He'd fought his way past two more Shadow Warriors and a handful of Thirsters, had leapt down the stairs, burst into the room and all he'd seen was a blinding flare of light and Cyrus silhouetted against it. And then he'd watched the light fade to nothing. *He hadn't been in time.*

And yet it didn't matter. Evie was still here. And he didn't understand how or why, but for the moment he didn't need to. He reached a hand and touched Evie lightly on the cheek, wiping away a tear with his thumb.

'How could Cyrus do that?' she asked, staring at the wall, her face pale, her lips ashen.

'He's like you.'

Lucas turned his head. It was Vero speaking.

'He was like you,' she corrected herself, her voice breaking as she fixed Evie with a dark-eyed stare. A trickle of blood ran like a fat red worm from her temple to her jaw. She was holding her elbow as though it might be broken.

'What do you mean he's like Evie?' Lucas asked.

'Cyrus was a child of two warriors too. A pure Hunter.' Vero's shoulders were shaking as she said it and Ash put his arm around her and kissed the top of her head, closing his eyes as he did. It was only then that Lucas became aware that Margaret was kneeling on the ground, keening to herself as she rocked back and forth, her hands clutched to her chest.

'How?' he asked, guilt pulling at his insides, even as his grip on Evie tightened.

'His father was a Hunter.'

'Who?' Evie asked in a stunned whisper, '*Who* was his father?'

'David. The man who was training your parents and Victor and Margaret.'

A long, otherworldly cry erupted out of Margaret's chest, silencing them all. Lucas stared at her, fighting the urge to shove Margaret against the wall and demand to know how she could have let them believe all this time that Evie was the one, that she was the one to be sacrificed, when all along it had been Cyrus. But as he got to his feet all the anger evaporated out of him. Margaret had only been doing what he himself had been trying to do – protecting the one she loved. He understood Margaret far better than he wanted to and the anger was washed away by a torrent of pity he knew she would hate if she ever became aware of it.

'How long have you known this?' he demanded in a quiet voice, turning back to Vero.

'Just since last night,' Ash answered for her. 'Victor told Cyrus who his father was. I think when you and Evie ran off, Victor thought he had a second shot at it. And Cyrus agreed. He was going to close it by himself – and then Evie showed up and volunteered.'

Lucas turned back to Evie. She was still kneeling on the floor, staring at the wall, tears dripping onto her lap. Her arms and hands were covered in red welts. He dropped to a crouch in front of her, feeling the ache in his broken rib, and put his hands on her shoulders, turning her gently to face him.

'Evie,' he said, 'come on, let's go.'

He helped her to her feet, putting his arm around her waist and leading her past the others, past Margaret who was still collapsed and rocking back and forth on the floor. Evie hesitated. She looked like she was about to say something to Margaret but then she decided against it and let Lucas lead her through the hole where the door had once been and where the costume hire sign lay smoking and twisted on the ground. They crossed to the elevators.

'No, not the elevator,' Evie whispered.

Lucas led her up the stairs, halfway up pausing to look back, hearing Vero and Ash making their own way across the bomb-blasted basement towards the stairs. Vero was helping Margaret stagger up the stairs, while Ash was clinging to the banister, his face contorting into a tight grimace with every step.

When they reached the atrium with the sunlight bursting through, Evie shuddered.

'It was never me,' she said in a whisper. 'The White Light, the prophecy. It wasn't me.' She shook her head. 'It never was. All this time ...' She broke off.

Lucas didn't say anything.

'Everything I've done, every time I didn't think I had a choice, that wasn't true,' Evie mumbled, her eyes scanning the lobby. 'I always had a choice. My parents were right after all.'

She looked up at Lucas with a confused expression. He looked away. The whole time he'd believed the prophecy was about Evie. He'd believed it because he had needed a reason for why he was so compelled to save her, even before he really knew her. And the prophecy had given him that reason. He'd been the one to convince her she was it, even back when she was ready to quit. He was the reason she was here. And the realisation of that was almost worse than the feeling he'd had when he thought he'd never see her again. He could barely look at her, was too afraid that any second she'd figure it out and would wrench herself from his arms. A part of him almost wanted her to. But when he dared to look back at her she was smiling at him with such softness and hope in her expression that the fear backed off.

Evie walked across the atrium, past the piles of ash and blackened walls. The doors they were heading to were thrown open just as they reached them and a dozen firefighters rushed past them yelling.

'Get out! Get out of the building! Can't you hear the alarm going off?' one of them shouted.

'Come on, let's go,' Lucas said, urging Evie through the doors, and darting a nervous glance towards the elevators. It would only be minutes before they started finding body parts and scorched remains. It would be better if they were long gone before then.

They fell out into the sunlight, tripping down the steps, blinking in the glare and deafened by all the fire trucks and blasting sirens. His first instinct in sunlight was always to look for the shadows, to know where he could fade without being seen but Lucas didn't do that this time. He didn't want to fade ever again. He started to weave his way through the crowd, needing to step into where the sunlight was broadest, wanting to get Evie away from whatever else might still be lurking.

They were past the fire trucks, two blocks down, holding each other tight, still too stunned to really talk about what had just happened, when without warning, Evie was suddenly torn from his arms.

Lucas spun around, leaping without thinking at the man who had Evie by the arm and was dragging her across the sidewalk. It was Victor. He'd appeared out of nowhere and with his one good arm was holding Evie against his broad chest, a knife pressed to her heart.

Lucas was between them in the next instant, his elbow coming up and jabbing at Victor's shoulder, over the wound he'd made earlier. Victor let go instantly grunting with pain, the knife clattering to the sidewalk. Evie danced out of his way.

'It's done. It's done,' Lucas shouted, glancing around to see if anyone was watching. The street was crowded but all the attention was on the burning building.

'What do you mean?' Victor asked, glancing at Evie.

'Cyrus,' Vero said, appearing behind Victor. 'Cyrus closed it.'

Victor spun around. Seeing Vero, Margaret and Ash standing bloodied on the sidewalk, he faltered. 'Cyrus?' He looked at the Bradbury building and seemed for the first time to notice the firemen bustling in and out of the entrance and the fire trucks lining the street.

With a scream, Margaret launched herself without warning on Victor, pummelling his chest. 'It's your fault,' she yelled. 'You told him! You told him.' She collapsed sobbing to the ground. 'I could have saved him,' she cried.

Lucas took Evie's hand and pulled her backwards, glancing nervously at the crowd building up on the sidewalk and now starting to stare in their direction.

'Evie, don't turn your back on me. You can't just walk away!'

Evie took a deep breath and, still clutching Lucas's hand, turned to face Victor.

'The fight's over, Victor. The way through has closed. It's done.'

Victor stared at her open-mouthed and then, quick as lightning, he strode towards her. 'There are still unhumans in this realm to kill. We don't stop until the last one is dead,' Victor hissed, staring at Lucas.

'It's not my fight anymore,' Evie growled. 'I would have given my life, Victor. Now, I just want it back.'

Victor opened his mouth, then shut it once more.

Evie started walking backwards, tugging Lucas with her as she went. Lucas cast one last look back at Victor. It was strange. He no longer felt any kind of anger towards him. He didn't need revenge and the loss of that feeling was unexpected. Revenge had been such a part of him and of his existence for so long that he'd feared its loss would change him irreversibly, would empty him of all feeling, but what it did do, which he'd never anticipated, was carve out a new space inside him, which filled all at once with hope as clear as glass and with a lightness that could have lifted him off the ground. The past didn't matter any more. Not now he had a future – one that he could choose freely.

47

Through the crowd gathered on the sidewalk Evie thought she saw a familiar white head and behind it two more familiar figures, one dark-haired and moving furiously, shoving people aside, batting them like flies, the other shimmering wildly. They were sprinting towards them. It was Flic and, following just behind, Jamieson and Issa. Evie tugged on Lucas's arm and pointed.

As they got nearer Evie could see they were yelling something, but from this distance, with the fire alarm still blaring, she couldn't make out what. And then it dawned on her. They were screaming Lucas's name. They were yelling a warning to Lucas. She turned at once towards Lucas and the whole world slowed. Lucas was half-turned towards Flic, his expression moving from surprise to a frown, and then his hand slid from hers suddenly and he staggered sideways. Evie grabbed for his arm.

'NO!'

Lucas dropped his gaze to his chest and Evie followed it. Lucas's black shirt was sticking to his chest. He pressed his hand against his abdomen and then lifted it away, palm outward.

Evie stared at the blood lacing his fingers. Lucas's eyes flew up to meet hers and they gazed at each other for several beats before Lucas took a half-step towards her and then fell. She caught him, sobbing his name, her knees smashing into the sidewalk as she broke his fall.

'You should have killed me back when you had the chance.'

Evie looked up. Victor was standing over them, his lip curled in a sneer. And then he vanished, backing off into the encroaching crowd.

Evie blinked, her breathing coming thick and fast and choking. She started to stand, her fingers closing around Lucas's shadow blade, when she felt Lucas tugging at her arm. She dropped back to her knees, letting the blade fall from her fingers and clatter to the sidewalk.

The world was closing in on her. She ran her hands frantically over Lucas's abdomen, pressing down hard, her fingers shaking, sticky and thick with his blood. She was sobbing, she realised, and she heard Lucas suck in a breath beneath her hands. She heard herself uttering prayers she'd never known she knew the words to, begging him to stay, pleading with him to hold on.

Because he was fading, she could feel it. He was slipping through her fingers. She was losing him.

'Lucas,' she said bending over him, her hair falling in a curtain over their faces, shielding them from the others who were pressing in – Flic, Jamieson, Issa, their voices screaming over the top of her head, their hands tugging and pulling. 'Don't leave me,' she whispered. 'I need you. I choose you.'

He reached a hand up and his fingers traced lightly over her lips. 'Shhh,' he whispered. His lips were bright red, the rest of him so pale. So, so pale, almost translucent. He stroked his finger along her eyelashes. She closed her eyes for an instant and felt his hand fell away.

Evie kept her eyes closed, squeezed them shut tight until she could see stars flying on the backs of her lids, until she thought her heart might burst out of her chest and explode into a million little pieces.

Because she knew that Lucas was gone and if she opened them there would be nothing more to see.

THE END

Acknowledgements

My wonderful husband John and beautiful daughter Alula who make everything worthwhile.

Vic and Nic – for a fourth time I've taken this lonely journey with my two best friends. It's a joy and a pleasure to share every step with you.

Hannah Nersasian and Tom Arnold, both great writers themselves who supported me throughout the writing process.

All you wonderful bloggers and reviewers who tweet and blog and generally make being an author so much fun.

Jenny Cooper who always has the right words and whose encouragement made me want to get this book out into the world.

Amanda, my agent, for the constant support.

About the author

Sarah is the author of the highly acclaimed Hunting Lila series, the Fated series and a number of standalone thrillers, including The Sound and Out of Control, (all published by Simon & Schuster)

As well a Young Adult fiction, Sarah writes New Adult fiction for Pan Macmillan under the pen name **Mila Gray**.

Her first novel *Come Back To Me* will be out in summer 2014.

Sarah lives in Bali with her husband and daughter. You can find out more by following her on Twitter @sarahalderson

www.sarahalderson.com

Printed in Great Britain
by Amazon